COURTING THE
COUNTESS

By the Author

Heart of the Pack

A Royal Romance

Courting the Countess

COURTING THE COUNTESS

by

Jenny Frame

2016

COURTING THE COUNTESS

ISBN 13: 978-1-62639-785-9

THIS TRADE PAPERBACK ORIGINAL IS PUBLISHED BY
BOLD STROKES BOOKS, INC.
P.O. BOX 249
VALLEY FALLS, NY 12185

FIRST EDITION: SEPTEMBER 2016

CREDITS
EDITOR: RUTH STERNGLANTZ
PRODUCTION DESIGN: SUSAN RAMUNDO
COVER DESIGN BY SHERI (GRAPHICARTIST2020@HOTMAIL.COM)

Acknowledgments

I think most authors would say they enjoy writing each book, but writing *Courting the Countess* was truly a joy. I've asked myself why I seem to have a particular emotional attachment to this story, and all I can come up with is that it has everything I love to write about, between the covers.

A huge thank you has to go to Ruth Sternglantz for helping me work out my idea for the book and for coming up with the title, which gave me a really romantic theme to weave throughout the story.

As always, thank you to Radclyffe, Sandy, Cindy, and everyone at Bold Strokes Books, for their help, hard work, and dedication to make every book as good as it can be.

Thank you to Amy, Christine, and Govita for their friendship and unstinting support.

Readers are why we write books, and I want to thank all the readers who've bought a book, sent me an email, a message, or a tweet. I appreciate every single one of you.

To my family, thank you for your help and support in every aspect of my life. I don't know what I'd do without you all.

Lou, you make me smile every day, make me laugh every day, but most of all make me feel like the most loved woman in the world every day.

Together with our beloved Barney boy, I live my happy ever after every moment of every day of our lives.

Dedication

For Lou
My very own happily ever after

CHAPTER ONE

Henrietta Knight looked around the hotel reception room they were using to host her father's wake and watched her mother, dressed in an elegant black outfit, complete with hat and black veil, play the grieving widow part to a tee.

What a hypocrite.

She snagged a glass of whiskey from one of the servers' trays and took a large sip. Harry hoped the alcohol might dull the anger and frustration she was feeling. This whole funeral was a farce from start to finish and she couldn't wait to get away.

Earlier in the day they'd had the briefest service she had ever observed at the crematorium, then back here for the wake where only ten people turned up.

The worst part was taking her place as the head of the family and giving a speech about a man she hoped would burn in hell.

I need to get out of here. Harry could think of many different— better—ways to spend the day of her father the Earl of Axedale's funeral. She finished her whiskey and was about to slip out when her mother, Lady Dorothy, came over to her.

"Harry, you must circulate and thank people for coming. You are the head of our family now. You are the Countess of Axedale, and it's your responsibility now, not mine."

"I am Dr. Knight, Professor of Archaeology, first and foremost, Mother. That will always be my top priority," Harry said with bitterness in her voice.

Lady Dorothy looked around anxiously, but everyone seemed to be happily engaged in conversation. "Keep your voice down, Harry. We don't want everyone to know our business."

Harry gave a wry laugh. "How do you do it, Mother? How do you keep up this pretence in front of everyone when we both despised Father? How can you be so hypocritical?"

In a low firm tone, Lady Dorothy answered, "Years of practice. Charles embarrassed me and humiliated me throughout our marriage with his countless mistresses, and the only way I could cope, the only way to minimize my humiliation was to learn to keep up the pretence of a strong marriage in the face of scandal. That's why. When I heard that Charles had died, I cried with happiness, but I will see him off with as little embarrassment and fuss as possible. Once this is done, I can live again."

Harry loosened the black tie that felt tight around her neck. "I can't do that. Look around, Mother. When ten people turn up to your funeral, and they include your doctor, your lawyer, and your banker, I think it tells its own story about your character and your life."

Lady Dorothy sighed, unable to counter that argument. "I thought Bridget might come, to represent her father at least."

Bridget, Harry's best friend whose father had been Lord Charles's friend, had wanted to come for Harry's sake, as she knew how hard it would be for her.

"I told her not to come. As I said, I think it's hypocritical. She didn't like him either."

They were both silent for a few moments before Lady Dorothy asked, "Are you going to Axedale Hall or staying on at Cambridge?"

"Both. I'm taking a year's sabbatical from Cambridge to refurbish Axedale. I promised Grandpa that when I finally took control of the estate, I would restore it to its former glory. Father has let it crumble and die, but once my promise is fulfilled, then I will be going back to Cambridge. I'm head of my department, and that is my world, my kingdom."

Lady Dorothy took a glass of sherry from one of the servers as he passed. "That's probably best. I'll be staying at my house in Monaco, if you need me for anything."

Harry felt her anger return in an instant. "Need you? When have I ever needed you, Mother? You left Axedale and me when I was thirteen years old to fend for myself."

A look of guilt flashed across Lady Dorothy's face. "You had Mrs. Castle to look after you. She always loved you and took care of you. Your father wouldn't have allowed me to take you, and you wouldn't have liked to move to the Continent."

"You left me trapped there with him, trapped in that house, on my own." Harry had never voiced these truths to her mother before, but today of all days she just couldn't hold back.

"Keep your voice down, Harry. I had to get away. I couldn't stay with him one minute longer. He destroyed who I was," Lady Dorothy said desperately.

"But you left your child, didn't you? I'll never forgive you for that, and I'll never forgive him for making my childhood a misery. I'm leaving now. I'm not taking part in this charade any longer."

As she went to walk away, Lady Dorothy said, "Don't make the same mistakes in life that I did." Lady Dorothy had drummed that into Harry for years. "Don't fall in love, Harry. Don't ever let someone have that power over you, or you may be in my place one day."

Harry turned around and sneered. "Love? I'm not capable of it. You and Father made sure of that."

She walked out of the room and went directly to the hotel entrance, where her Aston Martin was waiting for her. The doorman opened the door for her, and she tipped him.

"Thank you, m'lady. Have a good day."

Harry pulled off her tie, stuffed it into the top pocket of her black suit, and put on her sunglasses. "I will now."

She roared off into the streets of London to find the only thing that would relieve her anger and frustrations.

❖

Harry grasped her bed partner's wrists lightly above her head as she thrust into her. She looked down at the woman and felt a rush of power listening to her deep moans and groans as she kept her on the edge of orgasm. It was exactly what she needed today, to feel in control of everything and everyone around her, and to work her deep-seated frustrations and anger out with one of her casual lovers, Clara Fitzpatrick-West.

"Yes, Harry. Just like that. God, I need to come."

Harry's own orgasm was close, but as with everything in her life, Harry kept it under strict control and would not come until she was well and truly ready. She had been fucking Clara much longer than usual, working her up into desperate need. Her long, deep, slow thrusts were punctuated by a roll of the hips which made Clara grasp at the bed sheets.

"Make me come, make me come. I can't take it any longer," Clara said desperately.

Harry groaned in pleasure. That was all she needed to hear. Clara was a feisty, enthusiastic lover, and hearing her beg gave her almost as much pleasure as an orgasm.

Harry began to hasten her thrusts dramatically. They both groaned as they raced towards the edge. Harry pumped her hips into Clara a few more times until she heard the telltale sounds of Clara's impending orgasm and finally allowed herself to let go. She threw her head back and thrust all the frustrations of the day out into one long release.

They collapsed onto the bed and rolled apart, gasping for breath. There was no hugging or holding each other, that was not Harry's way, and those she met for casual sex knew the rules well. She had known Clara for the longest and she was the woman who could claim to be closer to Harry than the rest.

"That was inspired," Clara said, running a fingernail around the tattoo on Harry's biceps.

Harry was still regaining her breath but already thinking about making her way out the door. "I aim to please." She clutched at Clara's hand and pulled it away from her arm. "No touching, Clara. You know how this works."

"You're such a bore, Harry." Clara sat up in bed and lit a cigarette. "Not the usual way to spend the evening of one's father's funeral."

That was Harry's cue to go. She didn't want to talk any more than she had to about him, especially with Clara. She swung her legs over the side of the bed and stood, took off the strap-on she was wearing, and threw it on the bed.

"On the contrary. It is the perfect way to spend the evening after my bastard of a father's funeral. No one will miss him, least of all me."

She pulled on her boxers and the black suit trousers that she'd worn to the funeral, and gathered her white shirt and black tie.

"So? How does it feel to go from Lady Henrietta Knight, Professor of Archaeology at Cambridge, digging up your dusty Roman artefacts, to Countess of Axedale?" Clara asked.

Harry finished doing up her buttons and gave her a smile. "It feels wonderful to get my father's grubby hands off the estate before he destroyed it, but I will always be Dr. Knight. I'm only taking a year's sabbatical from Cambridge. Just enough time to get the estate back on its feet and restore the house to its former glory."

Harry put on her designer suit jacket, her tie still peeking out of her pocket.

"One whole year in the country," Clara said. "One whole year without your giggling students following you around, and falling into your bed. How will you cope, darling?"

"It's only Kent, Clara, not the back of beyond. I can come back to London to enjoy…some female company whenever I wish. In any case it's not much to give one year of my life to fulfil a promise to my grandfather. I restore the house and its grounds, and I know he will be looking down on me with a smile on his face."

"What about your mother?"

Harry gave an ironic laugh and picked up her watch from the bedside table. "My mother would dance on my father's grave if she could. She's released from all obligations now. She tells me she's going to Monaco to recover."

"Very nice."

She picked up her smartphone and was ready to go, but Clara reached out to touch her hand. "You fuck me and leave more quickly every time. I could feel used, you know."

Harry couldn't help but laugh. "Of course I use you, as you do me and all the other lovers you have."

Clara gave an exaggerated sigh. "Perhaps if I could cheer myself up with a little shopping, I wouldn't feel so used."

There it was. The real cost of no-strings sex with Clara. Harry took out her wallet. "How much?"

Clara put on her little-girl look that Harry suspected got her anything she wanted from most of the people she shared her bed with. "Well there's this darling little Chanel handbag at Harvey Nichols, but Daddy keeps telling me I need to stop spending so much. He's put a limit on my credit card."

Harry sighed and pulled some notes out of her wallet. "Just tell me how much. I'm driving down to Axedale Hall right now."

"Twelve hundred pounds? It's not that much really."

Harry threw some notes on the bed. "I don't carry that much cash. Here's three hundred, I'll transfer you the rest from my bank."

Clara grabbed the money and kissed it. "Thank you. You are the best, darling."

As Harry walked out of the door, Clara shouted, "Oh, and remember, when you're playing at being lord of the manor, don't get any maids from below stairs into trouble."

"Very funny."

It had been some time since Harry had driven down these long and winding country roads of Kent, heading towards the small village of Axedale. The late July sun filtering through the trees did make the rural scene beautiful, but the place of her birth filled her with such mixed emotions. It was where she'd spent time with her beloved grandfather, but also was home to the man she hated absolutely, the father she had buried today.

She looked into the driver's mirror of her Aston Martin and gave herself a smile. "He's gone, and Axedale Hall is mine."

Harry saw the entrance gates up ahead and turned off the road. She drove on for a few minutes through the large estate grounds before she saw the house come into view. She stopped the car and took off her sunglasses.

"Axedale Hall."

The large English Baroque country house looked dilapidated and unloved, but still had the same charm and beauty that her grandfather Henry had taught her to appreciate.

"I'll bring her back from the dead, Grandpa. You'll never know Father had his grubby mitts on the place."

CHAPTER TWO

Annie Brannigan stepped out of the taxi and gazed up at the huge and imposing Axedale Hall. Not only was the house large, but going by how long it took the taxi to arrive at the front door after entering the wrought-iron entrance gates, the estate must be vast.

The frontage was imposing to say the least. Two sets of stone steps led off from the left and right, up to the grand entrance. Six pillars supported a grand portico onto which the family crest was engraved, with a Latin inscription below it.

She had never worked as housekeeper in such a large home before, and even though she knew the owner only lived in one wing of the house at the moment, it was going to be a big undertaking.

"Wow, Mum. It's huge."

Annie looked down at her ten-year-old daughter with her beautiful honey-coloured hair so much like her own and smiled. "It is, sweetie."

As ever, Riley had a book in her hand, learning everything she could about everything they ever did together. She knew Riley hated moving schools because of her agency job, but she had been so excited at the prospect of living in this ancient playground, as she saw it.

"It says here that the Knight family came to England with the Norman invasion in 1066."

Annie pulled Riley in to her side for a hug. "Let's hope the current countess isn't as terrifying as them."

The taxi driver started to get their bags from the boot of the car.

"Oh, and guess what?" Riley said, nearly bursting with excitement.

Annie chuckled softly. "I can't wait to hear."

"The Romans were here…in Axedale. There's a Roman bathhouse we can visit."

Riley had always been fascinated by the Roman Empire, since she'd covered the topic at school—so different from other ten-year-old kids. From then on she'd devoured books on the subject. That's what made her daughter so special.

Annie paid the taxi and it drove off down the large drive leaving them standing at the bottom of the steps that led up to the front door. "You lift the smaller ones, Riley, and I'll come back for the bigger ones."

She struggled up the steps with a flight bag hanging around her neck and two heavy suitcases. She dropped them by the door and tried to get her breath back. Just then her attention was caught by a group of workmen standing around the bottom of a scaffold that extended down the east wing of the house. They were only a few hundred yards away and looking at some kind of plans while talking to another labourer sitting on the first level of scaffolding above them.

Annie was close enough to see she was a woman, and a tall, strong woman at that, wearing worn, ragged jeans, a T-shirt, and an equally well-worn baseball cap, with a black-ink tattoo on her right biceps. *She's gorgeous. I've got some eye candy at least.*

"Mum? Are you listening?"

"What? Sorry, sweetie." She looked up and saw that another workman in yellow jacket and hard hat had opened the front door. "Can I help you, miss?" he asked.

"Yes, I'm the countess's new housekeeper, Annie Brannigan, and this is my daughter Riley."

"Oh, that's right, Lady Harry did tell us to watch out for you. I'll take you down to the kitchen and tell the countess you're here. The indoor staff aren't working today."

When they walked into the entrance hall both she and Riley let out a gasp. The marble-pillared hall must have been about sixty feet wide, with Greco-Roman busts and statues inset to the walls at regular intervals around the room. At the far end of the room were archways which she presumed led to a grand staircase.

"This is so cool, Mum." Riley's voice echoed off the high ceiling. The wide-open space was too tempting for the ten-year-old, and she dropped her bag and set off at a run.

"Riley, be careful."

"It's okay, miss," the workman said, "it has a big effect on everyone when they first see it. I'm David, by the way, project manager of the refurbishment work."

Annie smiled and shook his hand. "Nice to meet you, David."

"You're going to have a huge job trying to get this place in order, Annie. There hasn't been a housekeeper here since I arrived, and the cleaners that come in from the village don't seem to keep the place too clean."

She looked around the huge room and saw, on second glance, that as magnificent as it all looked, it was extremely dirty. A thick blanket of dust and cobwebs covered the statues and decoration. "Well that's what I'm here for. Hard work doesn't frighten me."

Riley raced back to her side. "I love it here, Mum."

In all her postings, she had never seen Riley as excited as this. It looked like her stay here was going to be one big adventure.

David left the suitcases at the bottom of the main staircase and led them along a corridor and down stairs. "It's just down here."

She walked into the large kitchen. "Oh, my." She hadn't expected it to be tidy but the sight that greeted her was awful. It was a complete tip.

The workmen had been using it to make tea and heat up instant food snacks, pizzas, and other takeaway foods. The rubbish and endless stacks of dirty teacups strewn across the kitchen table and work surfaces were bad enough, but it looked like the kitchen hadn't been cleaned in fifty years. The floor was sticky and disgusting, and the cupboards that held the pots and tablewear were caked in dust.

"If you want to make a cuppa for yourself, I'll go and get the countess," David said before heading back upstairs.

Thanks but no thanks. She wouldn't have eaten or drunk a thing in this place but supposed the workmen were less discerning.

The kitchen was dominated by an enormous wooden table. Annie could imagine it would have been a hive of activity in the past, with cooks, maids, and footmen going back and forth with beautiful dishes of food and drinks.

She walked to the back of the kitchen and popped her head around a door there and discovered the scullery, where clothes would be washed, and further on through it looked like there was an adjoining boot room.

Riley came running over, practically bursting with delight. "Mum, I looked down the corridor outside the kitchen and found a butler's room and housekeeper's room. They have plaques on the doors. Can you imagine, you get your own special room?"

Excitement wasn't an emotion Annie was feeling at the moment. The sheer enormity of her task hit her full square in the face. This house was a relic from the past, a sleeping giant that took a great deal of staff to tackle, and now here she was, one woman taking it all on herself.

"This is going to be a hard job, Riley. Let's get started."

"Mum, I've found a cupboard with brushes and cleaning stuff, but there are cobwebs everywhere." Riley gesticulated wildly with her arms. "There might be a tarantula or something."

"Tarantula? Really?" Annie smiled and lowered a pile of dusty plates onto the kitchen table. "Well why don't you put all the rubbish in the bin for me then, and we'll get the other things out when we're settled." She looked down at the mess the plates had made of the front of her white blouse and black skirt and sighed. "Why didn't I get my apron first?"

She was sure it was in her holdall that sat just outside the kitchen. She walked quickly towards the door, smacked right into a tall, solid body coming through at the same time, and was knocked to the floor.

"Are you okay?" Riley rushed to her side.

Annie looked up and smiled when she saw the good-looking builder from outside. "You've swept me off my feet," Annie joked, but the woman above her did not crack a smile. In fact she looked rather annoyed.

"You need to be more careful—there's a lot of dangerous work going on here." She extended her hand and pulled Annie up.

The posh upper-class accent that came out of her mouth surprised Annie greatly, but even more shocking was the surly attitude she had. "It was just an accident. I'm waiting on the countess. Do you know if she's coming? I'm the new housekeeper."

The builder crossed her arms and looked at her with hard, steady grey eyes. "I am Henrietta Knight, Countess of Axedale, but I prefer to be called Harry."

Annie's stomach fell to her toes. She closed her eyes and prayed that when she opened them again, Lady Axedale—Harry?—would be gone, and she hadn't really smashed face first into her new employer.

She opened them and, sure enough, there was the countess. "Do excuse me, my lady. I had no idea who you were. I…"

How could she have been expected to spot a countess dressed up as a good-looking butch in worn jeans, muddy work boots, and baseball cap? It wasn't fair at all.

As her words died in her mouth, she felt Riley sneak to her side. "I…was going to get my apron out of my bag. It is a bit dusty in there."

"You'll have no need of it as you won't be staying," Harry said harshly.

"What do you mean? The agency—"

"I asked your agency for a live-in housekeeper, not a family. If you'll just get your things together and ready to leave, I'll telephone your agency to ask for a replacement, and I'm sure they'll give you another assignment."

Annie was shocked. She'd worked for some bad-tempered, surly clients, but no one had ever had this reaction to her and Riley before.

"Lady Axedale…"

"It's Harry. I already told you."

Annie was getting angry now. "There's no need for rudeness, Harry. My daughter is ten years old and is no bother to anyone. She can sleep in my room if you can't spare another."

"It is not a question of space. We have many and precious artefacts and antiques around Axedale Hall. It is not the place for a child. I'm sure your agency will find you a more suitable post. You may stay here until I contact them."

Harry turned and marched away to make the phone call.

"Please?" Annie called after her.

But the countess didn't turn around.

"Mum? What are we going to do? She doesn't want us here. I've left my old school and everything. Tell her I won't touch anything, I promise."

Annie held her daughter tight and kissed her softly on the head. "Don't worry, I'll sort it out. I always do."

This was not her usual reception. As one of the most sought after housekeepers on the agency's books, her employers were usually happy to retain her services. If she and Riley stayed, the Countess of Axedale was going to be a difficult woman to subdue.

CHAPTER THREE

Harry sat at her ornate wooden desk in her wood-panelled study getting increasingly frustrated with every passing second as she spoke with Annie's agency on the phone.

"That is not acceptable, Mrs. Hendry. I'm refurbishing one of England's oldest stately homes, a home with priceless artwork, artefacts, period features, and you send me a woman with a ten-year-old to run amok amongst them?"

"I can assure you, Lady Axedale, we've never had any complaints about Ms. Brannigan or her daughter, and in fact she is the most popular housekeeper we have. There's usually a waiting list for her services."

Harry sighed. "That may be, but Ms. Brannigan is entirely unsuitable for my home and my life. I value my privacy and a child running around the place would be inconvenient."

"If that is your wish, m'lady. I could have a replacement for you in…eight to ten weeks."

"Eight to ten weeks? You must have someone available before then?"

"I'm sorry, Lady Axedale, but all our staff have placements at the moment. Ms. Brannigan had just become available again and that's why we were able to send her at short notice."

Harry let her head fall back against her leather chair, pulled off her trusty baseball cap, and threw it on the desk. The east wing of the house, the wing she lived in, had become a complete mess.

It wasn't pleasant to work hard all day in the grime and mess of the refurbishment area, and return to equally messy living quarters. The two women who came in from the village to clean were far from experienced and didn't seem to be able to cope with the work needed. A live-in housekeeper was essential.

Mrs. Hendry punctuated the silence by saying, "You are free to try a different agency of course, but I doubt you will find one with such a good reputation and discreet workers."

Harry thought of her most prized possession, a Roman sword bought from an antiquities dealer by her grandfather, which sat pride of place in the centre of the library, vulnerable to a child's hands. And she thought of her need for clean clothes and food every day. Having never done her own laundry or cooking in her whole life before, she'd had many accidents while trying to take care of herself.

The decision was made. "Well it seems as if I have no choice, Mrs. Hendry, but I will be giving them strict rules for staying in the house, and I want you to contact me as soon as you have a replacement." Harry ended the call and threw her smartphone on the desk. She hated to be forced into anything in her life, but what choice did she have?

"A bloody child? Well, Ms. Brannigan, you'd better keep her under control or there will be trouble."

Annie struggled to keep up as Harry marched ahead of them up the ornate staircase to the back of the magnificent entrance hall. The marble theme continued with a few evenly spaced alcoves housing similar Greco-Roman statues, and four finely upholstered chairs at the half landing area.

She must be strong, thought Annie. She took a breath at the landing while Harry continued to climb effortlessly with two of their heaviest cases. At least she would get fitter in her new role.

But the most important thing was that she and Riley were allowed to stay. Annie had no idea what Mrs. Hendry had said to Harry, but when she returned and said they could stay for the time being, she made a promise to give Mrs. Hendry a hug the next time she saw her.

As they trudged up the stairs, Harry barked out orders like a sergeant major. "Your daughter is not to touch anything. Any breakages will come out of your wages. You both may feel free to use the grounds as you will, but do not distract or talk to my refurbishment team. They have a great deal of work to do and only a year to accomplish it."

Harry came to a stop between two bedroom doors. She dropped the cases unceremoniously and said, "These will be your rooms. The servants' quarters in the west wing are not refurbished as yet, so you'll need to make do with these two family rooms. I will warn you, they are neither clean nor are the beds made, so you will have to take care of that."

Riley took hold of Annie's hand clearly needing a bit of reassurance. Harry opened the door on the right and pointed in, "This will be your room, Ms. Brannigan…or is it Mrs.?"

"Ms.," Annie said pointedly. She was sure she could see a ripple of interest or amusement in Harry's eyes at that response. She clearly liked to be challenged, but Annie was sure few ever did.

"Of course, *Ms.* Brannigan. This is the green bedroom."

Annie could feel Riley squeeze her tighter in repose to the tension in the air. She peeked into the room and saw the most beautiful old oak four-poster bed, with green drapes embroidered with gold and light green walls with beautiful painted birds and trees. It was a bright, open room, and she could only imagine what the view from the window was like.

"It's a lovely room, thank you." She smiled, but Harry's face remained stern.

"Your room has a connecting door through to your daughter's room on the left."

It irritated Annie that Harry couldn't even return a smile. Even if she wasn't pleased with them being in her house, she could at least display some manners. "And where is your bedroom, Harry?"

Harry stood up straighter and asked in a higher pitched voice, "My bedroom?"

"Yes, of course. How else do you expect me to pick up your laundry and change your bed?"

Annie was sure she was onto something when she saw Harry search her face questioningly. Her employer couldn't work her out by the looks of it, and Annie liked it just like that.

But instead of a sharp retort, Harry pointed to the end of the hallway, and said in a compliant voice, "It's just down at the end."

"Wonderful. You can leave us to settle in then. Was there anything else you wished to tell us? Any other rules or…?"

Harry looked confused. She had lost control of the conversation and wasn't quite sure how to respond by the looks of it.

Annie had worked with all sorts of challenging clients, aristocrats like Harry, pop stars, movie stars, business people, and politicians, but she had always managed to find a way of making them calmer and more malleable. That was why she was the best at what she did, and the most popular and most sought after employee with her agency.

Mrs. Hendry said she should have been a psychologist instead of a housekeeper, but she had simply always been good at reading people's emotions, and it came in handy.

"I'll go and rejoin my refurb team and…leave you to it," Harry said gruffly.

As Annie watched her walk away she thought, *I'll work out how you tick, Henrietta, Countess of Axedale and have you house-trained in no time.*

"Come on, sweetie," she said to Riley. "Let's get ourselves settled."

Riley sat on her bed and held her head in her hands. She always felt sad when her mother started a new assignment and she had to leave friends she had only just made at school, but this time she had consoled herself that this new place would be exciting.

She loved history and reading about it, and thought she would have lots of fun exploring the house and the grounds. Instead she couldn't wait to leave. The countess was scary and didn't want her here, and wouldn't even look at her.

She stood up and went for a look around her new quarters. It was a grand room with yellow, gold, and white striped wallpaper, with a few landscape paintings hanging on the walls. The bed was a smaller version of the one in her mother's room, except colour-coordinated with the yellow walls, and a marble fireplace was a main feature of the room.

In the corner of the room, there was a desk, shelving, and a bookcase, and a large cork noticeboard on the wall. On the noticeboard were a few posters of Roman-themed films and gladiators from computer games. There were lots of history books on the shelves—more particularly, Roman history. Then she spotted something really interesting on the desk. She picked up a folder with plastic sleeves and little pockets. "This is amazing."

The pockets were full of coins, old worn coins. It was difficult to tell what period they were from as they were so worn, but on a few she could see an emperor with a crown of laurel leaves. *Roman, they've got to be.*

Whoever stayed in this room loved Roman history, just as she did. As she flicked through the pockets of coins, she could hear the countess's words ringing in her ears: *Do not let your child touch anything.*

With a sigh she put down the plastic folder and went back to sit on the bed. The last thing she wanted was to get her mum into trouble.

The connecting door to her mother's room opened and she came in. "How is your room, sweetie?"

Riley looked down at her toes and just shrugged.

Annie hurried over and knelt down beside her. "Riley? What's wrong?"

She needn't have asked. Deep down, Annie knew what the problem was.

Every time they had to move, she felt more and more guilty. She had joined the housekeeping agency five years ago, and in that time, they'd had to move once, sometimes twice a year, and every time Riley had to leave school friends and make new ones, which she had found more and more difficult as she got older. Annie knew from her conversations with Riley's teachers that she was becoming increasingly isolated, not fitting in with the already formed groups of friends. Over the last year or so, she'd started to not even try to make friends.

Annie's logical mind told her that she had no choice, that this was the best life she could provide her daughter. By serving the rich and sometimes famous clients her agency dealt with, Riley got to live in safe, affluent areas, and attend better schools, better than Annie'd ever had when she was young.

And that's what drove her, to give Riley everything she never had.

"I know it's always hard to move somewhere new."

"She hates me, hates kids. How can we stay here, Mum?" Riley said angrily as the tears spilled from her eyes.

Annie sighed. How could she explain to a child that their way of life was so much better than the alternative? She cupped Riley's cheek and used her thumb to wipe away her tears. "Lady Harry doesn't hate you. She's just not used to being around children. She'll come around. I promise."

Riley looked up at her with wide hopeful eyes. "You think so, Mum?"

"I know so." She stroked her daughter's cheek. "You are such an adorable girl, she'll have no choice but to like you. Now why don't you get your suitcase open and I'll get some clothes hangers from the wardrobe."

Annie breathed a sigh of relief when Riley gave her a small smile and got up to empty her case. She stood and surveyed the room. It was a bigger bedroom than Riley was used to. The decoration was grand, as in her room, but there were a lot of books in the bookcase that she was sure Riley would enjoy—although the film posters seemed out of place.

I wonder whose room this was? "Did you see all the books, Riley? Someone likes Roman history like you."

"Yeah, and there's a coin collection in a folder over there. I only looked quickly, I know Lady Harry doesn't want to me to touch anything."

She smiled and gave Riley's short ponytail a tug. "Relax, sweetie. Don't worry."

Riley handed her some shirts and jeans, and said, "Mum, on TV, big houses like this usually have great libraries. Do you think she might let me use hers?"

"I'm sure. I'll ask her if she stops scowling long enough," she joked. "I'm sure it'll be fine."

Riley gave her a huge hug. "Thanks, Mum."

When Riley went back to unpacking, Annie opened the wardrobe and was surprised to find posters of glamour models, actresses, and pop stars tacked to the inside of the doors.

Annie chuckled to herself. *Aha. We have someone who likes Roman history but loves to look at beautiful women...*

CHAPTER FOUR

Harry sat at her desk typing on her laptop with various texts by her side. As much as she enjoyed the hard manual work of restoring her family home during the day, she loved getting time to herself at night to work on her first love, Roman history.

During her yearlong sabbatical from Cambridge, she had committed to writing her second book on the Roman occupation of Britain. Excavating new Roman sites both here and abroad was what she loved best, but researching and writing was a nice change of pace.

There was a knock at her study door. "Come in," she called out.

The oak door creaked as it slowly opened and Ms. Brannigan walked in. "Could I have a word, Harry?"

Harry sat back in her seat, confident and relaxed. She always liked to make it clear who was in control. "Of course, Ms. Brannigan. You may sit."

"I prefer to stand, thank you," Annie said with an equally confident smile.

Something inside Harry jarred, and her self-assurance was disrupted for a second or two. This was happening each time she spoke to Annie, and she didn't like it. This was not how her game was played, especially with women. She could always have them eating out of her hand with a few words or even a look. And she knew how people reacted to her. Men were intimidated or impressed by her intelligence and station in life, and women were putty in her hands with her looks and charm, and commanding attitude. Clearly with Ms. Brannigan she would have to try another angle.

She crossed her legs nonchalantly and simply looked at Annie, hoping her silent gaze would unnerve her. Her eyes caressed Annie's curves, which she could see despite the slightly unflattering shape of the black tunic she wore on top, with white collar and edging. That along with her sensible black skirt and ballet flats were weirdly sexy on Annie, but the only jewellery she wore were a pair of gold stud earrings and a crucifix around her elegant throat.

Annie was a beautiful woman. Not like the glamorous women she normally mixed with. No, she had a simple, natural beauty, but there was something else about her that made her ever more attractive. Harry couldn't work out what it was, but what most unsettled her were Annie's eyes. She held her gaze with confidence, not with a penetrating stare like her own, but with an open warmth that made her feel emotionally naked and defenceless.

Harry knew she would have to up her game, because apart from being an archaeologist and a Romanist, women were her specialist subject, and Ms. Brannigan, a little different from the usual aged housekeepers, was not going to get the upper hand with her.

Annie lifted her notepad and pen and said, "I wanted to find out your daily routine, your likes and dislikes—"

"Where is your child?" Harry said sharply.

"Her name is Riley, and she's unpacking her things."

"Riley? A strange name for a girl, isn't it?"

"Oh? Do you think so, *Harry*?"

Harry couldn't help but smile at that reply. It was clear she was going to enjoy these verbal tussles between them. "Point taken. To answer your question, I have simple tastes, Ms. Brannigan, but I like things done well and to my specifications. Why don't we walk while we talk? I was remiss in showing you around."

Harry walked over to open the door and indicated for Annie to go first. "Shall we?"

"If you want. Call me Annie, by the way."

"Annie?" She tested out the name and liked the way it sounded. "Come this way, Annie."

❖

"My father lived his last years in the east wing, so it didn't need too much attention except to check the electrics and central heating system. I had that done before I arrived at Axedale. The rest is just cleaning and cosmetic."

Annie had difficulty keeping up with Harry's long stride but was determined not to show it. Their footsteps echoed on the old wooden flooring as they walked down the corridor leading from Harry's office, which she guessed led to the vast marble entrance.

"We've painted here and there, and polished the floors. Nothing too drastic."

The house might have been a bit dusty and dirty but the decor did look beautiful. The walls of the corridor were decorated in period red wallpaper embossed with gold to match the gold-painted cornicing.

"It looks like you've done a great job."

Annie's heavy breathing must have caught Harry's attention because she slowed until she was by Annie's side.

"You're going to have to get those little legs of yours fitter to work here." Harry gave her a smug smile that aggravated Annie no end.

"I'm fit enough to take care of anything you might need me to, believe me."

She saw whatever witty retort was forming in Harry's head die away after that reply and her trademarked serious facial expression returned.

They arrived in the vast entrance hall and Harry stopped in the middle of the space. "This is what I'm most proud of, I think. It's the most impressive part of the house, and a gateway to all the other rooms."

Annie looked around with the same awe as she had when she first walked in. "It is truly stunning. Did you have a lot of work to do in this part?"

"No, this part my father actually did keep in good repair, since it was the main entrance to the house. Now, you have two maids that come in from the village twice a week to help you with the cleaning, and of course as more of the house opens up, I will have to engage more staff to work with you—if you're still here and I find your work satisfactory of course."

"And if I find your employment satisfactory. I haven't said I'll stay yet," Annie said without missing a beat.

"You're awfully confident for a housekeeper under my employ."

"I'm confident in my work and its worth. I can turn this house around and make it a home, if I'm allowed to."

Harry scowled and took a step into her personal space. "I don't want a home. I want to discharge a promise to my grandfather to restore the house to its former glory and return to my teaching post at Cambridge."

"Everyone needs a home, Harry, no matter where life takes them."

"And where is your home, Annie?"

"My home is with Riley. We don't have a place to call home yet, but we will…one day."

Harry walked on and led her around all the rooms that she would be taking care of, and she began to see the enormity of the job. There was so much to do, and when she met the staff from the village they would need to come up with a plan of action.

She was led down a stone staircase to a lower part of the house. "At the end of the corridor is the poolroom. It's still having some cosmetic repair but it won't take long."

They walked through a stone archway at the end of the corridor and Annie gasped. The swimming pool was empty of water at the moment, but that didn't diminish the room. It gave the impression that you had stepped into a cave hewn from the bedrock below the house. "This is beautiful."

"Thank you. My grandfather had it designed to resemble a Roman bathhouse. It's always been one of my favourite rooms."

She could see why. The pillared walls were covered in Roman mosaic tiles with depictions of gods and goddesses that she couldn't identify. "Are these gods?"

Harry leaned back against one of the pillars and crossed her arms. "Yes, the female is the Romano-British water goddess Sulis

Minerva. The Romans already had their own water goddess Minerva when they arrived, and the Celts had Sulis. So instead of imposing a new goddess on a conquered populace, they put the two together to embody both cultures in one."

Annie looked at Harry and smiled. "Clever."

Harry pushed away from the pillar and stalked towards her with a smoky look in her eyes. "The Romans were always clever. They came, they saw, and they conquered, but they had one final trick up their sleeve."

She was standing just a step too far into Annie's personal space, and she could see that Harry would be a difficult person to resist if you interested her.

"Oh? What was that?"

Her heart started to thud when Harry reached out and touched her crucifix. She then trailed her finger down to the first button of her tunic, and then used an open hand to stroke the side of her face. "Hearts and minds, Annie. If you win someone's heart and mind, you can get them to do anything." Harry's voice was thick with sexual innuendo, but Annie was determined to remain cool.

"Some people aren't that easily swayed."

The tension between them broke when Harry laughed at her words. "In my experience, most people are, but we can agree to disagree." She took a few steps back and pointed up. "If you'll look up to the ceiling you'll see a painting depicting the birth of Venus from an oyster shell. It's a stunning view when you are floating on your back in the water."

Annie laughed softly. "I can imagine."

"It shouldn't be long till it's finished. Feel free to use it—your daughter too of course."

"Thank you." Riley would love to swim down here.

"Shall we?" Harry indicated for her to go first, and all the way back upstairs she was sure she could feel Harry's eyes on her body.

They ended the tour in the kitchen, and Annie got her notepad to record Harry's daily routine. "What do you prefer for breakfast?"

"I don't eat breakfast. I require only that you bring me coffee in the morning at six thirty."

"You don't eat anything? How can you possibly work—?"

"That is all I require Annie, so please do as I say. At lunch I like something simple such as soup and bread," Harry said sharply.

Annie noted that down and asked, "And your team?"

"What about them?"

"What do your team do for lunch?"

Harry looked at her as if that was a stupid question. "I don't know. They bring food with them or walk to the village for food at the pub."

Annie realized there was a lot that needed to be done to make things right here and she was just the woman to do it. "What time would you like dinner served?"

"I don't need dinner, just a sandwich at seven o'clock with coffee"

"You want a sandwich for dinner?" Annie looked at Harry's sturdy, tall body and wondered how she could survive on what she ate daily.

"I'm researching and writing a book in the evenings, so I need something I can eat quickly. I find food a distraction in general that keeps me back from the tasks I need to accomplish."

She couldn't help but sigh at Harry's reply. It was clear that she was starved both physically and emotionally if she thought food was an inconvenience. It seemed as if her life was as run-down and full of cobwebs as the house she was trying to rescue.

"Very well. Do you have an account at the village shop?"

"Yes, of course. They do send a box of food every Friday. It has been enough for me alone, but I would guess you will require more."

"Yes, I saw the box of food in the kitchen, and yes, I will need more." The box had been full of junk food and loaves of bread, obviously for the countess's sandwich each evening. She didn't think she had come across such a poorly stocked kitchen or someone in such need of taking care of as Harry, in her five years of housekeeping.

"Is there anything else you think I need to know?"

"Yes, the vicar will be dining with me every Monday."

"I'll take care of that. Is there anything you don't like, foodwise?"

"No, I'll eat anything. As I said, food isn't really important to me. Oh, before I forget, you have use of a car. I'll get the keys for you."

Annie finished writing her notes and thought perhaps now was the time to ask about the library. "Could I have your permission for my daughter to use your library?"

Harry said nothing but looked at her intently. "Why would a ten-year-old be interested in the kinds of books I have in my library?"

"Riley is...well she's different from most girls her age. She isn't interested in pop bands or film stars, she loves reading everything—science books and encyclopaedias—and her favourite subject is history, especially Roman history. She will be so happy to lose herself in a library like yours."

Harry's expression was stony.

"Would that be all right?"

"I have precious artefacts on display in the library."

"I promise she won't touch anything. She's a good girl."

"It's strange," Harry said with a puzzled expression on her face.

"What?"

"I told you I was an archaeologist? I'm also a Romanist. I specialize in Roman history."

"That is a coincidence." Annie thought about Riley's room upstairs, and its interest in all things Roman but with the secret pictures of beautiful women. Could Harry have given Riley her own teenage room?

"You both may use it, but if she breaks anything..."

"Don't worry, I know, but it will just be Riley who uses it. I only read romance novels and I doubt you have many of those among your leather-bound volumes."

Harry's eyes narrowed. "You would be right. I don't have any nonsense like that in my library."

Annie decided not to respond to that remark. From the looks of it, the Countess of Axedale wouldn't know love if it came up and hit her in the face.

CHAPTER FIVE

Annie woke with a start to the sound of her alarm. She looked at the clock and breathed a long sigh. "Four o'clock on a Saturday morning."

She normally wouldn't rise before six, but she had a great deal of work to do to prepare for the coming week. All she could think about was that first cup of morning coffee, but she wouldn't get that until the kitchen was scrubbed clean. She got showered and dressed quickly into the agency uniform before opening the connecting door to check on Riley.

Riley was sleeping soundly, but had kicked off her blankets as usual. Annie crept into the room and tucked her back in tightly. "Sleep well, sweetie. You'll settle here. I promise."

Annie gave her a gentle kiss and walked back into her room. She picked up her faithful carrying case containing all her essential cleaning supplies.

"Well, Annie," she urged herself, as she began her first-day-of-work pep talk, "it's time to turn this dusty crumbing house into a home, whether Lady Harry likes it or not."

❖

Two hours later, the kitchen was unrecognizable. Annie had scrubbed almost every inch of it. All that was left to do were the large cabinets where the family china was kept and displayed.

Annie poured herself a coffee and stopped to admire what she had done so far. She hadn't worked as hard as this in a long time. Most of the households she worked in weren't in such a sorry state, but even though it was exhausting, it was satisfying.

As she drank her coffee she thought about talking to Harry last night. She was certainly a puzzle. She seemed to charge through life just expecting others to fall into place behind her, and you could almost feel the barriers she erected around herself. They were tough, strong and Annie would bet that after a lifetime of practice no one got behind them. Then there were times Harry had faltered and stumbled, when Annie gave as good as she got. In those moments she saw a chink in her armour, a vulnerability in her eyes that needed soothing, and then there was the Harry whose passion came out in spades when describing the history of the house and the refurbishments she was making.

She was a complex puzzle all right, but Annie was confident she would work her out.

The back door opened and an elderly man with white whiskers popped his head around the door. "Ms. Brannigan? We heard you were the new housekeeper and thought we'd come and introduce ourselves. "I'm Frank, the head gardener."

Annie smiled warmly. "Please come in and take a seat. Oh, and call me Annie."

"Thank you." He took off his cap and ushered the two men with him. "This is my son, Will, who's under gardener and young Davey here is stable lad and doubles up as coachman looking after Lady Harry's cars."

"Come in, come in and I'll put the kettle on."

The three men sat down, and Annie started to make tea. Frank's son was a strapping big boy who had a baby face and thick blond hair. Davey the stable boy had red hair, and pale skin that flushed whenever she looked in his direction.

"It's a long time since Axedale's had a housekeeper, and such a pretty one too," Frank said.

Annie chuckled. "I don't know about that." She brought over the teapot, mugs, and milk jug. "Here we are. Nice hot tea."

"Thank you, Annie," Will said.

She gave Davey a smile as she poured his tea, and his cheeks got redder. "Did Lady Harry's father have a housekeeper?"

"Yes," Frank said. "Old Mrs. Crane. She had been here for years, ruled this house with an iron fist in her heyday. She died about six months before the late Lord Axedale. She would have a fit if she saw us drinking in the kitchen."

"Why?"

"We're outdoors men," Davey blurted out.

"Outdoors staff wasn't allowed to take tea or meals inside the house," Frank said. "Lower rank than inside staff, you see."

Annie was astonished. She thought that kind of service went out a long time ago. "She didn't enforce that, did she?"

"Oh yes. She was a very old-fashioned woman. Her husband was butler but you would have never guessed he held higher rank with her around. The late Lord Axedale encouraged it. He liked to preserve the social hierarchy."

"I'm glad I wasn't around then. Does Lady Harry?"

"Oh no," Will replied. "Harry is one of the boys."

"Will, remember your manners," Frank warned his son.

"Sorry. Lady Harry."

It seemed her first impression was right. Harry was unlike any countess she had ever heard of.

"You must give me a tour of the gardens sometime, Frank. I love flowers, and I've always dreamed of having a garden of my own."

"We would be happy to, wouldn't we, Will?"

Will took a big slurp of tea and joked, "Yeah, and if you want to pitch in with a bit of weeding, that would be good too."

"It's a losing battle I'm afraid," Frank said. "Two gardeners can barely keep things ticking over. If the house was fully staffed there'd be a whole team of gardeners."

"I feel the same," Annie said. "It's overwhelming. A whole house to keep without a staff."

Frank and Will finished their tea and said, "We better get going. If you need any help, you know where we are."

❖

Harry headed out to meet with her project manager and his team. They normally met for a meeting about the day's work ahead, while the workmen got on with their tasks. On Saturdays the workmen finished earlier than usual, so time was of the essence. She took a sip of coffee from the travel mug Annie had brought her earlier. She had passed the first test. She could make a good cup of coffee.

Harry walked into the temporary office and found David already waiting for her, looking at the plans on his laptop. He stood when he saw her and said, "Good morning, Harry."

"Morning." She took a seat beside him and powered up her own laptop. "What's on the agenda today?"

"We have the plasterers hoping to finish the rooms in the west wing. Hopefully they can be dried to start decorating midweek." David said.

Harry scrolled her mouse along the 3D plans of Axedale on her computer screen. "Make sure you push them quite hard on that, David. The sooner they get done in the bedrooms they'll be needed in the ballroom and breakfast room."

"Absolutely. The stonemasons have still quite a bit to do on the roof. The weather has really held them back so far."

That was something she didn't want to hear. The stonemasons were needed all over the house and on some parts of the grounds, so if they were delayed it threw the whole schedule out. "Let's reassess where they are next week, and if they're still well behind we might need to look at getting more bodies in."

Something caught her eye out of the office window, and when she looked, she found Annie standing at the bottom of the scaffold with a tray of tea, handing out some food bags.

"What the bloody hell is that woman up to?"

David turned quickly. "It's Ms. Brannigan. That's kind of her."

Harry felt rage surge through her body. "Who does she think she is?" She leapt up and stomped out of the office.

Harry stormed back to the house and went down the kitchen stairs ready to give Annie a piece of her mind. They were on a tight schedule, and every hour mattered if she was to get back to her real job at Cambridge as soon as possible.

She burst into the kitchen and said, "Listen here, it is not—"

Harry's sharp words died in her throat with the scene that greeted her. Annie was on her hands and knees up on a large display cabinet putting away the dishes. Harry gulped hard and felt heat low in her stomach as her eyes caressed Annie's pert bottom in her tight black skirt, and her legs in sheer black tights. Not to mention the white maid's apron.

To make matters worse, Annie was gyrating her bottom and singing along with the song playing on the radio. Harry had walked in to find her fantasy playing out before her, and she couldn't do anything about it.

She was used to seeing the most stylish women on the London social scene in the most revealing of dresses, but nothing had turned her on like Annie Brannigan did in this moment.

"Can I help you, Harry?" Annie had caught her looking.

"Ah…yes…" She was desperately trying to remember why she'd come into the kitchen, and why she was angry.

"Can I get you something to eat or—"

Then she remembered. "No, I told you, I don't eat anything in the morning. I want to ask you why you've taken it upon yourself to serve tea and sandwiches to my refurb team."

"I'm sorry I didn't have anything more substantial than tea and some egg sandwiches for them, but I'll have more when I go shopping."

Harry's anger was back. There was a small part of her that felt like she was losing control of her own house, and she didn't like it.

"I told you last night that I don't want my refurb team distracted," Harry snapped.

"Could you at least help me down before you shout at me?" Annie said, holding out her hand.

Harry sighed and walked over to her. She put her hands around Annie's slim waist and said, "Jump. I'll catch you."

Annie looked unsure. "You won't drop me? I'm not good with heights."

"Of course I won't drop you, and you call this a height? I've dug bigger holes than this. Come on."

Annie gave a little jump and Harry held her tightly, allowing her to slide down her body. As Annie's body slid down hers, it left a trail of fire in its wake, especially when Annie's arms wrapped around her neck quite naturally, and her ample breasts pushed just below her own.

Harry's hands slid down to Annie's hips. They felt so good in her tight black skirt that she desperately wanted to go further and grasp a handful of that pert bottom. The hunger she felt in that moment shocked her with its intensity. She wanted to lift Annie up, place her on the table, open the buttons of her tunic, and expose the breasts that teased her so much.

They held there in that position, looking into each other's eyes for what seemed like minutes but was probably only seconds, before Annie closed her eyes, pushed away from Harry, and with a shaky voice said, "Food is not a distraction. In fact I think you'll find they will be much happier in their work, and more productive. Now if you're quite finished, I'll get on with *my* work."

Annie hurried off into the storeroom and left Harry standing alone. She took a deep breath and braced herself against the table. What had just happened? Her body was burning and hungry, and felt totally out of her control. That was not how she worked. She was able to keep firm control and command of her body and whomever she was with, no matter how beautiful or sexy they were, and now her body decided to betray her with one quite plainly dressed, but stunning in her simplicity, housekeeper who was off limits to her.

She shook her head to clear it, and looked around the kitchen. Everything had been cleaned, tidied, and polished. Light streamed in the windows, freshly cleaned and sparkling. Harry had never seen the kitchen in such good condition since she was a little girl. The kitchen felt warm, like home, and strangely comforting.

She didn't understand it, but something had shifted inside, something was different, and her subconscious was screaming, get out, get out now.

And so she did, as fast as possible.

Annie leaned back against the shelves in the storeroom, and let out a long breath. She held the crucifix that lay around her neck, hoping to bring calm to her heart hammering in her chest.

It had taken everything in her power not to react to Harry in the kitchen. She could tell almost from the start that Harry used sex and her obvious charm to control and get what she wanted—the problem was she was so hard to resist. She was incredibly good-looking and knew it.

Annie had never met anyone like her before. Someone who could make her skin feel hot with just a look. Passion was not something she was overly familiar with, and her new boss was the last person who should awaken it in her. Her one brief and unremarkable sexual encounter had not prepared her for this intense feeling of lust.

She had to remember the housekeeper's golden rule: never get involved with your employer.

It wasn't as if employers hadn't tried their luck with her before, they had. Something about having a woman in service to you seemed to fuel their fantasies, but she had never felt anything before. Not ever.

"Pull yourself together, Annie." She smoothed down her apron and, hoping she had hidden in here long enough, went back into the kitchen.

❖

The gargoyles that adorned the masonry on the roof of Axedale Hall, were awakening from their long slumber. After years of neglect, the moss and grime had been cleaned off the stone, and the masons got to work making repairs to them and the other stonework around them.

They used to terrify Harry as a child, but now she wanted to see them as they were meant to be.

"They're looking good, Lady Harry."

Harry knelt down on the high scaffold beside one of the stonemasons and smiled. "They are. They gave me nightmares as a child. I always said—"

"There she is!"

Harry was interrupted by some of the refurb team gibbering about someone while looking over the side of the scaffold.

She got up and looked over, and saw the object of the men's excitement. Annie, walking up the main drive with a shopping basket over her arm and holding Riley's hand with the other.

"What a beauty," one of the men said, and was met with general agreement from the others.

Annie was certainly winning over hearts and minds.

Harry thought back to her reaction to Annie in the kitchen, and she felt it again now as she gazed at her from high above. It wasn't just sexual arousal—that, she was used to. It was a feeling of hunger, and it disturbed her.

The stonemason whom she had been talking to got up and looked over beside her. "I wouldn't mind having her take care of me, Harry. She's gorgeous, and she can cook. Perfect woman."

The men around her weren't being rude as they watched Annie, but something inside Harry didn't like it. "Enough, back to work."

She watched Annie stride away with confidence and surety, and felt something subtle had changed in the atmosphere around Axedale Hall. In her world, whether in her department at Cambridge or her social life in London, she was always in complete control. There were never any surprises or anything else to shake her firm grip on her surroundings, but for the first time in a long, long time, she felt a little bit out of control of her life, and though she'd never admit it to anyone, the feeling was a little thrilling.

CHAPTER SIX

Annie and Riley walked down the hill from Axedale Hall towards the village. It had been a beautiful walk so far, and Riley was skipping along beside her full of excitement. For two city girls who were used to noise and pollution, the fresh air, the twittering of birds, and the rustle of the wind through the trees made the country an exciting wonderland.

Riley turned and walked backwards as she read from her local guide book to the area. "It says here that after helping to win the Battle of Hastings, as part of William the Conqueror's army, Harry's ancestors helped subdue the Saxon resistance throughout the country and in 1115 were granted these lands as reward. Wow— 1115 is like…a long time ago."

Annie smiled at her daughter's enthusiasm, "You're a mine of information, sweetie, but stop walking backwards or you'll end up on your backside."

Riley pulled in beside her. "Sorry, Mum, but it's exciting."

"I can see that." Annie pulled her to her side and kissed her head. Most kids were more excited about the clothes they wore or the gadgets they had than about living in an old village, but that's what made Riley so special. "So what happened then? Tell me more about Lady Harry's ancestors."

"Well, when they were given this land and the title of Baron Axedale, they built a small castle a few miles away, and you can still see the ruins." She looked up from the book. "That is so cool. We have to go and look at that, Mum, as well as the Roman bathhouse." Riley could hardly contain her enthusiasm.

"Of course we will. We have lots of exploring to do."

"Anyway, they moved to the site that Lady Harry's house is on now, and had a manor there until the Knight family were given their neighbour's earldom and lands, for loyalty to Henry Tudor after the battle against Richard III."

Annie laughed. "Oh my goodness. Sounds as if the Knight family were good at picking the winning side." She looked up ahead and the beginning of the village came into view. "Look, Riley."

A river ran through the village and up ahead was an old bridge that would allow them to cross safely.

"Cool." As soon as Riley saw the bridge she was off running.

"Don't go too far ahead, sweetie." As Annie approached the bridge and saw the start of the village up close, she sighed with contentment. What a beautiful, quaint little place it was, as if it had been lifted from the pages of an Agatha Christie novel, or one of the historical romances she read with regularity.

She could see a sign for the post office on a building on the other side of the bridge and further down a sign for The Witch's Tavern, an old-world pub with benches and picnic tables on the side of the river. A few yards down from the bridge, a group of eager swans and ducks were feeding on some bread thrown to them by a mum and little boy on the side of the bank. It was truly beautiful here. If she could only house-train the lord of the manor, then it would be a beautiful place to spend the next twelve months.

"Mum, hurry up. Let's play Poohsticks."

Annie laughed and hurried down to the bridge. *Winnie the Pooh* had always been her favourite children's story. Her grandmother had read it to her as a little girl and she did the same with Riley.

They each chose a racing stick, and held it ready to drop. "Okay," Annie said. "After three?"

Riley had a look of determination on her face. "One, two, two and a half…three."

Annie allowed Riley to drop her stick first and then they both raced to the other side and peered over.

"I see mine, Mum." Riley sounded thrilled.

"Well done, sweetie. You're too good at this."

They hadn't had the opportunity too often to play the silly game, living in the urban places they were used to, but it looked like the village of Axedale was giving them a chance to experience some of the simple things in life.

❖

By midmorning the roof repairs were going well so Harry decided to check in on the repairs in the west wing rooms. As she walked across the marble hallway, she heard her name called. She turned around and sighed when she saw Mrs. McRae by the front doors. Mrs. McRae was an elderly, conservative looking lady, with a bun piled on top her head and thick black glasses. She had been her father's social secretary, and Harry agreed to her staying on in that capacity. Harry had made clear she wouldn't take part in the usual social role as countess, but Mrs. McRae wouldn't let it go, continually haranguing her about one event or another.

"Lady Axedale? If I may."

Harry put on her best false smile and said, "How can I help you today, Mrs. McRae?"

"I have some invitations I would like you to consider, m'lady."

Harry crossed her arms defensively and watched Mrs. McRae search for the invitations in her handbag, dropping most of its contents on the floor.

"There's quite a lot coming up in the next few months, m'lady. It's an important time of year. There's the county flower show, the agricultural show, the charity gala, and of course the village winter festival."

Harry looked her straight in the eye and said simply, "No."

Mrs. McRae stopped dead and looked at her questioningly. "No? No to which one?"

"To them all. I told you when I arrived here that I wasn't interested in taking part in the social life of this county. "

"I thought that would just be until you got a chance to settle in."

"I will never settle in here. It's not my world." Cambridge was her world, a place where she ruled her own little kingdom. "Perhaps this will teach you to take my word as the truth."

Mrs. McRae was flapping, unsure of what to do next. "But it's your duty, m'lady."

That made Harry angry. How dare she be told what her duty was. "Mrs. McRae, let me explain something to you. The title of Dr. Knight will always mean more to me than Countess of Axedale. I'm here to discharge a promise to my grandfather and no more. Is that understood?"

Mrs. McRae said nothing but nodded. Harry walked away with lingering resentment. *I will not be trapped here.*

After Riley had beaten her fair and square at a few rounds of Poohsticks, they wandered down to the side of the river to look at the ducks and swans.

Annie closed her eyes and took a deep breath. She thought it truly beautiful here, and couldn't think of anywhere else she had ever felt so settled.

"Mum, Mum, look."

When she opened her eyes she saw Riley a few yards away standing at a strange looking wooden contraption by the side of the river. She caught up with Riley quickly, and saw that up close it was a rudimentary crane with a legless chair on the end. A plaque beside it said: *Witch's ducking stool.*

"My guidebook says they used it on scolds and witches. What's a scold, Mum?"

"A woman who speaks her own mind. I think I would have ended up in that chair."

Riley laughed and said, "There must have been a lot of witches in Axedale. Do you think they're still here?"

"I doubt it, and if there are, I'm sure they are just good white witches. Come on."

They walked up to the market square and in the centre was a small covered pavilion that served as bus stop—and horse stop, going by the looks of it. There were two horses with their riders there now, and the riders were allowing their mounts to drink from an old stone trough.

"Look, horses, Riley." Annie pointed up ahead.

Riley had a permanent smile on her face with each new thing they saw.

"There's the village shop." Riley indicated across the street.

"It's like a shop from a chocolate box."

They walked through the door and a bell rang. It was as if they had stepped back in time.

Annie couldn't imagine that Axedale was supplied from this little quaint shop. All the food and other products were kept on shelves behind the counter, along with a whole wall of sweets in glass jars. Riley would love them.

"Can I go and look at the magazines?"

"Okay, but don't leave the shop." The woman behind the counter—the postmistress, according to an official-looking badge she wore—was talking to someone who would have looked more at home back in London. She had on a black leather biker jacket, a figure-hugging black skirt, and a pair of the highest chic designer heels she had ever seen. She didn't seem to fit the country village mould at all.

Annie took a breath. Time to meet the locals.

As she approached the counter the postmistress looked over the leather-jacketed woman's shoulder and gave Annie a big smile. "Hello, my dear. Can I help you?"

"Yes, I hope you can. I wondered if Axedale Hall gets its food and supplies from here."

"Oh no. We only carry some day-to-day essentials. The supermarket a few miles away handles Axedale. Well, I say supermarket, it's really just a large grocer's." The shopkeeper's eyes darted towards the other woman, who was now leafing through the local newspaper.

Annie sighed. She would need to walk back and get the car. "Thanks. I'm just trying to find my way around."

"Are you new here?"

"Yes, I've just moved here with my daughter." Annie pointed over to Riley who had her nose buried in some magazine or another. "I'm the new housekeeper at Axedale Hall."

"Oh, my. Her ladyship has someone to take care of the place at last, Vicar."

Annie wondered who on earth she was talking to. There was no vicar here.

Then the leather-jacketed woman put down her newspaper and turned to face her.

She couldn't believe it. The woman was wearing a vicar's dog collar under her biker jacket.

"So it would seem," the woman replied, "Well, well. You will certainly brighten up Axedale, Ms....?" The unconventional vicar held out her hand.

Annie was lost for words for a second. Not only was the vicar strikingly beautiful, with her perfectly styled bobbed hairstyle and bright red lipstick that matched her nail polish, but she felt herself being openly appraised, not in a way that made her feel uncomfortable, but not how you would expect a vicar to look at a woman.

"Brannigan. Annie Brannigan."

"Delighted to meet you, Annie. I'm Bridget Claremont, but everyone calls me Bridge, and this is Mrs. Peters, our indomitable postmistress and chairwoman of the local women's guild."

"It's lovely to meet you both." Annie pointed over to Riley. "And that is my daughter Riley over by the magazines."

Mrs. Peters came from behind the counter, "I bet she'd love some sweets. Would that be all right, Annie?"

"Of course. Thank you."

Annie watched as Mrs. Peters walked over to Riley, put her arm around her, and guided her over to the vast array of glass jars with old-fashioned sweets.

"She loves children," Bridget said. "She and her husband were never blessed with any themselves, so they are now grandparents to every child in the village."

"That's wonderful. It really is like stepping back in time, coming here."

"Where are you from, if you don't mind me asking?" Bridget asked.

"Of course not. I'm originally from London, but I've moved around a lot for the last five years. Cities mostly, nothing like this."

"A city girl like myself. I think you'll find life here runs at a much slower pace. It can take some getting used to for some," Bridget said.

"I like it already."

"And how are you getting on with our Lady Harry?"

Annie pursed her lips and considered her words carefully. "I would say we are currently testing each other's boundaries, but it will soon settle down I'm sure."

Bridget laughed. "A very diplomatic answer. I'll look forward to seeing you both together on Monday at dinner. She may seem bad tempered, and to tell the truth she is, and quite controlling in her way, but she couldn't be kinder to those she cares for."

The vicar seemed to know Harry better than most. "How long have you known the countess, Bridget?"

"We went to boarding school together. The fearsome, young Lady Harry rescued me from a group of bullies, and the rest is history. That's why I became vicar here. The late earl was friendly with my father and offered me the parish when it became available."

"She has one friend here at least then?"

"Oh yes, but do you think that encourages her to use her family bench at church on Sundays?"

"I would guess no." Annie watched as Bridget's eyes travelled down her neck and lingered on her throat. She automatically moved her hand to her crucifix.

"You'd be right. I see you're a Catholic."

"My grandmother brought me up as a Catholic, but I haven't been practising for a long time. Faith still brings me comfort though."

"As it should. God never forgets us, even if life pulls us away from him. I hope you will come to church on Sundays. All denominations are welcome in my church, plus it will give your daughter a chance to make friends with some of the village children, before school starts again in September."

Annie smiled. It seemed surreal but refreshing to be talking to such an unusual woman of God. "We would love to, but I can't come tomorrow—there's just so much work to do up at the house to make it liveable. But I should have cleared my feet by next weekend."

So much work and a countess to tame.

❖

Annie took her last cake from the oven and set it on the kitchen table to cool. After a day of cleaning yesterday, today was baking day. She had been busy baking from the crack of dawn, and now the table was groaning with scones, small and large cakes, cookies, and freshly baked bread. A day's baking was always one of her first tasks when starting a new position. To Annie, a home wasn't a home without the smell of warm bread and the comforting feeling of knowing that the cupboards were full of tasty treats to feed a family.

Just then Riley came bouncing though the door. "Hey, Mum. Can I have some juice?" Her eyes went huge when she saw the table. "Baking day? *Yes.*"

"Take a seat, sweetie." She took a bottle of orange from the fridge and poured out a glass. "So? Have you had fun outside?"

"Lots. I'm going back out in a minute. I found this book in the library, about the estate, and it says that there's been lots of Roman finds on it before, and there might be a Roman building underneath Axedale Hall. Can you imagine, Mum? So I've been field walking, and look what I've found." Riley fished into her pocket and pulled out a few square blocks of plaster. "They are bits of mosaic floor, I think."

"You're the expert in this family. That's wonderful, sweetie." It filled Annie's heart with warmth to see Riley so happy and excited. The Axedale estate was fast becoming some version of Disneyland to her daughter. She only hoped she could make some friends when she started school. She was too isolated.

Riley gulped down her juice, and reached for a cake. "Can I?"

"Yes, and take a cookie for later."

"Thanks." With that she sped back outside.

This was the kind of small village life that she had dreamed of when she'd had Riley. A place where she could run and play outside safely. Something she could have never done in the city.

Now if she could pacify her ladyship, and try not to want to kiss her every time Harry looked at her with those brooding eyes, Annie and Riley could perhaps enjoy their time here.

Annie made a cup of tea and cut a slice of Victoria sponge cake. "Let's see if you have a sweet tooth, Lady Harry."

❖

Harry was in her study deeply engrossed in the research for her new book. Her desk was covered with thick tomes. Each had numerous Post-it notes peeking out from the pages.

She lifted one book and thumbed through the musty pages. Although a lot of her research could be done from online resources, there were some books that could only be viewed in their original hardback form and a few that had to be specially ordered, they were so rare.

As she found the particular chapter she was looking for, she sat back in her seat and let out a long sigh as she let go of tension she didn't know she was holding. There was something about the solitary pursuit of reading that made her content. The musty smell from the pages took her back to days spent with her grandfather wandering around their own library or the British Library in London searching for one book or another.

Happy days, Harry thought.

She took a pencil that had been resting behind her ear and began to take notes as she read down the page. Then something moving past the window caught her gaze. She looked up and saw Riley walking back and forth in front of her study window.

"What is she doing?" Harry got up and walked to the window to get a closer look. She was sure the girl was holding a book from her library. Every so often she would stop and pick something up. "Strange child."

There was a knock at her study door. "Come."

Annie walked in with a cup of tea and cake. "Harry, I thought you would like a cup of tea."

Harry walked over to her desk and sat on the front edge. "Did I ring for tea?"

"No."

"Well, why bother me?"

Undeterred Annie walked over to her and set the teacup down. "I thought you would like to taste freshly made cake. I've been baking all morning."

"Isn't this supposed to be your day off?" They had agreed that Annie would have every Sunday off. Harry crossed her arms defensively. She couldn't help but eye the cake greedily.

"Well I've only just started, it seemed silly to start with a day off, and in any case, I love to bake. I'm never quite settled in my surroundings unless I have lots of fresh bread and cakes."

Harry looked at Annie silently, searching for any signs that her penetrating stare unnerved her, but it didn't seem to. It appeared that Annie was quite immune to all her normal methods of gaining the upper hand.

"Will you try the cake? It will be worth your while."

Annie held out the plate like the snare to bait a trap, and Harry found herself taking it. She ate a piece with the cake fork and immediately wanted another. It was delicious. It reminded her of the cakes Cook used to make when she was a little girl.

"I wanted to talk to you about the washing machine and tumble dryer. You really need to get new ones—that is, if you want well-laundered clothes."

Harry placed the plate down on the desk, and reached out and traced a finger down Annie's cheek. She felt her shiver. "What a frightening woman you are, Ms. Brannigan. You stalk these halls with your cleaning tools like weapons, creating order out of chaos, and bribing your enemies with tea and cakes."

"Is that what you think I'm doing? Bribing you?" Annie said.

To Harry the air was thick with tension, sexual tension, pulling Annie to her.

"I'm not sure…yet."

Annie smoothed down her apron. "So? May I replace the appliances?"

Harry held her gaze for a few seconds, then went to sit behind the desk. "Order what you need and I'll give you my credit card."

"Thank you."

"Hmm." Harry looked out of the window. "Can you tell me what your daughter is up to, walking up and down?"

"She's field walking, looking for Roman artefacts. She found a book in your library saying that there are a lot of Roman sites in this area."

Harry remembered doing the very same as a child. She'd combed the grounds staring at the soil and earth, looking for anything remotely Roman. She could still feel the excitement of pulling her first Roman coin out of the ground.

Grandpa! Grandpa! Look what I've found.

Her grandpa had lifted her and swung her around before hugging her tightly. When he'd died not long after, she had no family left that gave her the warmth and love she craved.

Riley was different. She had Annie, and Annie radiated warmth and love. The kind that drew you in like a beacon, and that was not something she wanted to contemplate.

"There are, but she won't find much there," Harry said dismissively.

"Funny then, she's found pieces of mosaic tile."

CHAPTER SEVEN

B loody infuriating woman," Harry grumbled as she walked around the well-stocked wine cellar.

It was Monday and a new work week for the refurbishment of Axedale Hall. She had three teams working on the house today, one finishing off the roof, the second making repairs in the pool room, and one making a start on the once magnificent ballroom. They were rushed off their feet with work, and yet downed tools with regularity to partake of Ms. Brannigan's breakfasts, tea, coffee, and cakes at break time. What could she do but allow it, or it would seem as if she had lost control of her own staff.

Harry pulled out a bottle of red wine, looked at the label without really taking it in, and moved on to the whites.

"Then to top it all her child is running around the estate like it's a playground."

At least tonight she could have some normal conversation with the vicar.

Harry picked a white wine and walked upstairs. She strode across the hall on her way to the kitchen. As she got closer, she heard Annie and Riley singing along to a song on the radio. She was stopped in her tracks when the happy laughter and smell of dinner cooking filled her senses.

It triggered a memory, a memory she had tried to forget. A little girl ran past her, covering her ears and crying. She ran down into the kitchen and straight into the arms of the cook.

Cook lifted the little girl in her arms and set her on the table. "What's wrong, Lady Harry?"

Little Lady Harry had big fat tears rolling down her red cheeks. "They're arguing again, Mrs. Castle. Papa is shouting and Mama is crying."

Mrs. Castle and the kitchen maid exchanged a look. "Don't you worry about them," Mrs. Castle said. "Jessie, I think this big girl needs some apple pie and ice cream to dry her tears."

"Yes, right away, Mrs. Castle."

Harry watched the little girl eat her ice cream, and receive hugs from her cook, and remembered how much she'd needed the warmth and love of the kitchen staff, especially Mrs. Castle.

A warm voice brought her back to the present, and she saw Annie instead of Mrs. Castle standing beside Riley, who was polishing cutlery at the kitchen table.

"Is everything all right, Harry?" Annie said.

Harry slipped seamlessly back into her cool and together persona. "Of course. I have the wine for tonight. If you could put the white in to chill, I'll decant the red."

"Of course." Annie took the white and placed it in the fridge.

The aroma in the kitchen was wonderful. Whatever Annie was making smelled delightful. "What's for dinner?"

"Boeuf bourguignon, garlic mashed potato, and green beans. Do you think the vicar will enjoy that?" Annie said with a smile.

Harry's mouth immediately started to water and her stomach grumbled. She was so used to grabbing sandwiches, slices of pizza, and instant meals when she could, she had forgotten what a joy a home-cooked meal could be. It wasn't just the food. It was the aroma that filled the house, the physical warmth from the cast-iron range, matched by the emotional warmth she felt at being taken care of. The only place she had felt that before was in this very room, bestowed by the kitchen staff who gave her the love and safety that she should have received from her parents, and now it was happening again.

That warm feeling she felt as a child was building up slowly, and threatened to spread throughout all the cold places inside of her.

Harry cleared her throat and said, "Yes, I'm sure she'll love it."

She held Annie's gaze for longer than she should have. There was something in Annie that was pulling her closer, as if she was out in the cold and Annie was the warmth drawing her in close. Again a little voice inside told her to run, to get out of the situation that was all too cosy.

She paced over to the other side of the kitchen, and from the cupboard above she took out a candle, a crystal decanter, a mini bottle of wine, and a corkscrew. As she arranged them, she heard whispering behind her.

Harry turned around and raised an eyebrow towards Annie who was listening to her daughter's whispered question.

"Riley wants to know what you're doing. She thinks it's some kind of magic trick."

She looked at the collection of objects before her and smiled. To a child it must look a bit strange.

"It's no trick. Come and I'll show you," Harry said.

Riley looked worriedly back and forth from her mother to Harry, but with a slight push of encouragement from Annie she walked over.

Harry frowned inwardly. Riley was wary of her. She supposed that was her fault for barely even acknowledging her presence since she arrived, but a woman with a child had been a huge surprise for her. Harry's world was an adult one—she never mixed with children at all. The nearest she got were her first-year students at university, and although they sometimes behaved like children, were physically far from it.

It was the only frame of reference she had, and she quickly went into teaching mode. "I'm going to decant this wine from the bottle into the decanter to let it breathe. Can you guess why we do that?"

Riley shook her head but said nothing, still looking really nervous.

"Well, when the wine reacts to the air, many people think it improves the taste, but we can't just pour it straight into the decanter. First we take some leftover or cheap cooking wine and pour it in the decanter."

Harry unscrewed the little bottle of cooking wine and handed it to Riley. "Pour it in then."

Riley's eyes went wide with more than a little fear. "Me? I…"

"Pour it in. We don't have all day." Harry saw her look over her shoulder to her mum for support and then she lifted the small bottle and poured it in. Harry then swirled the cheap wine around. She didn't explain or say a word, hoping to encourage Riley to ask her own questions. It seemed to be working. She could see Riley shifting around nervously, trying to build up her courage to ask a question.

"Um…Lady Axedale?"

"Yes?"

"Why do you do that?" Riley said in a whisper.

Harry wondered if it was just her that made the child nervous or if she was like that with everyone. "This is called seasoning the decanter. There might be dust or something of that sort in there, but we can't wash it out with water because that would affect the taste of the wine. So we use an everyday wine to wash it."

After emptying the wine down the sink, she started opening the bottle she would be drinking.

"Now comes the interesting part. This red was bottled in 1982, long before you were born, and because it's old, it might have some sediment gathered at the bottom, and we don't want to drink that. So, pass the matches."

She lit the candle and picked up the bottle. "We place the neck of the bottle just over the candle, and as we pour we can see the sediment as we get to the end of pouring. As soon as we see it about to get too near the neck of the bottle, we stop, and that's it, all done and dusted."

Riley smiled for the first time. "Thanks for showing me, Lady Axedale."

Before she could tell herself all the reasons why this was a bad idea, Harry put her hand on Riley's shoulder and said with a smile, "Call me Harry."

A long forgotten memory burst into her mind. She was a few years younger than Riley, and their butler had shown her the very same trick. When her mother and father were hosting a dinner party at Axedale, and pretending they were a happily married couple, she would spend her time in the kitchen, with the people who cared for her, where she tried to help and most likely got in the way.

Too much. She had to get out of here, and escape these feelings.

"I'm going to dress for dinner," she said gruffly and stomped out of the kitchen .

❖

Bridget was thoroughly enjoying her evening already. Every time Annie entered the dining room, Harry bristled and Annie's eyes roamed over her boss. Bridget could feel the tension between the two.

Annie cleared away the starter and left the room.

"What a beautiful woman Annie is, and she can cook. What a lucky countess you are, Harry."

"Oh yes, very lucky indeed," Harry said sarcastically. "She's a bloody annoying woman, that's what she is. She's taken over my house in the space of a few days. Acts like she owns the place, feeding and watering my refurb team without even being asked."

Bridget smiled. *Sounds like she's gotten under your skin, Harry.* "From what I can see, she's making the place warm and comforting so far. Her food is marvellous, and you can't deny how utterly delicious she looks."

Harry shook her head and brought her glass of wine to her lips. "You do realize you are a vicar, don't you, Bridge? You should be talking to me and not lusting after my housekeeper."

Bridget picked up her wine glass and held it up in a toast. "I know very well that I am a vicar, and as a woman of God I'm simply admiring the beauty that God has made."

"Well if she's so bloody perfect, Vicar, ask her out."

Harry said that like a bad tempered child, and Bridget had to stop herself from laughing out loud. "I don't think I'm her type, Harry. I wish I was."

"Oh? And you can tell that from having two conversations with her?" Harry sneered.

Bridget tapped her painted fingernails on the dinner table before her. "No, I can tell from observing her body language, her reaction to the people around her, and reading her emotions." *Not to mention her eyes are riveted on you every time she comes into the room.* "I'm too femme for her. I think she prefers the handsome, rugged type."

Then Bridget had a thought that might provoke a reaction in her old friend. "Oh, perhaps I could introduce her to Sam McQuade of lower farm. I know she would like to meet someone."

"My tenant farmer, McQuade?" Harry said with surprise.

"Yes, why not? She's a rugged, strong farmer. I know she would like to meet a nice girl and I'm sure Annie would like to make a family for her child."

Harry did not look happy. "Could we change the subject from my housekeeper please?"

"Of course. Mrs. Castle has been asking for you. I know she'd really like to see you."

She watched Harry stare into her glass of wine absently.

"I'm extremely busy at the moment. Maybe in a few weeks."

Bridget couldn't understand why Harry was avoiding meeting her old family cook. She knew that Harry was fond of her. "Just be sure and see her soon, Harry. She hasn't been too well of late."

Harry just nodded but said nothing.

She decided to change the subject. "Do you think you might make it to Sunday service this week? What if I promise the sermon will be short?"

Harry sighed. "You know why I don't go. I would be a hypocrite."

"Not that praising God is unimportant, but in a small village parish like this, it's about more than that. The church is the hub of the village. The place people feel a part of something bigger, part of the community. Your role as lord of the manor is to go to church and take your place as the leader of that community."

"I would be struck down if I walked into church. You know God and I haven't been on speaking terms for most of my life. If he was like the Roman gods I would have more time for him."

It was Bridget's turn to become annoyed at the conversation. "Oh, here we go. You and your bloody Romans."

"Well at least they didn't pretend to be pious and holy. They lived, they drank, they loved, and they had lots of sex…that's what I call a god."

Bridget picked up a piece of the home-baked crusty bread and threw it at Harry, in a move reminiscent of the many food fights they'd had at boarding school.

Just as Harry picked it up to throw back, Annie entered with the main course. "I'm sorry. Should I come back in a few minutes?"

"Not at all, Annie. The vicar was just regressing to childhood."

Bridget stuck her tongue out at Harry for that comment. "That smells delightful, Annie. As much as my own housekeeper, Mrs. Long, takes good care of me at the vicarage, your good cooking and delightful company would be a joy to have every day. Perhaps I could steal you away from the bad-tempered countess over there?"

"Give me a month and I'll let you know, Vicar." Both she and Annie giggled and Harry gave them a hard stare.

❖

The next morning, Annie made breakfast for herself, Riley, and the refurb team. On the kitchen table was a choice of bacon, sausages, fried mushrooms, bread rolls, and crusty bread. All she had to do now before the men and women descended on the kitchen was scrambled egg, whilst keeping an eye on the pot of porridge for the more health conscious among them.

It was going to be a busy day ahead. The two regular cleaning staff were coming in today, and it could be an awkward experience if they were uncooperative with her and resistant to her new methods, but she was certain she could get them onside with time.

As she cracked the eggs into the pan and started mixing, her mind wandered back to last night. The dinner party had been fun, even for her as she went back and forth to the kitchen. Both Harry and the vicar seemed to enjoy their food, going by the thoroughly empty dishes.

Bridget was great fun too. Every time she came into the room, Bridge had a smile for her, and some harmless flirting. She was unlike any vicar she had ever heard of, and could give as good as she got with Harry.

Every new day that passed brought out another complex side of Harry's personality. Yesterday she had been bad tempered and surly because Annie had given food to the refurb team. Yet later, she took the time to teach Riley something new.

Harry's attention had meant the world to Riley. She'd gone to bed happy, armed with a notebook to write down all the questions she wanted to ask Harry, but Annie knew it would take more than one brief talk like that to stop Harry being so emotionally distant. When she watched Harry place a gentle hand on Riley's shoulder, the sweet gesture had made her heart ache, but just as suddenly, Harry appeared to get scared and ran.

Annie spooned the eggs into the serving dish and heard the kitchen door open. She knew who it was by the warmth spreading throughout her body.

"Good morning, Harry. Give me a second and I'll pour your coffee."

"Good morning. Thanks," Harry said.

When Annie turned around her stomach clenched in excitement. Harry was astoundingly good-looking even in her workwear of ripped and well-worn jeans, boots, and baseball cap. She was so far away from what you would expect a countess to be, but that made her even more exciting.

Annie handed over the coffee in the travel mug Harry used, and she took a sip. "Hmm, this is delicious. You are better at making coffee than me."

"Thanks." Annie saw Harry's eyes greedily look over the food on the kitchen table. "Could I offer you some cooked breakfast? Riley will be down soon and—"

"I told you, I don't eat till lunch, and then only some simple soup," Harry snapped.

Annie concluded it was only stubbornness that was holding her back, and decided to back off for the moment. "If that's what you want, but if you ever change your mind, the kitchen is always open to you."

The words appeared to resonate with Harry and she nodded. "It looks great in here now, after all the hard work you've done."

Annie smiled. She imagined compliments did not easily trip off Harry's tongue, so she took it that she was loosening up. "That's kind of you, thank you."

"Just speaking truth." Harry took a step towards Annie without even realizing she'd done it. When she was in Annie's company she was drawn to her unconsciously. She should have been angry that her request that her team not be fed from the kitchen had again fallen on deaf ears, but getting angry at Annie was becoming hard.

Last night as she tried to go to sleep, her unconscious kept conjuring up images of Annie and Riley out having fun with her tenement farmer, McQuade, and she didn't like it. She cursed Bridge for bringing it up in the first place, not to mention the blatant flirting she was doing with Annie.

She envied Bridge that happy, easy manner she could call on to talk to Annie. Harry could coax any woman into bed with her slick charm and looks, but Annie was different. She sensed that a woman like Annie would not be so easily charmed into bed.

It was time to leave, but the force pulling her to Annie was hard to resist. Her eyes settled on Annie's red lips. She wasn't one for soft tender kisses, she used kisses to take and show who was in charge, but Annie's lips were made for slow kisses. Harry could imagine being happy to simply kiss Annie for hours without needing more.

The silence between them was finally broken by Annie. "I wanted to thank you for being so good with Riley last night, she enjoyed learning from you."

"I'm not a monster, you know. I can be nice to a child, without you needing to thank me." It annoyed Harry that Annie had such a low opinion of her.

Annie placed a hand on her forearm and said, "I never once thought you were a monster, Harry, just not used to being around children. You made her happy last night."

Harry stared at the hand on her forearm, and felt the skin underneath it burn. "I...uh..." What was it about this woman that disrupted and changed her to a jabbering idiot?

Lust, lust, it's just lust. She tried to console herself. It had been weeks since she'd had sex and Annie was the nearest attractive woman. That was it.

They were lost in each other's eyes until Harry heard running towards the kitchen door.

"That'll be Riley," Annie said.

Harry quickly stepped back and said, "Thanks for the coffee."

Riley walked into the room. "Morning, Mum—hi, Harry."

"Good morning," Harry said, without even looking at Riley, and walked to the kitchen door.

Riley pulled out her notebook and followed her. "Harry? Harry, can I ask you some questions? About your work? About the Romans?"

"No. I'm busy," she said dismissively and left Riley behind her.

Annie walked into the entrance hall to meet the cleaning staff as they arrived, and found Riley sitting on the staircase staring at her notebook. In this huge marble hallway, she looked so small and lonely.

Annie sighed. The moment that she had shared with Harry in the kitchen had been both hot and angry. Harry only had to look at Annie to make her ache for her hands on her body, but no matter how much she yearned for her, she would never expose Riley to someone who would be in and out of their life.

After a heart-wrenching experience with her first lover, Annie had decided to wait for the one perfect partner she was certain was out there for her. Someone who would want to make a family for Riley. Looking at the sadness on Riley's face at the moment, and the anger she had felt at Harry's total dismissal of Riley, that someone would never be Harry Knight.

"What's wrong, Riley? I thought you were going to spend some time in the library, and then go looking for more Roman things?"

Riley shrugged, "Don't want to any more."

Annie sighed. She knew this was about this morning. Riley had been so excited with her notebook and the hope of striking up a friendship with someone who, it seemed to Riley, knew everything worth knowing.

Then she remembered how hot her body had been when she had touched Harry. Well if she was honest she felt that just being near her. How could she feel that for someone like Harry, someone who could dismiss her child as if she wasn't there and be generally bad tempered?

That was the conundrum about Harry. Annie might be wrong, but when she looked in her eyes, she saw someone whose emotions were mixed up, someone who struggled to relate to others.

She sat down beside Riley and put an arm around her shoulders. "Sweetie, I get the impression that Harry would like to be our friend, but doesn't know how."

Riley looked up at her with confusion writ all over her face. "How can you not know how to be a friend?"

"Well, I think she has been alone a lot throughout her life, and she was at boarding school all the time she was growing up. That means she lived away from her family most of the year."

"That's scary. I wouldn't like to be away from you, Mum."

"I know, I couldn't be without you, sweetie, but that's the thing—I don't think Harry knows how to be around a family. She needs to get used to us, and when she does, I think she'll want to be your friend."

The smile was back on Riley's face. "Do you really think so?"

"I do. We need to just give her a chance, okay?"

Riley jumped up abruptly. "Okay, I'll go and do some more research in the library. I'll be ready for Lady Harry when she wants a friend."

She watched Riley run off and prayed that she was right, for both their sakes.

❖

When the two members of staff arrived, Annie took them to the drawing room to talk. She asked them to sit and stood before them, assessing them. The younger of the two, Julie, was bright, smiling, and eager to learn, but the older woman, Beverly, looked to be on the defensive from the first moment.

It was time to get everyone onside. "Thank you for coming to talk to me this morning. I know it will be different for you both, working with a housekeeper."

Beverley said under her breath, "You think so?"

Annie chose to ignore it. She got the feeling that Beverly thought she should have been housekeeper, and it would take some diplomacy to make it better.

"First of all I can see what a difficult job this has been for you. It must have been a thankless task for two people to clean this huge house, and only two days a week? Impossible."

"It has, hasn't it Bev?" Julie nudged her colleague.

"You could say, yes." Beverly uncrossed her arms and relaxed her defiant posture and Annie gave a silent *yes!* to winning the first battle.

"Not to mention a house that is being refurbished, and has builders' dust and grime throughout the rooms. But I have a plan. First of all, if you are agreeable, I would like to make you full-time staff."

Julie's face was wreathed in smiles. "You mean a proper job, every day like?"

"Does her ladyship know about this?" Beverly asked.

She didn't, but Annie was sure she could persuade Harry of her plans. "Not as yet…but I'm hoping to have her go-ahead soon."

Beverly chuckled. "Good luck with that, Ms. Brannigan. Her ladyship isn't the most cooperative of people. Won't even come and attend to her duties in the village. She hides up here like she has nothing to do with us."

Annie had gotten that impression. Not that she knew much about the duties of the aristocracy, but she did assume the countess had many duties to perform in her particular area. The village was apparently another one of the many things in Harry's life that she had distanced herself from.

"Maybe she needs some encouragement, Beverly. But we can talk about that another time. Now, eventually I want to have a larger workforce, but in the meantime, I think between us, we should concentrate on the public areas of the house. If we take a room at a time, and deep clean it, thereafter they will only need light cleaning on a rotation. So, what do you think? Are you both interested in some hard, but full-time work?"

Julie replied enthusiastically, "Oh yes, Ms. Brannigan."

"And you, Beverly?"

She kept quiet for a second, and then a smile crept over her face. "Call me Bev."

❖

Harry retired to her study to do some writing while she ate lunch. She was glad to close the door and have some time to herself. Ever since this morning's kitchen encounter with Annie and then Riley, she had felt uneasy. At Cambridge she didn't need to sugar-coat her answers or explain herself. She had never thought of the effect her straight talking could have, but this morning after dismissing Riley so out of hand, she had felt bad for the first time.

She looked at the picture that loomed large above her fireplace. Her father had had his portrait painted as soon as he'd inherited his title and estate. Most of her ancestors had *family* portraits painted upon ascending to their family seat, but her father had shown in a nutshell just what his priorities were.

He may have been dead, but his very gaze from above the fireplace could still make the anger bubble in her stomach. People had often remarked how much they looked like each other, something she hated. Had she the same capacity to hurt and destroy people who cared about her? Deep down that was what she had always feared.

A brief knock at the study door brought her back from her disturbing thoughts. Anticipating that lunch was on its way, she got up and opened the door for Annie. "Hi."

"A light lunch as requested," Annie said with an edge to her voice.

Harry shut the door and walked over to sit at her desk. She soon realized that the tray containing her soup was far from simple.

The first thing she noticed was the small vase with three purple flowers. "I…" Words failed her.

Annie pointed to each item on the tray and almost dared Harry to complain. "Spiced carrot and lentil soup, rye bread, rocket, cherry tomato, and pine nut salad, and a piece of the lemon drizzle cake you would have gotten at tea break this morning if you had come down to the kitchen with your team."

Harry didn't think she'd ever been reprimanded in such a nice way. In fact no one had ever tried to. She knew from Annie's tone that her guilt was not unfounded.

"And the flowers?" Harry raised a questioning eyebrow.

"Crocuses. Frank the gardener gave them to me."

No one had ever given her flowers before. That was usually her role, not that it had happened often, and they were always to members of the family.

"Well this all seems wonderful. Thank you. Listen, about Riley this morn—"

Annie put her hands on her hips, annoyance pouring off of her. "She only wanted to ask you about your work. Riley is really interested in what you do."

The anger had the opposite effect than Annie probably intended. All Harry could think of was kissing her to shut her up.

Annie's hands slid slowly down and over her thighs, mirroring Harry's eyes on her. She had headed to Harry's office determined to reprimand her, and to discuss the staffing situation with her, but Harry's hot gaze threatened to make her forget everything. It was an all-encompassing heat that could only be quenched by Harry's touch.

She was well used to a level of sexual frustration. She had been tempted over the years, but tempted was not a word she would use to describe her attraction to Harry. Harry was someone who could make her blood run hot with just a look. She tried hard not to imagine what a kiss from her would feel like.

She's your employer, Annie repeated like a mantra, and breathed deeply.

"I will try to be more considerate of Riley. I'm just not used to children."

"Thank you."

Harry took a spoonful of soup and hummed in appreciation. "This is delicious."

As Harry was happily digging into her food, Annie thought perhaps that this was a good time to bring up her new ideas. "I wanted to talk to you about the staff, Harry."

"Okay." She ate a chunk of the rye bread, and said, "The bread is wonderful. You really make this yourself?"

"Yes, fresh this morning." Yes, maybe this was the perfect time. "I met with Beverly and Julie this morning. I've come up with a plan to get the house in order, but I want your permission to make them full-time staff."

Harry stopped eating midchew and placed her spoon down on the tray. "I see. You bring me a delicious lunch and then ask for more. First new appliances then full-time staff? Where will it end, Ms. Brannigan?" Harry said in half-serious tone of voice.

Annie leaned over and placed her palms on the desk. She saw Harry's eyes zero in on her cleavage that was exposed a little by her position.

"It will end when you have a clean, comfortable house. I have no idea how the house has gone so long without proper daily staff. We have so much catching up to do that three people working daily probably won't be enough, but I'm willing to start at that and see how they go. It's only going to get worse as you finish the banqueting hall, swimming pool, and then the rooms in the west wing. I'm the best housekeeper you could get, but I'm not a miracle worker."

Harry gave her sexy smile. "You're the best, are you?"

"Absolutely," Annie said without hesitation.

Harry hesitated for a few seconds and said, "Very well. I'll get my estate manager to draw up two full-time contracts for them, and we can review staffing in a month's time. Good enough?"

Annie stood and smiled. Harry wasn't that scary or unreasonable if she was handled correctly. "Yes, thank you. Enjoy your lunch."

She turned and walked out of the study, confident that plans were coming together nicely.

CHAPTER EIGHT

A few weeks later life was settling into a pattern at Axedale Hall. Annie had made her mark on the running of the house, much as a general taking command of an army, and Harry had learned it was best not to interfere with her new regime.

Each day she received a delicious lunch with a small vase of flowers, which she still found strange, but all she could think about was the next time she could spend time in Annie's company. As the day went on she would find herself missing Annie, and seek her out on some pretext to simply be in her company.

Harry had never wanted or needed anyone's company before. It was an exciting new emotion when she didn't think about it too deeply, but when she did, it was frightening. Her mother had warned her many times about never giving anyone power over her heart. She hadn't given Annie her heart but if she were to leave tomorrow she would feel…she wasn't sure what exactly, but it would hurt.

She had tried to appear more open to Riley, but the girl hadn't come near her after their last encounter, and she simply had no idea how she could breach that sort of gap with a child.

This afternoon Harry was on her way to the estate manager's office for their monthly meeting. The office was a stone building next to the stable block. It used to be such a hive of activity when she was a child—the noise of the horses, the grooms going about their business, and the sound of hunting dogs barking in the adjacent kennel block. Yet another area of the estate her father had let slip.

She walked in and saw Stevens, the estate manager, waiting for her. He stood as she entered. "Good afternoon, m'lady."

"Afternoon, Stevens. How are you today?"

Leonard Stevens had been working on the estate for five years. Her father's lawyer had suggested him when he'd found that the estate was failing as her father's money was running out.

It was Leonard who had immediately advised phasing out the stable and kennel block, and concentrating their efforts on the farms and tenants on the land. Most of the staff had already been let go in a previous cost-cutting exercise which left the estate in the state it was today.

"I'm very well, m'lady."

Harry had given up asking him to call her by her name. A man schooled at Eton forty years ago did not take easily to change. "Good, good. Shall we?"

Harry took off her baseball cap and sat at his desk while he brought over the necessary files. The window straight across from her gave a great view of the stable yard, and she could see Davey was in the process of cleaning her cars, now the groom's only job.

Leonard sat and took a pen from the pocket of his tweed jacket. "Where would you like to start, m'lady?"

"How about give me an overview of where the estate is at and we'll go from there. I'm not a farmer, Stevens. I'm an archaeologist, so I'm going to be relying heavily on your advice."

"Of course, m'lady. Overall the estate functions just about. We're not quite in the red but we could be doing so much better. Your late father, the earl, did not have the means in later years to do anything but keep things ticking away, but I hope with your ladyship at the helm and with your maternal grandfather's money, we will be able to make great strides."

Harry smiled. Stevens looked almost gleeful at the thought of spending her money, not in a bad way, but after years of not being able to do his job properly, it would be a relief.

Her mother's father had been a self-made man, a rag-to-riches story, really. From great poverty he rose to own one of the biggest refrigeration companies in the world, and he wanted his daughter to complete the final rung in his social climbing, a title.

He wasn't a stupid man, and on his daughter's marriage he settled a large sum on his new son-in-law, and a separate amount on his daughter. That way he ensured his daughter and his money were protected.

The bulk of his fortune was to be kept in trust after his death, until Harry was twenty-one. Harry thanked God he'd done that, or her father would have left nothing for her to bring the estate back in order.

"Yes, we will spend what we need to get the estate back on its feet," Harry said. "And the tenants?"

"The tenants we have are excellent. No problems on that score. We have two vacant farms and numerous cottages. I haven't been able to let them as yet because they need a great deal of work done on them."

Harry made a note in her notebook. "That is something that needs to be addressed. We can't expect young people to stay in the village or local area if they don't have comparable living arrangements to town."

"My thoughts exactly, m'lady. I'll start to get quotes on the work required, with your permission of course?"

"Certainly. What's next?"

"The other huge problem we have is staff. A great estate like this needs a big staff just to keep it ticking over, especially if you wish to repopulate the stables and kennels."

Harry felt her chest constrict and her breathing grow shallower. Her worst fear was being trapped in the place that had brought her the most pain and unhappiness in her life. The bigger the staff got, the more demands would be made on her time, and the more it would pull her away from her life of safety in Cambridge.

I will not be trapped here, she vowed to herself.

"Perhaps we can address that at our next meeting when we have all settled in together and see how the house is running."

"Indeed."

Harry noticed Stevens's attention was taken up with something in the stable yard. She followed his gaze and the tight coil of fear in her stomach dissipated and changed to the now-familiar tingle of excitement, when she saw Annie laughing and talking to the groom outside. By the looks of it she had brought him a cup of coffee and he was doing his best to keep her chatting, and was entirely too close to her for her liking.

Bridge had assured her that Annie was gay, but what if she liked men, or both? *Great. Now I have overeager grooms as well as rugged farmers to worry about.*

She couldn't believe what she had just thought. Why on earth would she be worried about it anyway? Annie was her housekeeper and could see who she wanted, but the very thought made anger boil up inside.

Harry was only half listening to what Stevens was saying, but she caught this: "I understand Ms. Brannigan has been a wonderful addition to the staff, and is making great strides in the house."

"Yes, she is." Harry wanted to walk out there just now and get Annie away from the groom. It was ridiculous and childish, she knew, but nevertheless that's what she felt.

"Let's finish this up tomorrow, Stevens."

He looked surprised that their meeting was cut short. "Of course, m'lady. I'll be available anytime you need me."

Instead of going into the stable yard and tearing Annie away, she stomped off to her study and slammed the door.

After lunch Riley headed to her favourite place in the whole house, the library. For someone who loved books, it was heaven. She opened up the heavy, old oak door and took a deep breath. Riley loved the comforting smell of old books. It made her feel safe when she felt uneasy, nervous, or scared.

The library was a beautiful room. The bookshelves ran down either side of the room, with a sliding wooden ladder to aid anyone wishing to reach the top shelves. On the ceiling were some beautiful classical frescos to inspire the library's occupants.

Down the centre of the room was a long wooden table and chairs, as well as display cabinets holding all the Knight family's prized objects.

Riley walked over to the bookshelves and put back the book she had taken out, before running her finger along the spines until she found the one she was looking for.

Rome: Rise and Fall by Dr Henrietta Knight.

She took her book over to the table and sighed as she sat down. Lady Harry was such a cool person with an amazing job, but she was also scary. She wished that she liked kids and wished she could be her friend.

Her mum had told her that Lady Harry was sorry about not talking to her in the kitchen, and since then Riley had seen Lady Harry looking over to her. Riley'd thought she was going to talk to her, but then Lady Harry would just walk away. Mum said to give her time, but Riley was convinced she just would never like kids.

Riley opened her book and flicked through the pages. It would be a tricky book to read, and she'd have to look up lots of words that she didn't understand, but it would be worth it.

It struck Riley how super brainy Lady Harry must be to have all this information inside her head.

She started to read the first page, while swinging her legs under the desk. She got to a part that described Roman armour, and her eyes were drawn to the Roman gladius on display in the library. It had been calling to her since she'd first used the library, but she didn't want to incur Lady Harry's wrath.

It wasn't in a sealed case, which made it all the more enticing. The ornate leather and gold scabbard was in good condition and displayed below the sword. The sword was not in as good condition. Rust covered the blade, but the gold handle was shiny and Riley wanted to touch it badly.

Just once couldn't hurt.

She walked over to it and looked to the doors behind her, checking the coast was clear, before lifting her hand towards the gladius.

Riley's fingers lightly touched the handle and she gasped. It was amazing to think that a Roman soldier once held this in his hand, and probably fought and killed with it too.

She was so taken with the sword that everything else around her receded.

"What are you doing? You were told never to touch anything!" Harry's voice boomed from behind her.

Riley jumped in fright and her hand knocked the sword from its resting place. Everything seemed to happen in slow motion. The sword tumbled to the hard wooden floor, and Riley did the only thing she could think of. She ran.

The clatter of Annie's shoes on the wooden flooring mirrored the hammering of her heart as she stormed through Axedale's ancient halls in search of its countess.

Harry had gone too far this time. When Riley had run into the kitchen and her arms, sobbing about Harry shouting at her, Annie's temper had broken. The time for treading carefully around Harry, and trying to break down her walls gently, was over. It was time for some home truths and if it cost Annie her job, then that's just the way it would need to be.

She couldn't find Harry in her study, and the refurb crew hadn't seen her outside, so Annie headed up to her bedroom.

Annie knocked on the door with her fist.

"Go away."

That only made Annie more infuriated. She barged in, and found a surprised looking Harry, nursing a glass of whiskey, over by her bedroom window.

Harry walked over to meet Annie in the middle of the room.

"How dare you shout at my child. I don't care how important or priceless one of your dusty relics is. Riley is a little girl. A little girl who despite your best efforts since we arrived thinks that you are great and yearns for your attention."

Harry put her hand out to touch her arm. "Annie, I…"

Annie wasn't interested in what Harry had to say. "No, there's no excuse. Do you want a child to be scared of you? Is that what you really want?"

Annie could see a wave of emotion drift over Harry, and she put her head down solemnly. "No, I don't."

Annie was surprised. She'd expected a fierce, angry Harry, who would argue with her and then dismiss her. This Harry almost looked as sad and upset as Riley did. She exhaled a long breath and her anger began to fade.

"Well, I've made my point. If you want me to leave—"

Harry's head snapped up and she grasped Annie's hand. "No. I don't want you to go, either of you. I just…I don't know how to do this, Annie. I'm confused. Tell me what to do, I don't know how to make things right."

Annie realized that Harry had taken a step towards her and had hold of both her hands. It was an emotional step as well as a physical one. Harry looked as if she was desperate with need, a need for emotional comfort, like a child almost, and a need for physical comfort. Her arms ached to give her that comfort, but with the look of turmoil on Harry's face, this was rapidly turning into something else entirely, and she had to get out of here before they both did something they would regret in the morning.

"I need to go." She pulled away and hurried to the door.

As she went to turn the handle, Harry said, "Will you tell Riley that I'm sorry, and there's no damage to the sword?"

She looked back and said, "Tell her yourself, m'lady."

Harry moved to follow Annie but the door slammed shut. It felt like Annie had given her a physical blow, just by leaving. She deserved it. Why had she shouted? The sword wouldn't have fallen if she hadn't startled Riley and all this angst could have been avoided.

As a youngster she had done many similar things, worse actually, and she had felt the wrath of her father's temper.

I'm just like him.

The realization hit her hard. She downed the glass of whiskey in her hand and walked over to the mirror on the wall. Her father's looks stared back at her, and she felt a dread deep down inside her. She was turning into him. It was her worst fear. And just like she had run away in fear of his temper, Riley had run from her.

The only difference was that her mother never stood up for her the way Annie did for Riley. Annie, she was sure, would stand up to the devil himself for Riley.

Harry held her head in her hands. How could she fix this? Why was this so hard?

She left her bedroom and walked down the hallway. Harry had no idea why she was drawn to her nursery, but something in her said this was where she would find some answers to her confused thoughts. Harry opened the door and entered.

The nursery had largely remained untouched since she had left it years before, her small bed in the corner, her many toys strewn around the room. She half smiled at the pile of dolls in one corner of the room in nearly pristine condition, despite her nanny's and mother's best efforts to get her to play with them. Ever the tomboy as a child, dolls were only used to stand in for imaginary foes.

Harry walked over to the built-in wardrobe in one corner of the room, and ran her hand across the door. She recalled the many times she had sought refuge in this wardrobe trying to get away from the screaming and shouting of her parents.

Today had been one big mistake. She had been feeling frustrated and more than a little jealous after seeing Annie talking with her groom. Then she had walked into the library and taken her frustrations out on Riley. It wasn't the ancient relic, as Annie called it, which was important, it was the fact that it had been her grandfather's pride and joy.

Her namesake Henry Knight was a warm, loving man, who'd adored her. She'd spent her childhood walking the grounds of Axedale, listening eagerly to everything he wanted to teach her.

Strictly speaking, the Roman sword should have been in a museum, but he had bought it from a somewhat shady relic hunter, and it had been in the library ever since.

Of course as a young child not much younger than Riley, she'd wanted to play with it. To keep her little hands off, her grandfather had a wooden sword and shield made for her.

Of course. Harry pulled open the wardrobe doors, and there, sitting in the corner, were the sword and shield he had made for her. She got down on her hands and knees and picked them up.

They still gave her the same thrill as they had when she was a child and Grandpa had called her his little centurion.

Harry stood up and stood in front of the mirror to look at her appearance. She had changed so much from the girl who'd held this sword. She had become hard, cynical, and was held hostage by her memories. Perhaps it was time to make some new ones?

At around midnight, Annie walked wearily up to her bedroom. She was tired and her feet were aching. It had been another long, weary day, but despite everything it had been a productive one.

She, Bev, and Julie had made great strides with the house. All the fragile William Morris curtains had been taken down from the public rooms, and packaged up ready for the specialist curtain cleaners tomorrow.

As she rounded the corner to the hall in which her bedroom was located, she saw Harry place something at Riley's door, and then creep back to her bedroom.

When Harry shut her bedroom door she hurried up the hall to see what she had left. She smiled when she saw a wooden sword and shield with a note addressed to Riley.

To Riley,
I'm very sorry that I upset you today. Rest assured that you didn't break anything, and even if you had it wouldn't have been

*worth upsetting you over. I know you want to be my friend, Riley.
I'm not good at making friends, but I hope both you and your mum
will teach me how. This gladius and shield were my own when I was
about your age. Please enjoy playing with them.*
    Your friend,
    Harry

Annie felt her heart flutter as she read the note. "I knew you
had it in you, Harry."

She stuck the note back onto the shield and went to bed with
Harry's words filling her thoughts.

CHAPTER NINE

Harry walked out of her estate manager's office and made her way back to the house. She had put off seeing Annie or Riley long enough. She hadn't even had her usual strong cup of coffee this morning because she was worried about their reactions, either good or bad.

As she approached the large stone steps at the entrance to Axedale, she saw Riley sitting with her gladius and shield, and a book in her lap. She wondered how it was that she could talk to large lecture halls of people, mix with other aristocracy and royalty, and yet this one ten-year-old made her nervous.

Riley looked up as she approached and smiled. "Hi, Harry."

"Hi. How are you today, Riley?" she said nervously.

"I'm great. Thank you for these. They are the best present ever."

Riley's enthusiasm was infectious and she couldn't help but smile. "You're welcome. They were mine when I was little. I had lots of fun with them."

"I know, it says your name on the shield." Riley turned the shield over and Harry smiled at the inscription she had scratched into the wood as a youngster.

This belongs to Centurion Henricus, aged eight.

"My grandfather had it made for me. I think he was getting fed up with me trying to play with the one in the library."

"You tried to touch it too?" Riley asked with surprise.

"I did indeed, and I had forgotten about that until last night when I did some thinking about things."

"Harry, I'm sorry I knocked over the sword yesterday. I know I'm not supposed to touch anything."

Harry took a chance and sat on the step beside her. "It was my fault. If I hadn't shouted, you wouldn't have jumped out of your skin and knocked it over. So I'm sorry. Can we start again?"

She offered her hand to Riley and she shook it. "Yes, Mum always says that it takes a strong person to say sorry, and a strong person to forgive."

"Your mum is very wise."

"She is. She's the best," Riley said confidently.

Harry was beginning to see that with each passing day. *Annie? Why are you in my head?*

They were silent for a few seconds before Harry said, "I forgot what it was like to be a child living in this big place. It's an exciting place to explore."

"Yeah, it's great. We've never lived in a place like this. Mum doesn't usually let me go far outside. She says it isn't safe, but here I can explore everywhere."

Harry never considered what a big life change this was for two people used to city life, to suddenly be in a little country village, and she wasn't making it any easier for them to adapt, especially Riley, who clearly wanted some friendship from her. It was time to think about how her behaviour affected others, and not just expect them to follow in her wake. This wasn't Cambridge, and Annie and Riley were not her students.

She looked down to the book by Riley's side. "So what are you reading?"

Riley closed the book so she could see the cover, and said proudly, "Your book, Harry. I found it in the library."

"That's a really grown-up book for someone your age. Are you managing okay with it?"

"Uh-huh, I always read books like this. I just look up the tricky words in the dictionary. Can I ask you something?"

"Of course. Fire away."

"My mum got me a guidebook for Axedale and it says there's a Roman building somewhere under the estate. Is that true?"

Harry immediately relaxed. This was something she could talk about with no problem. "Yes, somewhere. My grandfather and I dug some test pits when I was younger, but we only found some Roman coins."

"The ones in my room?" Riley asked.

"Yes, that's them. I do mean to organize an archaeological investigation of the grounds in years to come. I'm determined to find it."

Riley fished in her jeans pocket and pulled out a collection of tiny mosaic blocks. "Look what I found. Are they Roman?"

Harry lifted a block from her hand and examined it carefully. She knew exactly what it was and started to feel the excitement that came when she was on the verge of a discovery. "They certainly are. They're called tesserae mosaic blocks. Where did you find them?"

"On the grass just before the start of bluebell wood. Are they a good find?"

Harry looked at all the others and gave Riley a big smile. "I think they just might be."

She stood up quickly, her mind whirring with possibilities, and rubbed her hands together with glee. "Okay, first things first. We'll go to the stable block and get my toolbox, and you can take me to where you found these."

Riley leapt to her feet, and holstered her gladius. "I can show you."

❖

"We're finally getting somewhere Ms. Brannigan," Beverly said.

Annie carefully climbed down the ladder they were using to clean the large windows. Today they were working on the family breakfast room, and its seemingly endless windows.

"It's not looking too shabby is it? And it's Annie, remember?"

After an initially frosty reception Beverly and she were getting on well. Well enough that she could delegate duties to Beverly and leave her to direct their younger employee, Julie.

"If you insist, Annie."

Annie looked around the room and was pleased with what she saw. The curtains were off being cleaned, the large rug was steam cleaned, and the fireplace was dusted and chimney swept, and Harry was having the floor refinished at a later date.

"Yes, I think it's going to look beautiful when it's finished," Beverly agreed.

Julie came in carrying two buckets of water and placed them at the bottom of the ladder. "Well done, Julie," Annie said. "Now, four windows down, eight to go."

She and Beverly moved the ladder over to the next window, and Annie started to climb up. "Are you sure you don't want Julie to take a turn, Annie?" Beverly asked.

Annie stopped to take a breath and looked down at Beverly. "That's okay. I've got a few more left in me yet. Julie? Turn up the radio. I can't work without my music to sing to."

She smiled and turned back to the task in hand. When she did she was astonished to see the sight of Harry walking across the estate grounds with what looked like a toolbox in hand, and alongside her, Riley.

"What are they up to?"

"Sorry?" Beverly asked.

"Oh, nothing really. I'm just watching Harry with my daughter. They seem to be on a mission somewhere."

Beverly said, "She is? It's not like her to mix with people, especially children."

Hmm, are you turning over a new leaf, Harry? Annie started to clean the window, and kept her eyes on Harry and Riley until they moved out of sight. "Do you know her mother, Bev?"

"Yes. In the first couple of years of her marriage, she was a fixture at all the usual village events. Church committees, women's guild, village festivals, that sort of thing. She wasn't born into the aristocracy, her father was a working class man made good, but even so she learned what she could and tried to fit in to village life."

"What happened then?" Annie asked.

"I can only tell you what I've heard. After Lady Harry was born she had bad postnatal depression, not helped by the reports getting back to her about the earl's many infidelities. Now there's a man who wasn't well liked. After a while we saw less and less of her, until she moved back to London, leaving the earl to do as he pleased."

Poor Harry. She had the urge to pull the countess into her arms and hug her until she felt better.

❖

"This is it." Riley stopped in an area where the grass perimeter ended and bluebell wood started.

Harry dropped her toolkit and the spade and looked around at the landscape. "Well there is running water near here, so it could be a good spot for habitation." She took off her baseball cap and put it on back to front, one of her little rituals while working on a dig. She clapped her hands together and said, "First things first. Come over here, Riley."

Riley smiled and hurried to her side.

Harry pulled out a smartphone from her pocket and handed it to Riley.

"Wow, this is amazing. I've seen these in adverts on television but never up close."

"You haven't used one of these before?"

Riley held it gingerly with both hands. "Uh, no. What do you want me to do?"

Harry leaned over her shoulder and opened up the camera app. "We're going to cut a few corners since this is my land, but I want you to record anything we find okay. Lots of pictures, lots of evidence, okay?"

"I can do that," Riley said gleefully.

"Excellent."

Harry opened up her toolbox and took out her tool roll. It contained everything she needed for a dig: her trusty trowel, which she called her right hand, brushes of every size, and other digging tools.

"Next we get GPS coordinates, and take note of them so we can find the precise site again." Harry picked up her GPS tool and switched it on. "This sends the coordinates to my laptop and smartphone, and afterwards we can map what we find."

She then picked up the spade and began cutting a rough square in the turf. As the spade cut around it hit off something solid.

"It's hitting something, Harry."

"I hear it. Just don't get excited too quickly. It could be anything. Old garden features or something of the sort."

Harry cut away the top square of turf and threw it to the side, then began digging out the topsoil. As she did she spotted something in the dirt.

"Riley, get me a finds bag from my toolbox."

She got one and hurried back. "What have you found?"

Harry pulled a small round object out of the soil. The thrill of the dig was back, and she was enjoying sharing it with Riley. "Some good dating evidence. A coin."

Riley jumped up and down. "A coin? A coin? Is it Roman?"

She loved Riley's enthusiasm. It reminded her of her own enthusiasm at that age. To someone so young, a dig was glamorous and exciting. It was only as she grew up that she realized how slow and hard going the job could be. She'd lost count of the hours she had spent on her hands and knees, knee deep in mud, to find nothing, and then learning that sometimes finding nothing is a good thing. It eliminated possibilities and opened up new lines of inquiry.

Ideally, they needed water to clean the finds, but she did her best to wipe the grime from them. "It's Roman all right. Emperor Septimius Severus, somewhere around AD 193."

"Yes!" Riley held open the finds bag and Harry dropped the coin in, and patted Riley on the shoulder.

"Your first find, Riley. Congratulations. Why don't you keep that as a special memory?"

"Really? Thanks!"

"Now, I want you to take some pictures, and then once we're finished with this pit, you can search this discarded topsoil for other finds."

She took her trowel and scraped the dirt from the hard surface below and it quickly became clear they had something good. "It's part of a mosaic floor. I think we have a building." Harry held up her palm and Riley gave her a high five.

"Yes!"

❖

Harry watched as Riley ran ahead of her to be met by Annie at the front of the house. She was full of excitement as she told her mum about her Roman finds, and Annie hugged her tightly with obvious pride on her face.

Annie met her eyes and mouthed the words, *Thank you.*

Harry had felt the familiar panic grip her chest. Everything was all getting a bit too close, and so she quickly excused herself, and went to hide away in her study.

She had enjoyed today more than any she could remember for a long, long time, and that was what had frightened her. They had found a part of a mosaic floor which suggested a building of some sort lay beneath her estate. It was the building that her grandfather had dreamed of finding, and yet all she could think of was the joy on Riley's face and Annie's smile as Riley reported their exciting news.

Now she was back here in her empty, lonely study, and she wished she had had the guts to stay and enjoy the conversation she now imagined was going on around the kitchen table.

It was strange. She had never felt her study to be empty and lonely before, but she did now. If she was brave she would go and find Annie and Riley and enjoy their company, but she wasn't brave.

Harry leaned her head against the desk. "What is happening to me? I want to be with them, I want to be with…Annie."

For someone who was so used to being in control of everything, feeling so out of control was frightening.

Her smartphone rang and she answered without looking at who was calling. "Harry Knight."

"Oh, so formal. Hello, Harry Knight."

It was Clara. "Hi, how's London?"

"Oh, you know busy, lots of parties, dancing, and debauchery. How's country life m'lady?"

"Oh, you know, tea, cakes, and not much scandal."

Clara laughed. "Well you know what to do, come back to London."

Maybe that's what she needed, to get away and vent some of her sexual frustration. She was sure that would quiet her attraction to Annie. Harry stood up and walked to the study window. She spotted Annie and Riley on the lawn out front, and Riley appeared to be talking her mother through the rudiments of a Roman soldier's fighting strategy with her sword and shield. They were smiling and laughing, and Annie pulled Riley into a big hug. She had never seen two people hug as much as Riley and Annie did. It was so strange and alien to her, but yet at the same time she ached for that kind of intimacy. She had to get away from here.

"Harry? Harry? Are you listening to me?"

"What? Sorry." She had been so caught up in yearning for Annie, that she had forgotten she was talking on the phone. "Sorry, Clara. What were you saying?"

She heard Clara sigh and say, "Jasper is having a marvellous party in Sloane Square on Saturday." She named an exclusive club. "I thought we could have some fun at my place, then you can take me shopping, then on to the club at night, and some more fun for you after. What do you think?"

She wished it was the weekend so she could get rid of some of this frustration now. "I think…"

Her words died in her throat when she saw Annie and Riley turn towards her, smile, and wave. Without thinking she found herself waving back and smiling like an idiot.

"Harry? You think what? You're awfully distracted today."

She was distracted. Distracted by the most beautiful woman she had ever seen, and the most wonderful child she knew. "I think

I'd better stay in the country, Clara. I've uncovered some evidence of Roman occupation on the estate. I really need to make plans for that, and the repair teams need me here too."

"You are very boring, Harry. I had planned on letting you buy me this perfect little dress," Clara said with sharpness in her voice.

Now she was angry. She was starting to feel like a portable cash machine for Clara. It had annoyed her before, but never made her angry. She thought of Riley who had never even held a smartphone before, never mind owning one. Annie clearly didn't have much left over for luxuries, but they were the happiest, most positive two people she had ever met. Clara and her other friends seemed so shallow in comparison. "Well I'm sure you can find another one of your close acquaintances to buy it for you."

There was a silence and then Clara said, "Have you met some girl down there? You never turn down sex."

Yes, I have met someone, her mind said silently. "Of course not, but maybe it's time I did turn it down. Goodbye, Clara."

Harry ended the call, and threw the phone on the windowsill. She watched Annie and Riley walk back into the house, and she had the insane urge to go and find them. "No, don't get involved. Just keep your distance."

She forced herself to walk back to her desk and start working on her book.

❖

Annie looked into the oven and inhaled the aroma of the shepherd's pie baking. It was one of Riley's favourites, and hers too.

"It's going to be a good one, Riley."

Riley smiled at her. "It smells so good, Mum." She was sitting at the kitchen table, busy drawing and full of excitement. Her shield was at the kitchen door, but her sword still hung at her waist.

Annie was just cutting some ciabatta for Harry's dinner time sandwich, when she noticed Harry standing silently in the kitchen door with a book under my arm. "Oh, you gave me a fright. Can I get you something?"

Harry looked almost terrified to come in. "No, not really. I just came to—"

Riley jumped up. "Harry? Look, I'm drawing a plan of the Roman site." She pulled Harry over to the table and showed her the drawing. "This is the house and the grounds, this is the test pit we dug and its GP...What is it called?"

Annie couldn't help but smile at Riley stumbling over the technical terms.

"GPS," Harry said.

"Yeah, GPS numbers, and then when we find the perimeter of the site, I can add that later, and I marked where we found the coin."

"That's an excellent idea. A good archaeologist always keeps detailed plans." Harry put an arm around her shoulders and then quickly pulled back.

Annie caught the gesture and immediately tried to stop Harry from retreating completely. "Riley, set the table for me."

She packed up her drawing things and went to get plates and cutlery. Harry stood gripping her book so hard her knuckles went white.

"What was it you came in to say, Harry?" Annie asked.

Harry simply gazed at her, but the look in her eyes was so different than the penetrating one that made Annie's skin burn. It sounded ridiculous, but Harry looked like a lost soul reaching out for safety but afraid to take it. This must be the Harry who hid behind those walls.

But in an instant that Harry was gone, and the confident, cultured, controlling Harry was back. "I was walking back from the library and there was a lovely aroma from the kitchen."

"It's shepherd's pie," Riley said as she started to set the table. "Mum's is the best."

Harry gave Annie a devilish smile. "I bet it is. I thought I would have some for dinner instead of my usual sandwich."

"Of course," Annie said, as Harry had already turned to leave the kitchen. "It will be on the kitchen table at six thirty sharp. Riley? Set three places at the table."

Riley looked overjoyed that her new friend would be joining them, but Harry stopped dead and turned back to Annie.

"No. I would like it served in my study as usual," Harry said flatly.

Annie walked towards Harry until they were just a foot apart. "You can't eat comfort food on your own. It has to be shared around the table with companionship and conversation, and comfort food this certainly is. Warm, hot, and bubbling."

She could see the fire return to Harry's eyes, and her jaw flex with tension. Annie knew Harry knew she was teasing, and enjoyed it. It was nice to know that someone as unattainable as Harry Knight, Countess of Axedale could have want in her eyes when she looked at her.

"You do realize that you work for me, and not the other way around?"

"I'm painfully aware of that fact, Harry. Are you going to dismiss me?" Annie said in a low teasing voice.

Harry took another step towards her and upped the ante. "No, but I want it in my study. I always get what I want, Ms. Brannigan."

"Not with me," Annie said with more than a double meaning. "You can have it in the kitchen."

Annie could feel a crackle of energy between them. Her reaction to Harry was primal in its intensity. Harry's eyes travelled slowly downward from her lips, to her neck, and then settled on her cleavage. Annie parted her lips and wet them in response.

She had to suppress a gasp when she felt the back of Harry's hand softly stroke down her forearm. Her breath grew shallow, her heart pounded and matched the steady beat lower down in her sex. Annie was caught in Harry's spell and she was slowly melting into her.

No, don't do this. I can't...I...

Annie stood, desperately trying to control the energy between them, but the spell was broken when Riley said, "Yes, please have dinner with us, Harry."

Harry broke away and inhaled a long breath. "Not tonight, Riley." She gave Riley a small smile and turned back to Annie.

"In my study, Annie." Then she walked off.

"Kitchen, six thirty sharp, *Harry*." Annie gasped. This time Harry didn't stop, and left the kitchen.

Annie immediately went to the fridge for a cold bottle of water, and tried to calm her hammering heart. She thanked God that Riley had been there, or they might have literally jumped on each other, and that was so far from her usual personality, it was scary.

"Mum? Maybe you shouldn't have said that. We might get in trouble, she might send us away."

Annie put down her bottle and opened her arms for Riley's embrace. She hugged her tightly and placed a kiss on her head. "Don't worry, sweetie. She'll be back. I have a hunch that she wanted to come and eat with us when she came into the kitchen. I'm just giving her a little push in the right direction."

Harry read the first line in her notepad for what seemed like the hundredth time and threw her pen down on the desk. Bloody woman. Annie would come. Of course she would come. No one told Harry Knight what to do.

She tried to stop her eyes from wandering to the clock on her laptop screen, but she couldn't. Twenty-five past six. Harry started to drum her fingers on the desk. *Bloody woman. She'll come.* No one told Harry Knight what to do.

She jumped to her feet and began to pace. "Oh, this is ridiculous." Maybe she could go this once. Not for her own sake, but Riley would want to talk about the dig.

Harry brought her hands to her head and rubbed her temple. No, Riley would get too attached.

Even as she thought those words, she knew she was lying to herself. It was she who was getting too attached to them both, and the longer she spent in Annie's company the more she could feel warmth spreading slowly through her cold heart.

But as ever her mother's warning came floating across her mind. *Don't make the same mistakes in life that I did. Don't fall in love, Harry. Don't ever let someone have that power over you, or you might be in my place one day.*

But she couldn't stop thinking about Annie. How much she wanted her, how hard it had been to tear herself away from her in the kitchen. It was raw, passionate, and she was frightened that she could become addicted to her.

Harry's eyes drifted up to the painting of her father. She could almost hear him laughing at her, and she remembered how he would hide in this very room away from his family. The only time he spent with her was to punish her for being naughty. He would look at her and say, *Your mother couldn't even give me a boy. The first girl to inherit this title in two hundred years, and it has to be my child.*

She looked at his image in the painting and snarled, "I will never be like you."

Before she could change her mind, she walked out of the study.

CHAPTER TEN

Harry. You came," Riley shouted.

Annie looked up and saw Harry standing in the doorway with a bottle of wine in hand and a rucksack on her shoulder.

"Come in and sit down. Everything's just about ready."

"I will. I've something for Riley first."

Harry pulled out two radios and handed one to Riley. "As director of our dig I need to be able to contact my assistant wherever she is, and vice versa. Would you like that?"

Riley threw her arms around an obviously surprised Harry. Annie held her breath, thinking she might run, but she didn't—in fact, she visibly relaxed. And Riley's face lit up.

"This is brilliant, Harry, thanks."

In all of her previous assignments, Riley had never become friends with the owner of the property, but Harry was different in so many ways. Despite Harry's best efforts, Riley hero-worshipped her, and if she would only relax a little more, Annie was sure they could have a good relationship.

It would be nice for Riley to have an adult to talk to, other than her. Annie always felt a little bit of guilt that Riley didn't have a second parent, who would bring a distinct influence and give her the rough-and-tumble kind of experience that she would never be able to.

She had faith that one day they would find that someone, but as she had watched Harry and Riley walking back from their dig earlier today, covered in mud and smiling brightly, she wished it could be someone like Harry.

But they wouldn't be here forever. Maybe in another life, Annie thought sadly.

They settled in to dinner and Annie was delighted to see Harry wolf down her food.

"The food is fantastic, Annie. You're such a good cook."

"Mum is the best cook I know," Riley said.

Harry took a sip of her wine and smiled at Riley's pride in her mother. Annie was clearly someone who didn't take easily to compliments, as her reddening cheeks were testament to. "I'm sure."

It was a strange but wonderful sensation to be sitting eating dinner with a family like this. Of course she ate together with people at Cambridge, at society events, and occasionally when she took a group out to dinner, but this was so different.

Harry tried to remember when she had last eaten a home-cooked meal around this kitchen table, and struggled to come up with anything. As a very young child she ate meals in the nursery but as she got older she joined her mother and father in the large formal dining room. That was not a warm family setting.

It was severe, cold, and distant, nothing like this, nothing like… then Harry remembered when she'd last eaten here. The scene burst into her mind with the warmth, light, and smells of the food they had.

My sixteenth birthday.

Lady Dorothy was out of the country and her father was off with some mistress or another, and she was alone, but the staff at Axedale were her real family. Mrs. Castle made her favourite dinner and a cake for them all to share. They made it a special day for her.

The warmth she felt that day was returning to her heart, which was thawing with every passing second spent in Annie's and Riley's company.

She was fascinated by watching Annie listening to Riley tell her about her day. She didn't just pretend to listen, she really did, and then asked questions to get Riley to explain something. Then every so often Annie would stroke Riley's hair or clasp her hand.

Annie must have had a wonderful family to have turned out to be such a wonderful mother.

The warmth around the table was just as Annie had predicted, and Harry loved it. Although she didn't say much, she felt part of it, and was so glad she'd forced herself to come.

"So, Harry, are you going to excavate the whole Roman site?" Annie asked.

"Possibly, we're going to dig some more test pits first to establish the perimeter of the site. It may not be doable on our own, but with Riley helping we can get a good picture of what's happening, no matter what."

"Yeah, it's going to be great, Mum," Riley said.

Annie smiled at her warmly. "Just for that you can have apple pie and ice cream, m'lady."

Harry's heart started to thud hard in her chest. "I'd like that."

After dinner they continued talking while Riley worked on her drawing. Annie brought over coffee for them.

"What's the book you're writing?" Annie asked.

Harry held the warm cup in her hands and took a drink. "It's about Roman Britain. Very detailed, very dry," she joked.

"I'm sure nothing you write could be dry. You seem to be a passionate person. Is that true?"

Harry looked to the side and Riley was humming away, completely taken up with her drawing.

She leaned forward and clasped her hands together. "You could say that."

Harry smiled smugly when Annie's cheeks went ever more pink, and she played with a strand of her hair nervously.

"Ah…did the woman that called earlier get you on your mobile phone?"

"What woman? You mean Clara? Clara called the house phone?"

When her name was mentioned, Annie lost her flirtatious manner and became tense. "Yes, Clara. She was quite insistent about talking to you, but I explained you were out in the grounds."

The thought of Annie and Clara talking made her shudder, and she wasn't quite sure why.

"Is she your girlfriend?"

"God, no. I don't have girlfriends. We just sometimes meet and—"

"That's fine. Riley, are you finished with your ice cream bowl?" Annie stood abruptly and the warm, comforting feeling dropped away like a stone.

"Yes, all finished, Mum."

Annie got all the dishes and started to pack up the dishwasher loudly. Harry went to her, and asked, "Is everything okay with you, Annie?"

She couldn't possibly be jealous, could she? God only knew what Clara had said on the phone. There was a part of Harry that was happy Annie appeared to feel a little jealous. It wasn't adult or mature, she supposed, but still, there it was. No woman could ever have been said to have a claim over Harry—she would have been horrified and put a stop to it straight away—but where Annie was concerned, everything was slowly changing.

Harry took a chance and placed her hand gently on the small of Annie's back and heard her inhale sharply. "Dinner was wonderful. Would it be all right if I have dinner with you more often? I love your company, and Riley's."

Annie turned around making Harry's hand slide onto her waist, and she didn't move it. Annie's hands started to reach out to Harry's waist but she pulled back quickly.

"Of course you can. Riley would love that. There's always enough food."

"And what about you? Would you like it?" Harry let her hand slide down Annie's waist to her hip.

The skin on Annie's upper chest was glowing rosy red. Harry knew she was having an effect on her. She clearly enjoyed her touch, and a hot burning fire spread through Harry's body.

"I would. I like talking to you. It's nice to have an adult conversation for a change."

Harry took her hand away and saw the tension Annie had held in her body release. "I'll just say goodnight to Riley, and I'll see you tomorrow."

Annie just nodded and turned back to her dishes. It couldn't be clearer, they wanted each other badly, but it was impossible. Annie was her employee, and anything Harry could offer Annie would be a temporary affair, and she was sure Annie would expect a lot more.

❖

Annie pulled the curtains shut and turned around to find Riley jumping in her bed in her pyjamas.

"Into bed now, sweetie. You're up late as it is."

Riley scrambled under the covers. "I can't help it. I'm excited. Harry is my friend and I'm her assistant."

She was delighted to see Riley happy for once, but she was also concerned that she might get too attached.

Riley grasped her radio from the bedside cabinet and held it close. On the other side her gladius lay beside her teddy bear Mr. Snuggles.

"Sweetie, you remember when mum talked to you about how Harry wasn't used to being around a family and kids?"

"Uh-huh." Riley snuggled into her quilt cover.

"I don't want you to get too attached to her."

Riley scrunched up her face. "But why? Harry is my friend now. We taught her how to be friends like you said, Mum."

Annie stroked her daughter's hair gently. "I just don't want you to be disappointed, to expect too much from her. We won't be here forever."

"We never stay anywhere forever. I like it here." Riley turned on her side away from Annie, and clutched her radio close.

She sighed and gave her a kiss on the head. "Goodnight, sweetie. I'm sorry I have to work like this, but it's for the best. Believe me." Riley didn't reply and pretended to be asleep.

I'm a bad mother.

She got up and walked to the door, turning off the light as she went. Just as she was about to close the door, she heard static come from the hand-held radio.

Annie strained to hear what was coming from it, and then she heard Harry's voice say, "Harry to Riley. Come in, please."

"Harry? It's you. Riley here."

"Hi, Riley. I wanted to thank you for your hard work today. You're a great field assistant, and I think we'll have a lot of fun together."

Annie couldn't believe it. Harry was full of surprises. It was such a kind thought to talk to her before bedtime.

"It'll be great, Harry. I really love having fun with you."

"I do too. You have a good night's sleep, Riley. I'll see you tomorrow. Harry out."

"I will. Nighty-night, Harry."

Harry. Annie thought. Was she just pulled in by her obvious charm and good looks, or could the ache that she felt in her body and her heart mean more?

Harry stood by the fireplace in her study nursing a glass of whiskey. She leaned against the mantel and stared into the flames, searching for comfort in them. With only a small lamp on in the room, the shadows of the flames danced on the walls, creating a cosy atmosphere.

She took a long sip of whiskey, but found her thoughts were not eased by the alcohol or the flames.

Annie. The name and her image seemed to be permanently etched on her brain these days.

In the kitchen she had wanted Annie, wanted her like she had never wanted anyone. Annie had not only invaded her house, but also her body, and taken control.

If it was just about sex, she could have gone to London and taken care of her needs, but she hadn't. No the object of her affection was here and there was no hiding from it.

"Oh God. The one woman in the world I want and I can't have her." That sort of thing never happened to her. She could always get who she wanted, but the more she couldn't have Annie, the more she wanted her.

She held her glass up high and said, "Thank you very much, God. Thank you for making the perfect woman for me untouchable.

I blame Bridge. She probably prayed for this, to get me back for not going to Sunday services."

Harry heard a knock at the door. "Come in."

Annie popped her head around the door. "Do you mind if I have a quick word, Harry?"

"Of course. Sit down please." She indicated the leather couch that faced the fire. "Can I get you a drink?"

Annie looked hesitant.

"A small nightcap then?" Harry said.

"Okay, just a small brandy, maybe." She supposed she could use the courage.

Harry poured the small brandy and a larger one for herself. "Here you go."

Annie let Harry sit first and took up position at the other end of the couch, staying away from temptation.

The silence between them was deafening.

Finally, Harry asked, "Is Riley asleep?"

"Yes, thank you for saying goodnight to her." Annie pointed to the radio sitting on the mantelpiece.

"I wanted to. She's a good, intelligent child. A testament to your parenting skills, I'm sure," Harry said.

Annie chuckled. "Oh, I don't know about that. She's far more intelligent than I was at her age. Actually I wanted to thank you for the whole day, for reaching out to her and being kind to her. She doesn't have many friends, and she really likes you."

"I like her. I know that I—"

Annie cut her off. "I wanted to say, if she gets to be too much for you or you want to be on your own, just tell me and I'll take care of the situation. Please don't tell Riley."

Harry looked at her with disappointment in her eyes. "You don't have a high opinion of me, do you?"

"It's not that. I just have to protect Riley."

"I understand, and I know I haven't shown you or Riley my best side since you arrived, but I want you to know that I like what you've done to the house so far. You've made it warm, comforting, and I should have said thank you before now."

Annie took a small sip of her brandy and said, "I don't go out of my way to aggravate you. I'm just trying to make everything more of a home for you."

Harry stared into the fire. "It's never been a home to me. My parents were very unhappy here, and my mother moved to Monaco when I was thirteen. I was at boarding school since I was five, but came back for holidays, and my father and I generally tried to ignore each other as much as we could."

"Your mother left you?" Annie asked with shock in her voice.

Harry then realized how much she had said, and grew tense. Why was she talking like this to someone who was a virtual stranger to her? She never talked about her past, or articulated what she felt inside, for fear of appearing weak, but there was something about Annie that lulled her into a sense of calm and safety.

Suddenly Harry felt embarrassed and a little defensive. "My father drove her away. He was an angry, bitter man. He resented the estate, the money it took to run it, and my mother's unwillingness to constantly fund his lifestyle. She had her own money, you see."

Even as she said that, she knew it wasn't an excuse for her mother. She couldn't imagine any circumstances that would cause Annie to leave Riley.

Harry thought it best to change the subject. "It was different when my grandfather was alive. He was a wonderful man, and we did the sorts of things Riley and I did today. So you see, I'm not used to being around a family, but I am trying."

Annie reached out her hand, and Harry took it before Annie could change her mind.

"I think you're doing really well. It can't be easy to have your house invaded."

"I like it. It's different. Everything is different with you here, Annie." Harry rubbed her thumb over the back of Annie's hand, and she felt her heat enter her body.

Annie looked away.

Harry had said too much again, and she searched around for something to change the subject. She asked, "Is Riley's father still in the picture?" Almost immediately she realized her mistake. "I'm sorry. That's a personal question."

Annie smiled softly. "It's all right. I don't mind talking about it. No, he is not. I used artificial insemination. I wanted a child but…"

"You're gay?" Harry said with a hint of hope in her voice.

"Yes." Annie was sure Harry's hold of her hand got tighter. Perhaps this was a good opportunity to tell Harry what she expected in a partner. It might cool things down.

"I always wanted a child, a family. But there was no one in my life so I decided to have Riley myself, and wait for the one my heart wants. I'm a romantic, you see. I believe in waiting for the one I love, the one who will be my forever."

"Forever? Are you joking?" Harry pulled her hand away from her with annoyance, and Annie could almost feel Harry's emotional wall rebuild in front of her eyes.

"Yes, forever. The one who will love me, court me."

Again Harry laughed. "Did you just say *court*?"

Harry's reaction was what Annie had expected, but it still hurt to know that the one person her body and heart had reacted to in years felt that way.

"Yes, I did," Annie said sharply. "Anyone who wants to be in my life has to be serious about a relationship because I have Riley to consider. If someone takes the trouble to court you, then they are showing you they're serious about loving you, and they respect you. I've only been with one woman before, and when I discovered I was just another notch on her bedpost, I promised myself I would wait until I found my forever."

This appeared to anger Harry. She got up and leaned against the fireplace.

"Love doesn't exist. People fall in lust and mistake it for love, and lust wanes. That's why divorce is so prevalent. You're setting yourself up to be hurt deeply."

Annie put down her glass on the coffee table and simply said, "Love exists and I believe in forever."

Harry turned to face Annie. "Humans weren't built to love. We were built to procreate. The Romans had it the right way. Marriages were arranged for political reasons, not foolish notions of love. No, they were much more grown up about life and sex. They thought sex just jolly good fun. Women weren't prized for their virginity, apart from the vestal virgin cult. In fact they thought women were oversexed and lusty. It was only in later eras we learned to become ashamed of sex. I'm not ashamed. I enjoy sex for its own sake, and as often as I can."

Annie couldn't help but feel hurt, and tears threatened to fall. "But you won't know the pleasure of making love with someone who you're totally connected to. Someone you love. Anonymous sex can't compare to that."

"In your opinion—but I won't ever be in love so I'll enjoy sex as much as I can. Happiness is only temporary, Annie. While I'm here, I will give everything I have, and then I'll go back to Cambridge. That's all I can give."

The stony silence returned, until Annie stood up and said, "I think I'll turn in. Thank you for the drink." She could feel Harry's frustration from across the room. She now knew what Annie expected, and it obviously wasn't what she wanted to hear. Whatever feelings were bubbling up between them had no chance of becoming more. They couldn't be any more different from each other if they tried.

When Annie opened the door to leave, she stopped and said, "I feel sad that you believe that, Harry. Love is the most beautiful thing in the world, and if you don't have hope of finding it one day, well…" *And we'll both be hurt if we don't fight this attraction.* "Goodnight, Harry."

CHAPTER ELEVEN

Since that terrible night in Harry's study, Annie tried to keep busy and to not spend any time alone with the countess. It helped to quell their growing attraction. As promised, Harry didn't shy away from Riley, and as the weeks passed, they settled into a comfortable rhythm. Harry had gradually been pulled from the safety of her study to enjoy breakfast, lunch, and tea breaks with her team in Annie's kitchen. She ate with Annie and Riley most nights, unless it was a Monday, then the vicar joined them.

In the afternoons, and at the weekends, Harry took Riley to the dig site where, Riley reported, they did more painstaking excavating. And Harry had not left Axedale to visit London or Cambridge.

Harry admitted to Annie that the house was looking the best it had been in years, the swimming pool was finished, and every refurbished room was clean and fresh. Annie was getting to know the village and the villagers well, and was finally feeling settled in Axedale.

Today Annie was driving down to the village, leaving Riley to play at archaeologist. As she drove down the road out of the estate, she saw Harry and Riley over by the dig site, staging a mock swordfight, Riley with her gladius, and Harry with a wooden stick. She let out a long sigh. Harry had come so far in becoming their friend, and letting them in, but she was afraid Harry wanted more, and afraid if Harry touched her, she wouldn't be able to say no.

That was the biggest problem. Harry didn't think sex was a big deal, and she did. There was no choice. Harry would break her heart if she let her close. She had to be strong.

Annie's first stop in the village was to the school outfitters to pick up Riley's new uniform. Term started next week, and Annie knew her daughter was dreading it. She thanked God trousers were allowed for girls in this school, as they had had that fight countless times as she'd moved around. Trying to get Riley into a skirt was a no go.

She put the bags in the backseat and heard her name called.

Annie looked across the cobbled village road and saw the vicar waving with a warm smile, and standing next to her, Mrs. McRae, Harry's social secretary.

She walked across the road and greeted them warmly. "Vicar, Mrs. McRae, how are you today?"

"Very well, thanks, Annie," Bridget said. "I hear your house-training of our countess goes well."

Annie laughed softly. "I don't know about that. She has her own ideas about things, but we are getting on much better and the house is looking better."

"Not from what I hear. The staff say her ladyship is walking around with a smile on her face instead of scowling at everyone. I'd say that's a minor miracle. Now we need you to perform another."

Annie felt instantly wary. Harry's reputation went before her obviously, but no one had taken the chance to build a bridge to the countess.

"The invitations and requests for her to open events are piling up. There's the flower show, the agricultural show, and I know not what. Mrs. McRae here would like you to have a word with her."

"Oh, I'd be ever so grateful to you, Ms. Brannigan. She has many duties to perform as countess, but she's just not interested. Could you use your powers of persuasion?"

What did these women think she was, a magician? Or more likely a witch. "I'll certainly try but I think the vicar grossly exaggerates my powers."

Bridget laughed. "I don't think so."

"Any help you could give would be appreciated," Mrs. McRae said. "I'll be on my way then. Goodbye, Vicar, Ms. Brannigan."

"Bye." Annie said, and then gave Bridget a hard look. "Stop telling people I have some sort of power over Harry. Believe me, I don't."

"Oh, shush. You've got her practically eating out of your hand." Bridget looped her arm through Annie's and they began to walk. "Have you got some spare time, Annie? There's someone I'd love you to meet."

"Of course. It's a while yet to lunch. Where are we going?"

"To meet Harry's real family," Bridget said cryptically.

❖

Harry was kneeling in the second test pit she and Riley had dug so far. She leaned back on her heels and smiled at Riley, who was cleaning their finds using a bucket of water and a toothbrush. Riley was a great child, more grown up than any child she had known. Not that she knew any other children. But she was interested in everything, it seemed.

Something strange happened to her when she was around Annie or Riley. She became someone that she never knew she could be. She felt happy, loving, and protective of them both.

It was nice to care about them, to put other people first for a change. Maybe it didn't have to be a scary thing to care.

How different would her life be if Lady Dorothy had been even a little like Annie as a mother? Maybe she would actually be able to have an adult relationship.

Only in her quietest moments had she ever dared to dream what it might be like to be part of a couple, but as soon as she did, the memories of hiding while her parents would scream at each other, and her mother crying would burn bright in her mind, eclipsing any other thoughts.

She continued to scrape away the earth from the patterned mosaic floor. Whether the floor was simply patterned or depicted a scene they were still to discover, and that's what made it so exciting.

"Can you make out what the tiles are, Harry?" Riley asked.

"No, but I will soon."

They were silent for a while longer before Harry asked, "Riley, has your mum ever had a…" She struggled to find the words that a child would understand. "A someone who takes her out, or likes her or loves her?"

"You mean like a partner?"

"Yes, a partner."

"No, she went to dinner with a couple of people, but I never saw them. She said she was waiting for her knight in shining armour, but that would be a lady knight cause my mum is gay. That means she likes girls, you know," Riley said with great seriousness.

Harry smiled. *What a great child you are.* "So it does. And you're okay with that?"

"Uh-huh. It's just the same as liking boys."

"Well that's true." Riley was growing up in an age where being gay didn't matter as much, and that was wonderful.

Riley began to scrub her piece of pottery again and said, "I'd like her to meet someone nice. I'd like her to smile, and be happy. Someone to take her out and make her feel special."

"You are a really kind girl, Riley. What kind of woman would be good for your mum?"

"Um…someone who's nice to her, makes her smile, and likes kids, and…" Riley stared at her strangely for a second or two, then smiled. "That's about it."

"And what about you Riley? Would you like—"

"Another mum?" Riley shot off quickly.

Harry immediately wished she'd never brought it up. Why had she even asked?

"Yeah, I'd like that. If it was someone who wanted to be my mum as much as she wanted to be my mum's partner."

Harry stood up and brushed down her jeans, before climbing out of the test pit. "You really are a clever girl, Riley. I hope you find that person for you and your mum."

"I will, I know I will. I just don't want Mum to be lonely. I know she is sometimes."

When Harry thought of Annie being lonely, all she imagined was taking her in her arms, and never letting go. Her heart told her it was her place to do that, but her head said, *Don't even think about it.*

❖

The vicar took Annie to a beautiful little cottage on the edge of the village. "Mrs. Martha Castle used to be head cook at Axedale, and surrogate mother to Harry."

"Really? I'd love to know what Harry was like as a child."

Bridget knocked on the cottage door and walked straight in. "Martha? It's the vicar."

"Does everyone leave their doors unlocked in Axedale?" Annie asked.

Bridget nodded. "Of course, everybody looks out for each other, but they're also in each other's business too, that's the way villages work. A bit different from London, isn't it?"

That was the understatement of the year, especially the parts of London she'd grown up in. Her one abiding memory of living with her mother were the many locks and bolts across the front door, and the scary samurai sword that lay to the side, in case of any intruders. The worst thing of all was that the people who hung around her mother's flat were much more scary than any sword.

Riley would always be safe here, Annie thought.

Bridget led them into Mrs. Castle's sitting room. It was a pleasant cottage front room, with a roaring fire. Ornaments and pictures filled the mantelpiece keeping all her memories safe, and in the centre of the room Mrs. Castle sat in her armchair with a blanket over her legs.

"Afternoon, Martha. How are you today?"

Martha turned off the radio on the table beside her, and said, "Good afternoon, Vicar. I think those stiletto heels get higher every time I see you."

Bridget laughed. "Oh, shush now. They are much smaller than the archbishop's, but he only wears them in private."

This brought guffaws of laughter from Martha. "You really are bad, Vicar. Introduce me to your friend."

"Of course. Martha, this is Ms. Annie Brannigan. The new housekeeper of Axedale Hall."

Annie saw a frail old woman, but her face was bright and full of warmth and smiles. She could just imagine Martha creating a warm, loving environment in the Axedale kitchen for a young Harry to find some love and care.

"Pleased to meet you, Mrs. Castle. Please call me Annie."

"Then you must call me Martha. Come and sit, Annie." Martha pointed to the couch in front of her.

Annie could see why Harry would have loved this woman. She seemed a kind, grandmotherly figure with a warm and welcoming smile.

Bridget told them she would make tea and left them to talk. "So, Annie, how are you settling in at Axedale?"

"Very well. It was a bit of a culture shock at first. I've never worked in such a big house before, although we're only living in one wing of the house. It is beautiful."

Martha sighed happily, as if her memories were running through her mind. "I hear you've taken on more staff."

Did everyone know everything in this village? "How did you...?"

"There are no secrets in Axedale, Annie. You know, in its heyday, Axedale had over a hundred staff."

"I could believe it. Now there are three indoor staff trying to keep one wing of it in order." Two pictures caught her eye on the mantelpiece. One was of a young Harry and the other was Harry graduating from university. This woman clearly cared about her.

Martha caught her looking. "I treasure those. How are you coping with her? I know she can be difficult."

"We didn't have the best of starts. I have my daughter Riley with me, and Harry didn't like the idea of a family living with her, or me trying to turn Axedale into a home. But I have gotten her to eat properly at last. Before I arrived she was surviving on soup and sandwiches. Now she's eating a good dinner a day, at least."

"I bet you frighten her to death, Annie," Martha said smiling.

"Why do you say that?" Annie asked with surprise.

"Harry might seem the arrogant ladies' woman, but really she is a scared little girl, hiding in the kitchen from her parents. The earl and countess were dreadful parents. Harry's mother was a sweet, hopeful young girl when she arrived at Axedale, but that brute of an earl turned her into a hard, emotionless woman. The only time Harry has been loved and cared for was by myself and the staff, and now a beautiful young woman is taking care of her in the same way, but now she is all grown up. I'm quite sure she craves the attention you give her, and that will be terrifying to her, believe me. That's why she hasn't come to see me since she returned. She doesn't want to face her past, because it makes her feel weak."

When Martha put it that way, it all made perfect sense. The way Harry looked at her made her feel hot all over. But Harry wasn't capable of loving her forever, was she?

Martha reached out and took her hand. "Give her time, Annie. She is capable of so much more."

They were interrupted by Bridget bringing in the tea tray. "Here we are. I brought some of Mrs. McCrae's fruit cake, Martha."

They chatted and laughed for the next hour before Annie and Bridget excused themselves.

"I'll walk you to your car, Annie."

"Thanks. Martha is such a sweet woman."

Bridget pushed her hands into the pockets of her leather biker jacket and sighed. "She is. I keep trying to encourage Harry to come and visit, but she keeps putting it off, and she might not have much longer. Martha has a bad heart condition and her mobility is poor. We all try to muck in and help take care of her and her cottage, but we can't be there twenty-four hours a day."

They arrived back at Annie's car, and she got into the driver's seat. "Does she not have any health or care workers that come to see her?"

"Only once a month. It isn't good enough, but there are a lot of remote villages in this part of the country, and services are stretched. Don't get me wrong, Harry takes no rent for the cottage, and pays her a monthly stipend, but an old lady with no family needs more than mere material comfort. Unfortunately that's all our countess can offer anyone."

"I'll try and have a word with her."

"Thanks."

Annie keyed the ignition and it made a terrible screeching noise.

"Uh-oh," Bridget said. "That doesn't sound too healthy."

"No, it doesn't. That's all I need," Annie said.

Bridget looked up and waved across the road. "Oh, lucky us. Help is at hand in the form of a handsome, rugged butch."

A woman matching Bridget's description came bounding across the street with a warm smile on her face. "How can I can help you ladies?"

❖

"I can't believe this," Harry said.

"You never, ever found anything like this with your grandpa?" Riley said as she watched Harry start to backfill the test pit.

Unlike the mosaic at the first pit, where they found a nice but predictable border pattern, the mosaic they found here was special. After scrapping back the soil and rocks, she sponged down the tesserae tiles, and what emerged bit by bit was a blond woman's head, and just the hint of an oyster shell behind.

"No, I never did. It's the birth of Venus, goddess of love and… other things." Harry hesitated with further explanation. "Hand me my phone, please, and I'll show you." She searched for a similar picture of the birth of Venus from a shell. "It's just like the ceiling in the pool room."

"Wow! She looks like my mum with her blond hair. She's pretty."

Annie, my goddess of love and sex.

"What are you thinking, Harry?"

God, even a little girl could see what she was thinking about Annie now. She needed to get this aching need under control. "Nothing. Let's get back up to the house. I've got to think and make some phone calls. This discovery is too important to take lightly."

"Why did we just cover it over again with the dirt?"

Harry gathered up her tools, and turned her baseball cap around the right way. "It's the best way to preserve what we've found until we can make better arrangements. You see, it's been protected well by the earth all this time, so it will be again for at least a while longer."

Riley packed up her bags of finds in her rucksack and emptied the bucket of water. Harry got her toolbox and said, "We can leave the bucket and larger tools here for the moment. I'll take your rucksack for you. Remember your shield."

"I won't forget, Harry."

Harry smiled at her. Riley was the sweetest child, both eager to learn and easy to please. Without thinking Harry reached out and took her hand, and said, "Let's go, centurion."

Riley beamed with happiness at the term of endearment and Harry gulped hard. *Why did I say that?*

Centurion was what her grandfather had called her, when she'd worn the sword and shield just like Riley.

One part of her told herself not to panic. It was just a friendly nickname to a nice kid who looked up to her. And another part of her told her to get away now, to get herself out of this situation because she was starting to really care for Riley.

Harry remembered Annie's words, *If she gets to be too much for you or you want to be on your own, just tell me and I'll take care of the situation. Please don't tell Riley.*

She would not allow her fears to win and hurt Riley, so they walked off hand in hand across the grounds, and back to the house.

"I can't wait to tell Mum what we found."

"Yes, I think she'll be very proud of you helping to find such an impressive archaeological discovery."

"Look, Harry, a truck. I wonder who's that is."

As they got nearer she saw some woman she didn't recognize, and Annie in the passenger seat.

"She took the car to the village, why did she need a lift home?" Harry asked Riley.

The driver got out and Harry immediately felt her stomach churn. The woman was tall, broad, and butch and wore farming clothes. The vicar's rugged farmer. Bloody hell.

When they got up to the driveway the scene got ever worse. The farmer helped Annie out of the high passenger seat of the Land Rover, by holding her waist and letting her slide down her body. Just as she and Annie had done in the kitchen. The simple act that had sparked the fiery want in her belly.

Annie's laughter at something the farmer said made her feel even worse.

"Annie," Harry called, "is there something wrong?

They walked around to the front of the truck and Annie said, "Oh, hello, you two. Sam, this is my daughter Riley, and this is my employer, Lady Axedale."

Employer? I'm just her employer? Harry was furious.

"Pleased to meet you both. Call me Quade, everyone does. We haven't met before, m'lady, but I'm one of your tenant farmers."

She held out her hand for Harry to shake and she had no choice but to comply.

"Ah yes, I'm sorry I haven't been able to get around all the farms to see how things are going, but I will do."

"No problem, m'lady. Whenever you have time."

"It's Harry," she said flatly. "Where's the car?"

"Oh, it wouldn't start and Quade here came to my rescue, like a knight in shining armour." Annie touched Quade's hand.

Harry felt a tight coil of jealousy slither around in her stomach. She looked at Riley, and remembered that she had used the very same phrase.

She had no right to be angry, and no right to be jealous, in fact she had never felt jealous over another woman in her life. But first she had felt it when Annie had talked to her groom, and now this. After all, she kept women at arm's length and expected them to have other lovers, but with Annie it was different. The thought of her being close to anyone else made her feel sick.

Acting on instinct, she took a few steps to stand at Annie's side, placed a hand on the small of Annie's back, and gave Quade a hard stare. "Thank you for looking after Annie for me. I'll send my groom down to get the car soon."

There was a tense awkward silence, and then Quade said, "I better get going then. Nice to meet you, Riley, Harry. Oh, and Annie, remember you promised to come to the pub quiz. My team needs all the help it can get."

"Of course I will. It'll be fun to have a night out for a change."

Harry couldn't believe her ears. She felt like she was losing Annie before her very eyes. Bridget said that Quade was looking to settle down with someone, and it looked like she had Annie in her sights.

"Goodbye then. We mustn't keep you," Harry said, dismissing her altogether.

Quade looked at her and nodded. "Of course. Goodbye then."

When she drove off, Annie said, "Why were you so rude? Quade was very kind."

"I'm sure she was. You could have called me. I would have come and picked you up."

"There was no need. Quade was there."

"Indeed," Harry said sarcastically. "Your knight in shining armour." Harry was so angry. She was going to say something she would regret, so she stormed off towards the house.

She heard Riley shout after her, "But Harry, we have to tell mum about the Venus mosaic."

That evening Harry decided a swim might clear her head, and after she had finished her lengths of the pool, she turned over onto her back and floated across the surface. On the ceiling above was the painting of the birth of Venus, the same classical image that was emerging from the ground beneath Axedale.

"I can't get away from you."

Harry swam to the side and smoothed back her dark, wet hair. She was so glad the pool room was finished—it was such a peaceful, relaxing space. With the imitation torches on the walls and marble everywhere, she really could believe she was in a Roman bathhouse.

She needed somewhere to collect her thoughts after today. Harry let her head fall back against the side of the pool and closed her eyes.

The scene from this afternoon kept playing over in her mind like a movie. *My knight in shining armour.*

The words tortured her. "I don't want to want her, and yet I can't think of anything else," Harry told the empty room.

Harry jumped when she heard the pool door open, and gasped when she saw Annie walk in, carrying a towel and wearing a black bikini. The incessant and inevitable beat started pounding between her legs. *God, I want her.*

Annie put her towel down and held her hand to her chest. "Oh God, Harry. You gave me a fright."

"Sorry. I felt like a swim."

Annie looked unsure of what to do, and said, "I don't want to disturb you. I'll come back later."

"No, please, come in. It's fine, honestly."

Annie held her arms crossed over her chest. She was feeling more than a little exposed. Harry was looking at her with that penetrating hot look that made her skin ache to be touched.

As she slipped into the pool, she knew this was a bad idea, yet there was no way of turning back now. She swam over to where Harry was, and leaned against the edge of the pool with her. There was an awkward silence that Annie felt obliged to fill. "So Riley tells me you had a good day today."

"You could say that. We found more mosaic floor, but this time it was far better quality than we found the first time, which tells me we're dealing with a villa or public building with slave quarters, kitchens, places where the mosaic doesn't need to be as good a quality, and the public rooms designed with the finer quality floor."

"Riley said it was a mosaic of Venus?"

Harry gave her a dark look that made her shiver. "Yes, goddess of love…and sex."

This was crazy. Annie could feel the sexual energy pulling them together.

"What will you do now?" Annie asked.

"That's the tricky part. If I report the find, like I should, I could lose control of the dig, and I promised Riley we could do it together. I might get a digger to make a full length trench and see how it goes. The site has the potential to be a truly magnificent building."

"What's been your best find in your career?" Annie asked. She thought keeping the subject on work might calm their libidos.

Harry moved in front of her. "Career wise, the Aqua Sulis villa in Bath. It's a palace-sized villa, and I worked on that from the first spade of dirt to the end. There's a visitor centre there now, I'm very proud of it, but the finds that mean the most are the small things. The everyday objects that connect you with the people that used them, like a child's shoe, a doll, or letters from back home sent to the soldiers based in the UK. When you hold something like a child's shoe in your hand, they aren't just a race of people from the pages of history so long ago. They are living, breathing people, with the same wants and needs as us."

Annie was captivated by Harry's answer. When she spoke with passion about her work, she lost her moody, arrogant side. There were so many depths to this woman. Martha was so right about her.

Annie touched the black ink tattoo on Harry's biceps, and saw her body shudder. "What does this mean?"

"It was my own piece of teenage rebellion. It's the Roman standard with an inscription meaning fight until death."

Annie found herself boxed in against the side of the pool, with Harry looking at her like she wanted to devour her whole.

"I've never met anyone like you, Annie," Harry said huskily.

"What do you mean?"

"Someone who makes me want to know more."

Harry's eyes gazed at her lips, making Annie lick them without thinking, and her heart beat out of her chest. "More than the women who fall into your bed?" she husked.

"Yes," Harry whispered and came in closer, preparing to kiss her.

Annie took a deep breath and remembered her promise to herself. "I won't fall into your bed, Harry."

"Why?" Harry's lips hovered inches from her own.

"Because I don't do that. I don't fall into bed with anyone. I've told you before, I need a committed relationship, I want forever."

"Forever doesn't exist. We have to take what we can, while we can."

"It does in my world," Annie said flatly.

Harry stared at her, lust pouring from her. "I can change your mind. I want you, Annie."

It was taking everything in her power not to give in, to Harry and to her own desire. "No you can't. Besides, I'm your employee."

Harry leaned in and their lips came together softly. The kiss was exquisite, softer than she imagined Harry could be. Everything about how her mouth felt, how her lips felt, was wonderful, like they had been made with the sole purpose of kissing her.

They broke apart and Annie stroked her finger down Harry's cheekbone in a loving, tender touch.

"Don't touch me like that," Harry said.

"What? Like this?"

Harry caught her hand. "Yes. It doesn't work like that for me."

"Why?"

Harry remained silent, but her eyes were saying so much more.

"So you can't feel anything more than lust? So you can't feel love?"

Harry turned away quickly and got out of the pool. Annie had clearly hit the nail on the head.

CHAPTER TWELVE

The next morning, Annie didn't see or hear from Harry. She never even came in for her coffee. This was becoming a pattern. After an emotional event, Harry ran away and hid from anything that disturbed her controlled façade. By lunchtime, though, she'd had enough and took Harry's lunch to her study.

She knocked on the door and heard a lot of shuffling with papers, and then Harry said, "Come."

When she walked into the room Harry didn't even look up at her. "You can leave the tray on the desk."

Annie gave a sarcastic laugh. "You must be joking. You hide away all morning and think I'm just going to leave the tray?" She put the tray down with a thump, and sat down.

Harry looked up and said, "I'm not hiding. I'm busy, okay?"

"You are hiding, because you don't want to talk about what happened. Well if I'm to keep working here, we need to."

This got Harry's attention. As scared as she was of her growing feelings, the last thing she wanted was to lose Annie, and Riley.

She put everything down and said, "Okay you have my attention. I don't want you to leave."

"Good. Now, last night happened because I think we are attracted to each other, yes?"

Attracted is an understatement. I want to kiss you, love every part of your body, and watch you come while I'm deep inside you.
"Yes."

"But we both want different things in life, plus you're my employer. So if we nip it in the bud here, we can carry on as friends. What do you think?"

What she thought and what she wanted were two different things, but Annie was right, if this was to work they needed to draw a line in the sand. "Okay then, friends."

Annie offered her hand and her beautiful smile, and Harry took them.

"Deal," Annie said. "Now eat your lunch."

Harry looked at her tray and smiled when she saw the usual vase with three flowers in it. "What are they today?"

"Pink camellias. Beautiful, aren't they?"

Harry wanted to say *Not as beautiful as you*, but she had a second chance to keep Annie and Riley here and she wasn't going to risk it. "Yes."

Annie furrowed her brow. "You don't really like flowers, do you?"

How else could she answer but with the truth? "I like that you take the time to pick them and give them to me every day—it means a lot. I usually *give* the flowers."

"I bet," Annie said with the merest hint of annoyance. "So have you decided what to do with the dig site?"

Harry swallowed down a delicious bite of homemade bread. "Yes, I'm going to keep quiet for the moment. It is my land and it's something I want to share with Riley, as long as we can go with it. I've ordered in some specialist equipment to help—a digger, an inflatable tent to protect the dig from the elements—but mainly it will be a recording exercise. I can't lift any mosaic flooring without a large team, so Riley and I will continue to dig test pits, find the limits over the area, record all the finds, and build a computer map of the building. Then in the future I can bring in a big team to uncover the ruins permanently. If I bring in a team now, Riley will be sidelined, and I don't want that. It's her discovery."

"Riley will be happy."

"I hope so. I really enjoy her company."

"I'll leave you to your lunch then." Just as Annie turned away, she added, "Oh, I almost forgot. Riley and I are going to church on Sunday and I wondered if you would like to come with us."

"Church? But I thought you were a Catholic."

"I am, but it's still God, isn't it? And besides the vicar asked us to come. I wouldn't like to let her down. There's a charity bakery sale afterwards, and I said I'd bring some cakes."

Me? At a bakery sale? Harry's thoughts were suddenly filled with Quade at church alone with Annie and Riley, and then her walking them home afterwards.

"I'll come."

Annie rewarded her with a big smile. "Thank you. I appreciate it."

As Annie left, Harry realized she had been manipulated in the nicest possible way, but she didn't care.

By Friday morning, Harry and the refurb team had finished the ballroom, and Harry was really excited to show it to Annie. When she had shown Riley this room earlier, she had excitedly exclaimed, "It's just like the ballrooms they have in Mum's romance novels—she sometimes reads me those bits."

Well, Harry thought, if Annie liked romance so much, then she would love this. She led Annie to the room, and told her to close her eyes. "Okay, keep them tightly shut—I mean it, Annie Brannigan." Annie stuck her tongue out at her, so she stood behind her and covered her eyes with her hands.

Annie giggled. "What are you doing?"

She placed her lips close to Annie's ear and whispered, "Keep your eyes shut, I told you."

Annie shivered in response.

"Okay, walk forward five steps, and open."

Annie's eyes opened and she gasped. "Oh my goodness. It's so beautiful."

Harry's chest puffed out with pride at Annie's reaction. "You really think so?" She was genuinely proud of the work done here.

The ballroom was one of the most highly decorated rooms in the whole house, with intricate plaster mouldings painted in gold, the ceiling painting that had to be carefully restored, as well as the many repairs needed to the large crystal chandeliers. Yes, she was proud, and she was glad Annie could appreciate it.

Annie lifted her arms in a dance posture and spun around in the centre of the room. "I can imagine a decadent ball here with brooding, handsome gentlemen and fine ladies dancing. It's truly stunning."

Harry folded her arms and leaned back on one of the marble pillars, and enjoyed watching her as she spun around the room. She looked girlish and carefree, and as she ever was, beautiful.

"Not bad is it? I bet it's just like a scene from one of your trashy romance novels," Harry teased.

Annie stopped and gave her a glare. "They are not trashy, but yes, it's just like a ballroom from a Jane Austen novel."

Harry pushed herself from the pillar and walked over to Annie. "There used to be great balls held in here all the time. My grandpa told me about them."

"It must have been a wonderful sight to see the room used as it was meant to, with all the couples dancing in sequence."

Harry smiled mischievously. "Shall we recreate the scene?"

"What dance?" Annie responded with surprise. "Do you know how to dance like that?"

"Somewhat. We had to learn at school, and practise with the other girls since there were no boys, and it suited me completely." Harry winked at her.

"I can just imagine, m'lady."

Harry took her hand gently, and said, "So? Shall we dance?"

Annie held her hand up. "Oh, no way. I'm not a dancer."

Harry leaned over and whispered, "Are you scared to dance with me?"

Annie held her gaze. "I'm not afraid of *you*."

"Then let's go." Harry took out her smartphone and started to play some Regency style music. She pulled a reluctant Annie to the middle of room.

"I can't do this, Harry."

"Of course you can." She hit pause, then led Annie a few paces away from her and went back to her place.

She hit play, and the music resumed. "Perfect. Now, are you ready?"

Annie gave her a cheeky smile. "Do you curtsy first and I bow?"

Harry put her hands on her hips and said, "Do I look like I would be the one who would curtsy? You curtsy, I bow. That's the way it is."

"Maybe it shouldn't be," Annie teased. "Maybe you should let someone else have a bit of control?"

Oh my God. I want her. I want her to beg me to let her come. Harry closed her eyes for a split second to regain control of herself. "I can do a lot of things, but giving up control is not one of them, and believe me, you wouldn't want me to."

Harry held Annie's eyes until she looked down and curtsied. She felt a ripple of pleasure run through her body, just for winning this first sexually tinged skirmish. If this made her feel this good, then God knew what making love to her would feel like.

She bowed and said, "Take my hand, keep looking in my eyes, and follow my lead."

They walked slowly in a circle, one way, then the other, and after a few repetitions, they were soon dancing in sync.

"You see how well we do together if you follow my lead?" Harry said as they moved around elegantly.

"Only because I let you lead me," Annie said, smiling.

Inside she knew that was true, and it was driving her crazy, and made her want Annie like crazy. She wanted to please her, to make Annie scream her name, and all because this woman let her. No other woman had ever made her feel this way.

"Am I playing the part of your brooding, handsome gentleman sufficiently?" Harry had meant it as a joke, but Annie didn't smile. She gazed into Harry's eyes with what she could only hope was love and want. She should have been scared of that, but in this moment there wasn't fear, there were just two people who wanted the same thing. Each other.

"Yes," Annie croaked, "you're the perfect brooding, handsome gentleman."

Their dancing slowed until they simply stood in each other's arms with the music playing, and Harry knew she was falling under love's spell.

Harry closed in on Annie's lips and whispered, "And you are my perfect lady."

Annie's eyes closed and her lips parted in invitation. Harry was just an inch away from her lips and she didn't care what the consequences were. She needed to kiss Annie more than anything in the world.

Harry heard the telltale creak of the ballroom doors opening and a voice say, "Oh, excuse me. I'm sorry to interrupt."

They sprang apart immediately and the spell was broken, and the harsh reality of real life was back. Damn.

It was Bev. "I can speak to you later, Annie."

"It's all right," Harry said, the feelings of panic spreading throughout her chest. "I've got lots I need you to be doing. I'll leave you to talk."

Harry was off and out the door before either could say another word.

❖

Later that night, Annie was getting ready for the pub quiz. She sat at her dressing table and applied her lipstick. She couldn't remember the last time she'd had an adult night out, but her heart wasn't in it at all.

Annie gazed at her reflection in the mirror and sighed. "What am I doing?"

When she had reminded Harry she was going out tonight, she had said nothing and plodded off angrily. Annie had hoped that after connecting this afternoon Harry might come and enjoy the evening with her, and just maybe open up to their growing feelings, but no.

Today when they danced together, she'd seen a different Harry. She wasn't frightened and her walls were nonexistent. They were just two people with a passion between them that was frightening in intensity, and who were simply falling in love. She had to face it, they were, but Annie's fear was Harry would never admit to it to herself or to her and run away.

Going by Harry's track record there should have been no hope that she could give more than one night of passion, but when Annie looked into her eyes, she felt deep down in her soul that Harry had a great capacity for love.

But instead of Harry spending time with her tonight, Annie was getting ready to go and meet with Quade, and her stomach churned with a feeling of guilt.

I'm kidding myself. It's impossible.

She was Annie's employer, and a night of passion here and there would never be enough when it came to Harry Knight.

"Mum?"

Annie jumped in fright but smiled when she saw Riley come into the room and sit on her bed. "Yes, sweetie?"

"I don't think you should go to the pub with Ms. McQuade. Harry looked sad at dinner."

Annie sighed. "She isn't sad, Riley."

Harry had been quiet and withdrawn, and she suspected she was the cause of it, but what else could she do? This was what Harry wanted. No relationship, nothing to tie her down. Well she was giving her what she wanted.

"How can I explain this to you?" Annie came over and sat on the bed beside Riley. "I like Harry and I know she likes me. She's my friend, but she doesn't want to have a girlfriend, Riley. She's wants to be single. Independent."

"No, she doesn't," Riley said angrily. "She likes you like a girlfriend."

"Riley, stop. I know you like Harry, but we're not going to be here forever and we can't afford to get attached to her."

"We always leave. I hate it." Riley ran out of the room full of anger and frustration.

❖

Harry was outside, walking the grounds, trying to work off her bad mood. She found herself walking in the direction of the secret garden. It was a gated part of the estate gardens where her great-grandmother had introduced wildflowers and plants to attract the birds and butterflies.

She opened the heavy grated garden gate and walked in. She had retreated to this little bit of tranquillity so many times when she was growing up, to escape her parents' arguing and unhappiness.

Harry made her way over to what she had described as her tree, when she was young.

She ran her hand over the rough bark until she found what she was looking for. Then she saw it, the words *Harry's Hideout*, carved into the bark.

She looked up and saw the boards that were the flooring for her tree house. This had been her sanctuary for many years, and maybe it could be again. Harry found the steps at the back of the tree and started to climb up. It was a lot harder now she was taller, as she discovered when she hit her head on a branch, but she got there in the end and swung her legs over the side of the wooden platform.

There was a fantastic view over the estate grounds and house. It was hard to believe this was all hers now—in fact there was a large part of her that didn't believe it, except that it was, and she didn't want it. Too many bad memories lived here, and at first she'd felt more like a custodian, bringing it up to scratch before handing it on to the next generation.

But then came Annie and Riley, who made the house feel warm and happy. Annie had promised that she could make the house a home for her, if she was allowed, and she resisted, but with each passing day she was getting in deeper. Axedale Hall was feeling more like a home with every new room they renovated, and Annie with her redoubtable manner was banishing the bad memories and making new ones.

Annie. In a parallel universe, where she was strong and wasn't petrified of relationships and commitment, Annie would be her new lady of the manor, and she would love her like no one had ever loved before, and Riley would make their little family complete, but in this universe she was hiding in a children's tree house while Annie was getting ready for a night out with someone else.

She felt a wave of emotion hit her. Sadness, frustration, and weakness.

The gate to the garden opened and she jumped, but soon saw it was Riley. The girl clambered up the tree and sat beside her.

"You've found my secret hiding place then?" Harry said to her.

Riley looked as down in the dumps as she felt. "Yeah, I've come to play here sometimes. Is it okay that I did?"

Harry slung an arm around Riley, and said, "Of course I don't mind. I came here a lot when I was a child. To think as well as play."

"What did you need to think about?" Riley asked.

"My mother and father didn't get along well, and it wasn't nice when they fought."

Riley sighed. "Mum's getting ready to go out."

"I know," Harry said sadly.

"Why don't you go too? You can have fun with Mum, instead of Ms. McQuade."

She wished she could. Annie insisted it wasn't a date but she was sure Quade thought otherwise. I mean who wouldn't try to catch Annie's eye and go out with her?

Me, Harry thought, *because I'm a frightened idiot.*

"No, your mum needs to have fun without her boss being there. She has to live with me all day, every day. I'm sure she needs a break."

"But she does like you. She smiles and laughs with you all the time. No one's ever done that before. Oh, and she always makes your favourite jam roly-poly and ice cream on Sundays."

Harry smiled at Riley's innocent view of love, and thought of the little vase of flowers Annie brought with her lunch every day. Even though flowers were not her favourite thing, she looked forward to them now. Annie didn't know that she treasured them so much that she kept one of each flower in her notebook.

"You like her, don't you, Harry?"

Harry sighed. "Things aren't as simple as that, Riley. I can't ever be what your mum needs. You'll understand when you're a grownup."

"I won't. You should be her knight in shining armour," Riley said angrily.

"I'm no knight, Riley."

Riley took her hand and pleaded with her. "I want you to be. It's not fair."

"Maybe, but it's the way it is. Let's get you back so your mum can drop you with Mrs. Peters." Harry went down the ladder first, and then Riley went down a few steps and jumped into Harry's arms.

"Why couldn't I just stay with you?" Riley asked.

"I have a lot of writing to catch up with. I've been having too much fun with you and your mum, and I'm way behind. Besides, you'll love being with Mr. and Mrs. Peters, she'll take you down to the shop and let you choose any sweets you like. They're nice people—they used to babysit me sometimes, or I'd just go into the shop and visit for a while."

Harry had almost forgotten all about those memories. Someone else who had been a big part of her life, and she had purposely shut them out, just like she did the whole village. The thought made her sad.

CHAPTER THIRTEEN

Annie wondered for the thousandth time why she had come tonight. It was stupid. She felt bad for leaving Harry and nervous about walking into the pub alone. She dropped Riley off at Mrs. Peters's house just down the road, and walked to the door of the Witch's Tavern.

She was just about to turn around and leave when Quade came jogging towards her.

"Hi, Annie, sorry I'm late. You look beautiful."

Annie looked down at her figure-hugging, knitted silver minidress and felt a bit self-conscious. If Harry had said that, she would have felt her skin grow hot. She chastised herself for comparing Quade to Harry. Harry was never going to be the person she needed, so she had to get her out of her head. Maybe a pleasant evening with Quade and the other villagers could do that.

"Thank you. You look nice too." And she did. Quade was ruggedly handsome, just like the vicar had described her. The perfect date for a woman like her. Even if she wasn't Harry.

"We better get a table before they're all gone," Quade said.

She ushered her in the door, and led her to a table. A number of the villagers she had met came over to say hello, and some new people were introduced to her.

Quade got them both drinks and registered them for the quiz night. They began to chat about their respective jobs and the village for a while, until Quade said, "Annie? Could I ask you something?"

"Of course."

Quade looked apprehensive as she prepared to ask her question. "Are you and Lady Axedale romantically involved?"

Annie nearly choked on her drink. "Of course not. She's my employer. Why would you think that?"

"Well for one, when I dropped you off the other day, she gave me the look."

Annie hadn't the first idea what she was talking about. "The look? What's that?"

Quade smiled and took a quick sip from her bottle of lager. "It's the *You're stepping on my territory here, mate, back off* look."

"I have never heard of that in my life."

"You're not meant to. We learn it at butch school," Quade joked.

Annie laughed. "You've got to be kidding? I know she was a bit rude but…"

"If it was only that, I wouldn't have said anything, but since you got here tonight, she is all that you have talked about."

Annie was taken aback. "That's not true, is it?"

Quade nodded, and Annie apologized quickly. "I'm so sorry. There's been a lot going on, and we're really good friends. We're attracted to one another but we're not together."

"Hey, don't apologize. I'm disappointed of course. You're a beautiful woman, Annie. But I'd never tread on someone else's toes."

"There's nothing going on," Annie said.

"But you'd both like there to be, so why don't we be friends and say no more about it?" Quade said.

There might not be anything going on but her attraction and care for Harry were clear, so she took the opportunity to keep things simple. "Thank you, Quade."

Just as she finished speaking the pub fell silent. They both looked over to the door, and saw Harry walk through the door. It was such a strange sight. This was Harry's home and yet she looked like the new cowboy in town.

She looked gorgeous in designer jeans, a tight T-shirt, and a black pinstripe suit jacket. Annie stood and tried to wave Harry over to them, but she just scowled and headed to the bar.

"She looks lost," Annie said.

Quade gave her hand a squeeze and said, "Don't worry. Let me go and talk to her."

The pub went back to its chattering but it was muted. It made Annie sad that Harry had absolutely no relationship with these people. She knew that Harry didn't have the tools to mend bridges and heal wounds, so she decided she would have to do it for her.

Harry might not be here forever, but she would be coming back and forth from Cambridge every so often, and she wanted Harry to always know she had a place here, and a support system in the village to help her.

Annie vowed that before she left Axedale, she would help Harry mend these bridges.

❖

Why did I come here? Harry asked herself as she stood at the bar.

When she walked in and saw Annie close to someone else, it hurt badly. All she wanted to do was turn around and go home, but with the whole pub staring at her she felt compelled to go to the bar and get at least one drink.

"What can I get you, m'lady?" She looked up and was amazed when she saw Mr. Finch still behind the bar.

"Mr. Finch? You're still here?"

The tall silver-headed man laughed softly. "I'm not dead yet, m'lady. My son runs the bar now but I help out at night."

Another piece of her past slotted into place. Mr. Finch had poured her first legal pint of lager in this very pub on her eighteenth birthday.

"It's wonderful to see you, Mr. Finch. You gave me my first pint, do you remember?"

"I also remember giving you a clip round the ear when you and Mrs. Gray's son stole four bottles of beer from the cellar." He poured out a pint of lager and gave it to her.

"Good God, I had forgotten all about that." Harry laughed and took a drink. "I got worse when I got home to Mrs. Castle, believe me."

Mr. Finch started drying some glasses while they talked. "Not your parents?"

"No, they probably weren't even at Axedale that day, Mr. Finch," Harry said with a bitter edge to her voice.

"I think you're old enough to call me Ted, m'lady. So, we haven't seen you in the village since you inherited Axedale."

"I've lost touch with everyone, Ted, and I know that my father wasn't well liked, so I thought it best to just leave things as they were."

Ted leaned across the bar and smacked her on the shoulder. "You are not your father, m'lady. It's time for a fresh start, no?"

Could it be time for a fresh start? A new life here in Axedale with—

"Hi, Harry."

Just what she needed, the bloody handsome, rugged farmer, but she put on a forced smile and said, "Quade, how are you?"

"Fine thanks, mate. Listen, I wanted to have a word about Annie. If I had known you were...you know...well I would have never asked her to the pub. I mean I would have asked both of you to join the team but...I just want you to know I'm not trying to step on your toes. We've agreed to be friends."

Harry was taken aback. What had Annie said to her to give her that impression? "I appreciate you saying that, Quade, but Annie and I aren't together."

"So she tried to say, but she hasn't stopped talking about you since she arrived, and you're not going to deny you gave me the look. Come on, you can join our team."

"Oh no, I couldn't intrude," Harry said.

"Mate, she's over there worried about you. Come on over and make her feel better, and anyway the vicar's on my team too, so we'll be even numbers."

Harry leaned against the bar and let out a breath. She had no idea what she was doing. Even other people thought they were together. Red lights of warning were flooding all over her brain.

She looked over to Annie's table and saw that Bridget had arrived, and Annie was smiling sweetly at her. Her smile promised everything that she craved and was terrified of. Harry thought of Riley and how much she cared about her, how Riley wanted her to be her mum's knight in shining armour, and felt the walls of the pub closing in on her.

"Quade, I have to go. Will you see they both get home safely?"

"Yes, but wait—"

It was too late. Harry walked out of the pub and forced herself not to look back.

❖

When Annie left the pub, the daylight was just starting to fade to a warm glow. When Harry had left the pub she wanted to run after her, but felt obliged to stay with her friends. She picked up Riley and drove back to Axedale. She put Riley to bed and wandered downstairs.

Everything was so confusing. One moment Harry acted like she wanted her badly, and the next she wanted to run. She went into the kitchen to make some tea and saw the kitchen door open.

Harry was standing outside looking up at the stars.

She walked up beside her and said, "Why did you leave?"

"I needed to think."

Annie shivered in the cool of the evening, and wished she had brought her cardigan from the bedroom.

Harry immediately took off her jacket and put it around her shoulders.

"Thank you." Annie pulled the jacket in tight and inhaled the reassuring musk of aftershave and Harry's own unique scent that filled her with warmth. She could feel the energy between them demanding she touch Harry, even from a few steps away, relentless and demanding, and so hard not to give in to.

The sounds of the countryside at night were the only noises to punctuate the awkward silence.

"Did Quade say something to upset you?"

Harry turned around and said, "No, of course not. Quade is a good and honourable person. You should see more of her. She'd be good for you."

Annie looked at her like she had gone mad. "Are you joking? You couldn't help but be rude to her when she dropped me back to Axedale, and now I should see more of her?"

Harry stuffed her hands into her pockets and her jaw flexed as if she was trying to control her emotions. "I've had more time to think about it, and after talking to her in the pub I see what a good, steady person she is. Quade would make a good partner for you, and a mum for Riley. I won't be here for long and it would be nice to know you were…taken care of. I don't like the idea of you and Riley going house to house all the time, always working for new people and never getting a home. Someone like Quade would give you the forever you're looking for."

Annie felt anger boil up inside to the point that she couldn't hold it any more. "One, I'm not a pet that you have to leave in someone else's care when you swan back to Cambridge because you're too afraid to face what you feel. I've been looking after myself since I was sixteen years old, so I'm not going to stop now. Two, you have no idea what forever means. It doesn't mean settling for someone safe, who will be with me forever because it's easy. Forever means finding the one who has no choice but to love me, and wants to make a family and a life with me, not because it's safe and comfortable, but because they need to be with me despite their fears, or the problems or inconvenience it would bring to their life."

Harry grasped her by the shoulders and pushed her up against the wall of the house. Her breathing was heavy, and her eyes were dark and dangerous.

"Do you know how many women I've had sex with? More than I could count. I love the thrill of the chase, getting anyone I want into bed. I've had great sex with beautiful women, even more than one woman at a time, but you know what? I have never ever wanted anything more than I want one simple kiss from you. I want to taste you slowly, deeply, tenderly, spending time learning exactly how you like to be kissed. But I can't ever have it. You have impossible expectations. No one can have forever, it's a fairy tale, and I will not have my heart broken in this house ever again. I had no choice as a child, but I have a choice now, and I will not give up that control to anyone."

The way Harry looked at her made Annie want to forget all about the reasons why kissing her was a bad idea. She had never wanted anything more than Harry's lips on hers.

Annie softly caressed Harry's face with her hands and whispered, "Kiss me. Just once?"

Harry's lips parted and moved close to Annie's, but before she kissed her, she held her parted lips inches from Annie's and breathed her in. If this was to be her last kiss with Annie, then she was going to savour it.

She gently cradled her face and placed a soft kiss on each of Annie's cheeks. Harry was poised to kiss the plump red lips that she yearned for when Annie whispered, "Tell me how you feel."

"You frighten me," she said honestly.

"Why?"

"Because when I'm near you, or touch you, I never know what's coming next. I have no control."

Annie's hands slid up and threaded into Harry's dark hair. "Then trust me that everything will be all right." She tugged her the final few inches into the kiss.

The first touch made them both moan, and Harry held back her instinct to make the kiss forceful. She wanted to take her time and give Annie the tenderness she deserved.

She softly swirled her tongue around Annie's, tasting her and learning what she liked and responded to. When she took her lip and gave it a soft bite, Annie grasped her more tightly. She imagined that Annie would enjoy similar tender bites to her throat, but if she went there, there would be no going back, so she returned to kissing her with all the passion she had for her.

Harry's heart thudded wildly and her lungs felt like she was running out of air but she didn't want to stop, but she did stop when she felt Annie's fingers slip under the hem of her T-shirt. They had to stop now. She was barely keeping control, and Annie's touch on her bare skin was too much.

She pulled back and rested her forehead against Annie's, gasping for breath. "Annie, I want you so much, I can't breathe when you touch me, but all I can offer you is sex. I don't have anything more in me. So you have to walk away, because I will hurt you."

Annie tugged gently on her hair and placed tiny kisses on her chin, nose, and finally her lips before whispering, "I know in my heart you're capable of so much more, but you're right, I'm not just going to have sex with you, no matter how much my body is telling me to. So, I'm going to walk away—for now."

All Annie could do was to take care of Harry every day and show her with each passing day how much she cared for her. With time, maybe she would trust in the love that was between them. But for now she had to calm the storm in Harry's eyes or she would become more distant.

She reached up and ran her fingers tenderly down Harry's cheek. "What we've shared here won't change anything. Tomorrow morning you'll come to the kitchen for your coffee, and at night you'll have dinner with Riley and me. Don't run away from us because you get scared. We can move on from this."

Annie gave each of Harry's hands a kiss and walked back inside the house.

CHAPTER FOURTEEN

The day Harry was dreading finally came. It was Sunday and she had promised to go to church. She had to admit that the walk to church with Annie and Riley was nice, more than nice, it gave her a comforting safe feeling. She looked down at her hand and saw Riley had gripped it tightly as she skipped along beside her. This must be what it felt like to have a family, and it wasn't as scary as her mind had told her it would be. This was okay, she didn't have to panic.

Harry thought about how many of her ancestors had made this same journey over many hundreds of years, and smiled. There was something good about continuity, about being part of something bigger than herself. Maybe Bridge was right, it wasn't just about going to church, it was about fulfilling her role as lord of the manor.

"What are you thinking about?" Annie asked.

"I was thinking about how many of my ancestors walked this path to church every Sunday. I used to come with my grandfather and grandmother, but not so often with my parents."

Annie squeezed her hand, "You're not your parents. You're your own person and can walk your own path."

Could she? There was a part of her that believed she would never get rid of the scars her parents left her with, but as long as she was here with Annie and Riley she was determined to enjoy these family times.

"Let's just hope I'm not struck down as I enter the church," she joked.

Annie laughed and said, "Just keep holding my hand. I'm on good terms with God, so you won't be struck as long as you're with me."

They did manage to walk into church with Harry staying in one piece. She felt every eye burning into her as she guided Annie and Riley to the Knight family bench at the front.

Bridge came out to the pulpit and gave her a wink and a smile, before starting her sermon. She had been carefully and skilfully manoeuvred by the woman sitting beside her to fulfil Bridge's request. Annie was the only woman who had ever been able to do that, and it was frightening. But not as frightening as she'd expected it to be.

The service went as expected until after the second hymn, when Bridge announced to the congregation, "And now to read the second lesson, our very own countess, Henrietta, Lady Axedale."

No, she didn't just say that. Harry looked from Bridge, who was waiting expectantly, to Annie, who had a knowing smile on her face. "You knew about this, didn't you?" Harry whispered.

"Yes, I did," she whispered back. "Would you have come if you'd known?"

Harry had no choice, and that was something she hated. She made her way up to the pulpit and Bridge pointed out the verse she was to read. She glanced to the side and saw written in Bridge's own notes, *Sermon theme—stewardship of the land and responsibilities— for Harry.*

Then as she scanned the first few lines of verse she was to read, she realized it too was related to the theme of stewardship.

It was a set-up. This whole church day was a set-up to teach and remind her of her many duties as countess, of the stewardship of the land and village.

She looked around at the expectant faces of the villagers and then her eyes were drawn to the many plaques on the walls, commemorating the Knights who had gone before, and she felt the heavy weight of expectation and the claustrophobic sensation of being trapped here, as she had been as a child.

Harry read the lesson as quickly as she could and sat stony faced throughout the rest of the service, her bad memories, thoughts, and fears churning inside of her.

As the service got to the end, Bridge said, "A few community notes before you all head off to enjoy the cake sale in the church hall. I ask you all to remember Mrs. Castle in your prayers as she remains unable to join us in church, and a thank you to Lady Axedale for coming to join us this morning. We hope that now she has returned to church she will take up her duties of church warden and chairwoman of the village committee that comes with her position."

That was the final nail in the coffin for Harry. As soon as the sermon ended, she told Annie she was returning home, and not to follow her.

Annie left Riley with Bridge to enjoy the cake sale and meet some of the other children, and hurried back home to Axedale. Each step she took made her a little angrier. Harry had left without any explanation and Riley wondered what they had done wrong.

She checked Harry's study, the library, and her bedroom and couldn't find her anywhere. With nowhere else she could think of, she walked down the seemingly endless west wing corridors. The east and central parts of the house were finished, and Harry's team had made a good start in the west wing, but it was nowhere near ready. She had to step over paint pots, discarded ladders, and tools.

The smell of plaster dust and mould permeated the air and somewhere further down the corridor she heard loud banging.

As she got closer she saw a cloud of dust coming from the doorway at the end of the corridor. Annie approached and looked in. She found Harry in old ripped dusty jeans, a sleeveless T-shirt, and a dust mask, knocking down a wall in the medium-sized room. Even though she was angry with Harry, she couldn't help but appreciate how sexy she looked. How she wished circumstances were different and Harry could push her up against the wall and kiss her, just like the other night.

The dust in the air made her cough, alerting Harry to her presence. She stopped and tore off her mask. "Checking up on me?"

Annie walked into the middle of the room. "You could say that. Why did you just leave like that?"

"Where's Riley?"

"At the cake sale. Bridge is looking after her. So? Are you going to tell me what made you run off and start smashing down walls, when you promised to spend the day with us?"

Harry dropped the sledgehammer, then pulled off her heavy duty gloves and threw them on the floor. "I wonder," Harry said, fuming with anger. "I wonder why I'm angry. Maybe it's because you and Bridge are trying to trap me here. This whole church visit was a set-up. You had me in front of everyone telling them I was taking my place on bloody village committees and as church warden. So now if I don't, I look like a complete and utter fool who doesn't give a damn. I will not be trapped here, by Bridge, you, or the people of this village. My mother's heart was destroyed here, and I was trapped here when she abandoned me to the care of a man who was devoid of emotion, and had a heart of stone. That will never happen to me again. I'm Dr. Knight. I am not Countess of Axedale and I never will be. "

Annie wasn't about to take this anger and attitude from Harry any more. It was about time someone stood up to her and laid it on the line.

She took a few steps towards Harry and said, "No, you're wrong. You wouldn't look like an utter fool, just a spoiled, rich brat."

"Excuse me?" Harry growled.

"Bridge and the people of this village have been pussyfooting around, trying to persuade you to do your duty, and I have been gently trying to help you, but enough is enough. You are the Countess of Axedale and you have a duty—"

"Duty?" Harry roared. "What would a woman from a council estate in London know about the duties of a countess?"

If Annie wasn't angry enough before, now she was raging. Harry had totally dismissed and belittled her in one sentence. "I know because I've been talking and learning from the local community, which is more than you've ever done. You have a duty and responsibility to these people. If you don't want it, then fine, but if that's the case then this big draughty house and large estate are nothing but a testament to your own wealth and position. This house and estate were meant to support this village. Do you know that the young people have to leave Axedale to find work? Quade told me how she struggles to get any labourers for her farm because of it. All the while this great big house sits here gathering dust like a white elephant. If you feel trapped by these people, by me, then please go back to Cambridge and never come back. Then you can watch the rents that these people pay you pile up in your bank, and you can count your money while this village dies."

Harry gulped and gave her a cold, hard stare. "You are just my housekeeper. Don't ever forget that."

Annie felt foolish and weak, but she couldn't help the tears that tumbled down her cheeks. "Believe me, m'lady. I won't."

Then she ran out of the room and didn't look back.

Harry closed her eyes and took a breath before knocking on the door to Mrs. Castle's cottage. When there was no reply, Harry opened the door slightly and called, "Martha? Are you in? It's me, Harry."

"Harry? Come in, come in," Martha shouted excitedly from her front room.

Harry's hands sweated and her throat went dry as she put her hand on the door to the front room. This was why she had put off seeing Martha, she was the link with the past. The one who had seen her at her weakest. But after her argument with Annie, Martha was the only one who she could talk to, the only one who could understand.

Harry walked in and was taken aback. Martha had always been a strong, sturdy woman and now she looked thin and frail, but her smile was as big and warm as she remembered.

"Harry? My little Harry, is that you?"

Martha held out her arms and after a brief hesitation, Harry leaned over and hugged her. Within moments she relaxed and felt the comfort she had done as a child.

"I'm sorry I haven't been before now. It's been—" Harry found it hard to admit her reasons, but as ever Martha read her fears and emotions and cupped her cheek gently.

"I know why, and it's all right. I understand."

Harry kissed her on the cheek. "You always did."

"Sit down, sit down. Now, look at you. You're so tall and broad shouldered too. So like your—"

"My father?" Harry finished for her as she took a seat opposite her.

"Oh no." Martha shook her head. "That wasn't what I was going to say. You will never be like your father, Harry. No, I was going to say you looked like your grandfather."

"Thank you. How are you doing, Martha?"

"Oh, I could do with a new pair of legs, but apart from that, not too bad."

Harry could see she was failing but as ever she was bright and never thought too much of her own problems.

"How are you getting on with Axedale? The vicar tells me there are great changes going on, and Mr. Edwards from number fifty-six says you're knocking hell out of the place."

Harry chuckled. The village gossip was certainly in full swing. "Things are going well. It's a lot of work and it won't be finished for a good few months yet, but we're getting there. It was in a sorry state after my father's neglectful stewardship, as you know."

Stewardship. There was that word again. The responsibility and duty that her father had shunned. Was she doing the same thing?

"I know, but you, Harry, are different. You are going to do great things with Axedale, and I hear you have a wonderful new helper."

Annie. "You mean my housekeeper?"

Martha gave her a knowing smile. "Yes, Ms. Annie Brannigan. The vicar told me how she was whipping the house into shape, and then she brought her in to visit me. A lovely girl, so pretty and kind."

Harry smiled. "She is kind, and hard working. She has a daughter too, Riley. She loves Roman history. So much like me when I was that age."

"It sounds like they are making Axedale a happy home."

Harry looked down at her clasped hands and said, "They are, so why do I want to run away?"

"Ah," Martha said. "That's the problem, is it? You care about her. I half suspected as much when she visited me. Why don't you pour us each a little whiskey and soda and we can talk properly. Everyone who comes in to see me makes tea, and as much as I like tea, some conversations call for a glass of whiskey. Am I right?"

"You are indeed." Harry got up and poured two whiskeys from the bottle on the sideboard. "Here you go."

Martha took a sip and said, "So, tell me what the problem is. You have feelings for her?"

Feelings? Is that what she would call this hunger? Not just an unquenchable hunger for Annie's body, but for the first time she hungered just to spend time in Annie's company. Doing tasks together, talking about nothing, spending time with Riley.

"Yes, and that terrifies me. I can't be what she wants me to be, and I can't be what the village needs me to be. Sometimes it gets too much and I feel trapped here."

"Tell me why, Harry. Tell me what scares you about loving this woman and why Axedale scares you. You know I will never betray you to anyone."

Harry gulped down the lump in her throat as her emotions threatened to overwhelm her. "I don't know if I can."

"You trust me, don't you?" Martha said.

She nodded. There was no one else, apart from Annie, who she trusted more. "Of course, but it's so hard to say it."

"Just take your time, and just say what comes to you."

Harry took a large drink of her whiskey and felt the burn trail its way down her throat. She had no idea how to articulate the black fear and self-loathing inside of her. How could anyone understand? "You know what one of my first memories is?"

Martha shook her head.

"We were getting ready for some village church event, I think I was around four or something. Father didn't want to go of course."

Martha snorted. "Did he ever want to do anything that didn't please him?"

Harry looked down into her glass and saw the memories that had shaped her. "There was a screaming argument that got physical. I went to mother and she was crying on her bed. I remember feeling scared, frightened, and I thought Father was a monster. We went to the village event alone, and everyone we talked to said I was so much like my father, and I hated it. People have told me that my whole life, and it's true. Every time I look in the mirror I see him."

"How does that make you feel?" Martha asked.

Harry stared into her glass. It was the fear she had never spoken of to anyone in her life, and hardly admitted to herself. She could feel tears start to well up in her eyes, and it made her feel weak and angry.

She stood up quickly and walked to the fireplace, so Martha couldn't see the emotion in her eyes. "I can't."

Martha put her glass of whiskey down on the side table. "Do I have to get you apple pie and ice cream to make you talk? It always worked when you were little."

Harry couldn't help but laugh, even though she was feeling anything but light-hearted. "Yes, it did." She took a deep breath and got herself under control before turning around to talk to Martha. "When I see him in me, I feel scared, scared that I'll hurt everyone I love and destroy everything good in my life, just like him. When he died and I became countess…it was like the final piece falling into place. I am my father."

"Oh Harry, Harry, Harry." Martha shook her head vigorously. "You couldn't be more wrong."

"What do you mean?" Harry asked.

Martha smiled and said, "Sit down."

She did as she was told, unsure of what was coming next.

"You don't know what your mother was like when she was younger. When your father was courting your mother and brought her back to Axedale, we all fell in love with her. She was beautiful, spirited, carefree. I think your grandfather Henry would have run off with her himself if he could have," Martha joked.

Harry could only listen in astonishment. She had never heard her mother described in those terms before.

"Of course," Martha continued, "none of us could understand how your father could capture a girl like that. He was never the nicest of children and grew up to have even fewer redeeming qualities. One quality he did have was good looks, and he could be charming if there was something to be gained from it. Then we learned that Lady Dorothy was the only heiress to her father's fortune and it all fell into place."

"Money." Harry snorted. "It was always his prime motivator."

"Very true, and he was on his best behaviour for their whole courtship until he got a ring on her finger, and then his true character showed itself. But Lady Dorothy made the best of it, even when the whispers of other women first came to her ears, and for the first year she brought life and laughter to Axedale."

Like Annie has.

"And I never saw a woman more excited and happy when she found out she was expecting you, but as time went on…"

"He destroyed her spirit?" Harry said.

Martha took a sip of her whiskey and sighed. "Yes, he suffocated the happy young woman inside her."

That was exactly the sort of darkness she feared was inside her. "I could hurt Annie, I can't love—"

"No," Martha exclaimed. "You've missed the point. You have the best of both in you. You might have his good looks, but you also have a great deal of that young, loving woman who came to Axedale all those years ago. That young woman had a great capacity for love, and so do you. Make your own life, Harry, don't be held back by the baggage of your past. Annie's a good woman. She could give you more than you ever thought you could have. You're not your father, and you're not the frightened little girl any more. Let down your defences and give love a chance, and make Axedale the living, working place your grandfather always intended it to be."

Harry gulped loudly. She allowed herself to imagine going back up to the house and declaring her love for Annie, but then she heard the shouts of her father and the tears of her mother, and fear gripped her heart. She jumped up and shook her head. "I can't, I just can't. I'll give Annie and Riley everything while I am here. That's all I can do, but I will make this estate great again. I promise."

CHAPTER FIFTEEN

Harry got into her Land Rover outside Martha's cottage and let out a breath. If her talk with Martha had taught her anything, it was that no matter how hard she tried she couldn't continue to live the way she had been living her life. Annie and Riley were more important because she loved them, and she couldn't hide from that, but doing something about it would be a terrifying step to take.

I need them in my life but I can't give Annie forever, I'm not capable of it. An idea that had been bouncing around her head ever since Annie and she had argued floated into Harry's mind. She felt bad that Riley and Annie always had to move from place to place all their lives, and even if she couldn't give them the family that they wanted, perhaps she could give them security and a home. Maybe she could show the stewardship that everyone needed, protect Annie, and keep her freedom.

Harry drove to Sam McQuade's farm. On her way she dialled her estate manager's number on her smartphone. "Stevens, I've got an idea and I want you to run with it and come up with a fully costed report for it, and I don't want it talked about. Top secret, Stevens."

"Of course, m'lady. What's your idea?"

After giving her estate manager the details of her plan, Harry drove into lower farm, and parked up.

Quade was outside just finishing up for the day. "Harry? How are you?"

"Very well, thanks. I wanted to talk to you about something. I have a proposal for you."

"Well you better come in, and I'll put the kettle on then."

Fifteen minutes later they were sitting in Quade's cosy farmhouse kitchen, enjoying tea and conversation.

"I want to make this estate a living, breathing entity. It was pointed out to me that I had forgotten the estate can't survive without the village and the county, and they can't survive without the estate. I'm going to be in Cambridge during term time, so I need people I trust to manage Axedale for me, people who are experts in their fields. I think if you worked with Stevens as assistant estate manager, we could really make something great here, something that will stop the drift of young families away from the village. What do you think?"

"Well, I don't know what to say. I mean it's a wonderful thing to do, for the community. It will bring so many jobs to the area but—"

"But?"

"Am I really the right person for the job? I don't have any formal training in estate management. I'm just a farmer."

"A farmer is the right person to do this. You know this land like the back of your hand, you know Axedale like the back of your hand, and the most important thing is that you care. I want to leave people running the estate who care. It's taken me too long to face up to my responsibilities, and now I want to do it right. I'll get you staff for the farm." Harry held her hand out to Quade. "What do you say?"

Quade smiled and shook on it. "You have a deal."

Annie pulled Riley's bedroom door shut, happy she was settled and drifting off to sleep, and sat down on her own bed. She couldn't have been gladder that today was coming to an end. It had started off so well. Harry was doing so well, being sociable and relaxing. Then at the first sign of trouble she ran.

"Well you can be sure I'm not chasing you any more." *She can do what she wants*, Annie thought unhappily.

She had been made even angrier when Harry hadn't turned up to dinner, and she was beginning to wonder if she could stay here for the year. Riley had already grown far too close to Harry.

Annie heard a crackling noise and looked to her bedside table. Riley had left her radio there. She picked it up to switch it off when she heard Harry's voice.

"Harry to Annie. Over."

Annie looked at it, trying to work out how to respond.

"Harry to Annie. Are you there?"

"Yes? What is it?"

"I wanted to apologize for what I said today. I didn't think you'd talk to me so I asked Riley to leave this in your room."

Annie couldn't help but smile. "Where are you?"

"In the kitchen. Will you come and see me?"

She didn't know if this was a good idea or not. Every time they seemed to make progress, they then took two steps back. "Okay, give me a few minutes."

She hurried downstairs, and got a surprise when she walked into the kitchen. Harry was standing by the kitchen table which held an opened bottle of champagne and two glasses poured, a big bunch of flowers, and box of chocolates.

"What's all this?"

Harry took her hand and guided her to sit down. "This is all for you. I wanted to tell you how sorry I was for my behaviour. It was inexcusable."

Annie hesitated, and Harry took her hand. "I'm really trying here, Annie. You've turned my world upside down, and sometimes I feel out of control and panic. Can you give me another chance?"

I just want to kiss you, and make it all better, Annie thought. "Of course I can."

"Great, please sit and have a drink with me." Harry gave her a glass of champagne and they both sat.

"Maybe I was a bit hard on you earlier," Annie said.

"No, I deserved everything you said. It gave me the kick up the backside I needed. I wasn't avoiding you all day, I've been busy." Harry gave her one of those slightly adorable smiles that made her want to kiss her.

"Oh, do tell." Annie took a sip of her champagne.

Harry drummed her fingers on the table. She was nervous, and more than a little scared about what she had let herself in for.

"I went to visit Martha—Mrs. Castle."

"Oh you did?" Annie smiled and covered her hand with her own.

"Yes, we had an enlightening talk, and I made some decisions. What you said made me realize that if I wanted to fulfil my grandfather's legacy, I had to do more than restore this house. As much as it isn't exactly what I'm used to, I need to be a countess in more than name, and the estate has to be a working, living thing, or it means nothing."

"So what does that mean? Are you going to stay here?" Annie asked.

Harry could hear a hopeful tone to Annie's voice. "No, but I'm going to make Axedale my base and stay in Cambridge during term time."

"I see," Annie said, her voice tinged with disappointment.

Can't she see I'm going as far as I can? "My estate manager is working on a plan to bring the estate up to full working order. I mean a fully working estate with horses, dogs, well-stocked rivers, refurb of tenants' accommodation, with a full estate staff. It would provide jobs for the local community, and bring in tourists to spend money here. We could provide a full range of country pursuits, for a premium price, and use the west wing of the house for accommodation, but keep the east and central parts of the house private. We could mark out walks around the estate woodland to bring in daily tourists, and their money would support the shops in the village."

Annie's smile returned to her face. "I knew you had it in you, Harry. You're doing a good thing."

"I hope so. I also called Mrs. McRae and told her I would be happy to attend the events I've been invited to. So it's your fault that I have to judge a flower show," Harry joked.

Annie stood, pulled Harry to her feet, and hugged her. "You are such a good person, Harry."

After a few seconds, Harry relaxed into the hug and went to put her arms around Annie's back but winced in pain.

"What's wrong?" Annie asked.

Harry rubbed the shoulder that had been giving her problems for most of the day. "I think I pulled a muscle when I was swinging the sledgehammer earlier."

"Take your jumper off and sit here." Annie moved the kitchen chair in front of her.

Harry's heart began to beat faster. "Why?"

"I'm going to massage your shoulder, of course."

This was a bad idea. She couldn't have Annie touching her, and not want her. "I don't think—"

Annie sighed. "Jumper off, and sit, your ladyship."

Harry reluctantly pulled off her sweater and was left in her sleeveless T-shirt. Annie put her hands on both her shoulders, and she had to stop herself from moaning.

"Okay, just relax."

Relax? How could she relax when Annie had her hands on her?

"Is it just the right shoulder?" Annie asked.

"Uh-huh." Annie started to dig her fingers into her sore, tired muscles. "Oh God, that's good."

Harry couldn't help but groan when Annie whispered in her ear, "I'm glad."

For such a small woman, Annie had strong hands and fingers, and they were currently making her shoulder and back muscles feel like jelly.

Don't think about how good her hands feel. Harry tried to think about some of the dry, dusty passages she was reading for her new book, but it was impossible.

"You have really strong muscles, Harry." Annie trailed her fingers from Harry's neck, down her shoulder, and caressed her tattoo.

"Excavation and digging will do that. I've got to keep strong for my job." As if Annie's touch wasn't bad enough, she heard Annie's breath hitch, and then her hands strayed into Harry's hair.

"I love your hair."

Harry's body thrummed with sexual energy. She had never let a woman touch her like this before, and she wanted Annie more than anything in the world, but she had to stop it before they went too far and she took Annie somewhere she didn't truly want to go.

What had been a soothing massage had changed into foreplay, as Annie stroked her hair, shoulders, and arms. The temptation was unbearable, as was the pressure building between her legs, and nothing could calm her until she was flesh to flesh with her.

It was made worse when Annie leaned over to speak into her ear, and Harry felt her breasts upon her upper back.

"Harry, I love the way you feel."

All Harry wanted to do was take her hand and pull her around to her lap, but if she did that, they would have sex, and Harry couldn't allow that to happen. For once in her life she was going to put someone else first, and if she had sex with Annie tonight, tomorrow she would break her heart. Harry couldn't bear that.

Without giving herself time to change her mind, Harry got up quickly, and said, "That's much better, thanks."

Annie's eyes were cloudy and wanting. "Harry, I—"

"You don't. I'm going to bed. Goodnight, Annie."

As she hurried out of the kitchen she wondered why she was being so noble. It wasn't like her. She could have had Annie so easily then, and yet she'd walked away.

Because you love her.

Annie grasped onto the chair for support when Harry left the room. Her heart was thudding wildly and her fingers were hot from touching Harry's skin.

As her body began to calm slightly, the realization of what she had just done and Harry's reaction to her started to sink in.

Oh my God, I threw myself at her.

She clasped her hands over her mouth and eyes and shook her head in disbelief. "What have I done?"

There was a small romantic part of Annie that still hoped Harry would come to her senses and discover that she couldn't live without her, but if she slept with her, then she would be giving her exactly the same as all the other women that passed through Harry's life, and there was no way she wanted to simply pass through.

Annie wanted to be everything to Harry, as much of a pipe dream as that probably was, and nothing else would be good enough. She had always believed her true love was out there waiting for her. Her grandmother had taught her to believe in that kind of love. But if she had any hope of making Harry believe in it, she had to stay strong. That meant not giving up her body without love being returned.

CHAPTER SIXTEEN

Harry stood at the bottom of the marble staircase waiting on Annie and Riley. It was Riley's first day of school and Riley was not happy about it. As Annie had explained, it was yet another school in another new place, and she was the perpetual new girl.

The nervousness was not confined to Riley. Harry felt nervous too. It was a new feeling to be concerned about a child. She wished she could spend the day with Riley, protecting her and making sure she wasn't scared.

Good God, you're on a slippery slope here.

Annie and Riley appeared at the top of the stairs and Harry thought, *I love them both.*

Riley trudged reluctantly down to meet her. Harry looked at Annie behind and she rolled her eyes.

Harry put on her biggest smile and tried to sound as upbeat as possible. "How are you this morning, Riley? All set?"

Riley shrugged her shoulder and stared at the floor. "I suppose."

Annie put her arm around her and said, "Come on, sweetie. Everything will be fine."

Riley shrugged her mother's arm off and said sharply, "It won't. It's going to be a horrible day and all the kids are going to hate me."

Harry took her hand and pulled her over to sit on the marble stairs. "Listen, centurion. I know how hard it will be for you today. I'm not going to pretend it won't, but it will get better, and I'll make you a promise. If you can get through the first week, I'll take you and your mum out this weekend. We can go and visit the Roman bathhouse site and the remains of the Knight family castle."

"Yes, and I'll make us a picnic," Annie pitched in.

"That would be wonderful," Harry said. "We'll make a day of it. What do you think?"

The beginnings of a smile were forming on Riley's face. "You mean it?"

"Of course I do. It will be great fun." Harry spontaneously gave Riley a hug. "Better?" she asked.

"Better. I'll do my best today."

Annie stroked Riley's hair and said, "That's my girl. Now go and pick up your lunch box from the kitchen."

Riley ran off and Annie grasped Harry's hand. "Thank you. That really helped. She gets so nervous, but you give her strength, Harry."

"I like being there to support her. She's such a good girl."

"She is. I want to spoil her, as much as I can afford, at her birthday in three weeks. I thought—"

"It's her birthday? You should have said. We'll do something special. I'll come up with an idea. What would she like for her birthday?"

"Well, she's been talking about wanting a metal detector and maybe an e-reader."

Harry's face lit up. "Perfect. I'm the one to advise you there, in fact why don't I pick them out? We can give it to her together."

"Wait. I think your budget and mine will be very different."

"Just let me worry about that."

"No, Harry."

"Yes, Harry. We'll pool our money. Please, let me?"

There weren't two more deserving people in the whole world to spend her money on. She was determined Riley and Annie were going to have a special day.

Annie sighed. "All right but I'm paying towards it. Okay?"

"Okay. Can I drive you and Riley to school?"

"Thank you. Riley would like that."

❖

True to her word, Harry did take them out at the weekend. First they visited the Roman bathhouse, which made Riley very excited, although it wasn't much more than a series of small walls. After Harry talked them through each room and what it was used for, they headed off to visit the ancient Knight family castle.

Harry drove them up a dirt track road until they emerged into a car parking area overlooking a large expanse of green field, and in the middle was the ruin of the castle.

"Woah, it's a real-life castle," Riley said from the backseat.

"Don't get too excited," Harry said as she switched off the engine. "It's only the outer walls that are left."

"It's still amazing. Knights in armour would have been here. Are there any ghosts?" Riley asked.

Harry looked at Annie for the okay to tell her about the creepier side of the ruins, and she nodded. "There is meant to be the ghost called the white lady who wanders the grounds in search of her lover, who was killed by her husband. Then there's the dastardly Guy Le Knight."

"Oh, sounds interesting," Annie said. She loved the amusement and joy that appeared in Harry's eyes when she was talking about something she was interested in. She supposed that was why she was such a good teacher.

"Yeah who was Guy Le Knight?" Riley was now virtually in the front with them, standing between the seats.

"Guy was the first Knight in England and started building this castle. He came over with William the Conqueror. He didn't come from a noble family and was actually squire to one of William's most trusted knights. The story goes that he took credit for saving the King's life when it had in fact been his master, who he killed in the midst of battle. William knighted him, and gave him the lands that would have been his master's, and he married his master's noble and extremely rich widow. The Knights are nothing if not opportunists."

Annie looked to Riley and saw the look of wonder on her face. Real history was better than any movie to her. "Sounds very dastardly. What happened to him?" Annie asked.

"He was stabbed to death by a group led by his son. It's said that his soul wanders these grounds tormented by the betrayal of his master, and hatred for his son."

Riley was bouncing up and down with excitement, and started to exit the car. "Let's go to the castle now, Harry. You be Guy Le Knight and I'll be your son who stabs you dead."

Annie folded her arms and gave Harry a mock look of annoyance. "It seems you are corrupting my child, your ladyship."

Harry leaned over to her and whispered in her ear, "That's the aristocracy for you. Corrupting women and children and stealing your neighbour's land."

Annie shivered and inhaled the scent of her aftershave. "You always smell nice, you know that?" *Why did I say that?*

Harry looked surprised at that comment but smiled with amusement. "I do?"

"Yes, and I love your hair. It's so...dark and thick." Annie wished she would just shut up. She appeared to have no control over what she was saying, or what she felt these days.

Harry moved closer and said, "Annie I—"

They were interrupted by Riley knocking on the window, while holding her wooden sword. "Harry, come on. I want to play."

"Oh, what it is to be popular," Annie joked.

"Duty calls."

After looking around the castle site, Annie set up the food at the picnic table while Riley and Harry play-fought around the castle walls. It was wonderful to see her daughter so at ease and having so much fun, and it was all because of Harry.

If only they wanted the same things. Harry would be a perfect second parent for Riley, but that was just a dream.

A while later, they both came running over in search of food. They devoured the picnic Annie had prepared.

"These are delicious. I've never tasted chicken salad sandwiches like these before," Harry said.

Annie took the used plates and stacked them away. "I aim to please."

"Oh, you do. Believe me."

Annie felt herself blush at Harry's words, but Riley seemed oblivious as she walked around the table to the basket.

"Can I have a super-duper cookie now, Mum?"

"Yes, take one and give one to Harry."

Harry took one of the dark chocolate cookies. "These are super-duper cookies, are they?"

Riley took a big bite of hers, and mumbled. "Uh-huh. They are so good."

They did look decidedly good and bad for you at the same time. Harry took a bite and groaned.

"Good?" Annie asked.

"Oh God, yes." They were so deeply and intensely chocolate flavoured that she felt quite decadent.

"Harry? Can I take some pictures with your phone?"

"Sure." Harry reached into her pocket and pulled out her phone. She saw a text from Clara on the screen. Immediately she felt guilty, and she had no reason to. Annie wasn't her girlfriend and she had no control over who texted her, but she felt guilty all the same. She quickly cleared the screen and handed the phone over.

"You be careful, Riley," Annie said. "That's a really expensive phone."

"She will." Harry stroked Riley's hair and she went off happily with her cookie and phone. "She's a wonderful child, Annie. You've brought her up so well."

"It's not always been easy, but I'm blessed to have her. I know some would say I should have waited until I was in a stable relationship but I just had this intense need to make a family."

Harry could tell there was something behind that need, going by the pain that was evident on her face. "It occurs to me that you know most things about my family going back to 1066, but I know nothing about yours. Would you tell me?"

Annie looked down at the table sadly and wrung her hands nervously.

"Look if it's too personal—"

"No." Annie grasped her hand. "It's not that. It's just difficult to put into words, but I'd like to tell you."

They both looked on as Riley stood at the castle wall taking pictures. "I was taken away from my mother when I was six years old."

Harry's head snapped back to Annie. "You what?"

"My mum was a heroin addict, and I was taken away from her by social services because of neglect."

That was not what Harry expected to hear, and her heart broke for her. She didn't care that they were meant to be keeping a professional distance, she just had to be close to Annie.

Harry moved up the bench and put an arm around her back, and clasped Annie's hand in hers. "Tell me."

"I don't remember a lot, just different snapshots of memories and lots and lots of feelings. Mostly I remember being scared and hungry. I was scared of the men who came around, and scared that I couldn't wake my mum up after she'd taken some heroin."

Harry brought Annie's hand up to her mouth and kissed it tenderly. "What about your father?"

"I didn't have one. Well, not one that I knew. There was just my grandmother. I found out later that it was Grandma that got social services involved, so she could get custody of me."

"Where did your grandmother live?"

"Kilburn in London. She was a good Catholic, and I think felt a lot of guilt that she couldn't help my mum."

Harry was astonished that someone who had been through so much could grow up to be so well adjusted, which made her feel a bit ashamed about her own childhood hang-ups. "What was it like living with her?"

A happy smile slowly crept over her face. "It was the happiest time of my life, until I had Riley, of course. She was the perfect grandmother, and I think probably tried to compensate for what I'd been through. She taught me to bake, and to cook, I did well at school for the first time. Everything was perfect until—"

"Until what?" Harry asked. What could have possibly gone wrong for someone who had gone through so much?

Annie wiped away the tears that were welling up. "She died when I was thirteen."

"Oh God, I'm so sorry, darling." Harry kissed her on the head and held her close. She didn't care that the term of endearment slipped from her mouth. Annie was what was important in this moment.

"I was taken into the care system, and I stayed there until I was sixteen. That's when I went to catering college. I lived in the worst area, I was always scared. That's what drives me to give Riley everything I never had."

Everything about Annie fell into place. Her intense drive to have a safe home for Riley, and a partner that would be there forever for them both. They deserved no less. No matter what she felt for Annie, she had to keep her distance because she loved her too much to ever hurt her.

Life was good as the next few weeks passed. Harry was getting a real taste of family life without the frightening aspect of a committed relationship.

This morning she was up on the scaffolding checking up on the work being done on the stone above the front entrance, bearing the family motto.

"It's amazing how well it's held up over the last three hundred years," the stonemason said.

Harry crouched down and ran her hand over the words that truly summed up her family line: *He who conquers will endure.*

"Yes, I—"

Harry was interrupted by the sound of Annie's panicked shouting below her. "Riley! Riley! Where are you?"

She looked down and saw Annie in an utter panic. "Excuse me, will you?"

She quickly climbed down and ran over to Annie. "What's wrong? What's the panic?"

Annie had tears welling up in her eyes, and could hardly form a coherent sentence. "The school phoned to say Riley didn't come back into classes at lunchtime. She's gone and I can't find her."

The thought of Riley being lost and alone made her feel sick, so Annie had to be feeling a million times worse. She grasped her by the shoulders and said, "Don't worry. I'll find her."

Annie's tears tumbled uncontrollably now. "What if we can't? What if someone has her?"

Harry pulled Annie close and held her tightly, trying to be strong and keep her own feelings of fear under control. "I promise I will find her. Stay here in case she comes back to the house."

Without thinking she gave Annie a kiss on the forehead. "Believe me, I'll find her."

Harry looked over to the refurb office and saw David walking towards them.

"Is everything okay, Harry?"

"Riley has gone missing from school. Can you get the team to search over the house and grounds for her?"

"No problem." He spoke into his radio, "Everyone meet at the office, young Riley has gone missing. I'm organizing a search party."

Harry caressed Annie's face and said, "You see? We'll find her. Stay here."

She set off at a jog around the side of the house but had no idea where to look first. Although she had tried to be positive for Annie's benefit, the estate was so large, Riley could be anywhere.

Panic gripped at her chest and started to overwhelm her, as her brain started to play the worst-case scenarios over in her mind.

"Riley? Are you there? Riley?" she shouted as she ran. Harry stopped and looked all around. "Think, think. Where would I go if I was Riley's age?"

Then it hit her. "I know exactly where I went when I was young and scared."

She ran to the secret garden, and as she approached the tree house and saw a pair of legs hanging over the platform, she experienced utter relief wash over her. She leaned her hand against the tree trunk and took some deep breaths.

How can I let them go, when I feel like this about them both? But no answers were immediately forthcoming.

Harry climbed up and sat beside Riley, who had her hands over her face to cover the fact she was crying.

"Riley? Look at me. Are you okay?"

Riley answered by throwing her arms around Harry and crying uncontrollably.

"Shh. It's all right now. Don't cry. You're safe, that's all that matters."

"I'm sorry. I couldn't stay at school any longer."

"Tell me what happened."

Riley wiped her tears away with her sleeve. "They all hate me and make fun of the way I talk."

"Ah, I see." In a small, insular village school with only one hundred pupils, a South London accent would sound a little different. "And they all do this? I thought you met a few at church who were nice."

"I did. It's not really all, just two. Mark and Sarah, they're brother and sister. They've been making fun of me since I started, but today they said a really bad thing."

Harry rubbed Riley's back tenderly. "What did they say? You can tell me."

"They said my mum…was the countess's whore."

Harry growled with anger. Probably someone she'd annoyed in the village and they'd talked in front of their children. "Did you tell the teacher?"

"No, I told them that you care about us, and you are my best friend. Then I hit Mark."

"I understand you were upset, Riley, but hitting him wasn't the best idea. I'm sorry they said that about your mum. You do know it's not true?"

Riley sniffed and dried her eyes again. "I don't know what that bad word means, but I know it's nasty. Nothing about you and my mum is nasty. You are her knight."

Harry sighed. Riley was already too attached to her, and couldn't shake this idea that her mum and she were this perfect couple, but she decided to let it go for the moment.

"Riley, give it time. You'll make friends."

"I won't, I don't try to."

"Why wouldn't you try? I'm sure there are some nice children at school."

"What's the point?" Riley said angrily. "Every time I settle somewhere and make friends, Mum moves us to a new place. I hate it."

That was why she wanted her new ideas for the estate to take off, so that maybe Annie and Riley could have a home. "Listen to me, your mum is doing her best for you both. I know it's not easy."

"You don't know what it's like," Riley snapped.

"Riley, do you know I was at boarding school since I was five years old? Do you know what boarding school is?"

Riley nodded. "It's like Hogwarts in Harry Potter. You stay at school not at home."

Harry could have burst out laughing, but was sure that would make Riley feel terrible. "Well, Hogwarts without the magic, adventures, warmth, and charm. I was only allowed to come home in the holidays and my parents were mostly abroad or with their own friends. I spent time with my grandfather, and during school time was miserable. When I moved schools, around about your age, I started to get bullied but it stopped…"

You can't tell her you beat up the bully.

She took a breath. "A bit like you, I snapped, only I fought with the girl involved. She was a few years older, and everyone left me alone after that, but the point is, I was still unhappy, but I met Bridge and had a good friend from then. You get to come home to your mum each day. I couldn't and I didn't have your sort of mum. So she's doing the best she can to make you happy, Riley. Give school a chance, and I'm sure in a few months it'll settle down."

"You think so?" Riley said hopefully.

Harry smiled and stroked her head. "Yes. I'm so sure in fact that I'm going to let you and your mum organize the party you wanted to have in the ballroom. We could make it a fancy dress party, and invite the people of the village and your school friends, which I'm sure you'll have lots of by them."

Riley threw her arms around Harry's neck. "Yes, a Jane Austen ball, just like mum's sappy romance books. It'll be great. Mum will dance with you and it'll be perfect."

Harry hoped it would live up to Riley's high expectations. "Well, for now we better get back to your mum. She's really worried about you."

❖

When they got back, Annie was furious with Riley, mainly because she was so scared. Riley was sent to her room until dinner.

Harry guided Annie into her study to calm down, but it was so hard. Apart from being scared witless, Annie felt guilty. She paced up and down, while Harry sat on the edge of her desk.

"I shouted at her. I shouldn't have done that. It's my fault, if I didn't take her from place to place, she would be happy, but it's so hard to know what's best. When she was a baby, I worked in restaurants, and all I could afford to rent was a dingy one-bedroom apartment in one of the roughest areas of London. I always said I'd give her a better life than I had, but maybe I'm not? I am a terrible mother."

Harry stood and pulled Annie into her arms. "Don't be ridiculous. You are a wonderful mother, the best I have ever seen."

Annie felt happy and safe in Harry's arms. It felt just right, and despite Harry's protestations to the contrary, she had a natural instinct for being loving and caring. If only she would allow herself to show it more often.

She wiped away her tears, and her eyes were drawn to a silver photo frame, face-down on the desk. Annie knew what picture it was, she had been in here dusting it often enough. She always propped it up and then found it face-down the next time she came to clean.

She lifted the frame and swivelled in Harry's arms so they were both looking at it. "Will you tell me more about them? They must have loved each other once."

"No," Harry said sadly. "Well my mother loved him at the start, I think. She said he played the perfect suitor until they got married. Then everything changed."

Annie saw the absent look in Harry's eyes and thought it best to get her to talk while they were both emotionally vulnerable. "Tell me about it."

"No, my childhood troubles are nothing to what you went through."

Annie squeezed her more tightly, "Everything is relative. Tell me."

"They fought on a daily basis, but one skirmish I can remember vividly happened in their bedroom. I had been playing in my father's dressing room, trying on his aftershave, playing at being grownup, trying on his ties and bow ties, you know the sort of thing, which I was not supposed to do. When they walked in I hid in the wardrobe. They had already been arguing, my father accusing my mother of being a social climber, my mother weeping over her broken heart."

As Harry recounted her memory, Annie had snuggled into the crook of Harry's neck, and was gently caressing the other side of her neck with her fingertips.

"That is the type of selfish people that the Knight family produces. My ancestors had the happy talent of marrying heiresses. Only my grandfather married for love, but she died when he was young. Maybe that's why my father was such an odious man. The Knights are selfish and individualistic, and because of that our family seat has prospered and kept in good financial health where others with large estates have gone bankrupt."

Was that at the root of Harry's relationship issues? Did she think she wasn't capable of a loving relationship because her ancestors weren't?

"I think we both have to let go of our pasts, Harry. Mine drives me to be this perfect mother, and that is unattainable, because nobody can be perfect, and you…Well you'll have to work that out for yourself."

Harry gave a big sigh and tightened her hold on Annie, burying her face in her hair. Her hair smelled beautiful, like home and safety, and it calmed her soul.

"Can't you just tell me? You seem to know best about everything."

Annie chuckled and said, "Can I quote you on that?"

"You can do anything you want, you know that. I'm happy with you and Riley here. Anything you need to do or change, or tell me, can only be good."

Annie never replied to that, and Harry didn't release her from her tight hold.

She had never held someone for the simple act of finding comfort, but she couldn't help but love it. It felt even more intimate than sex. When she imagined doing this with Clara or any of the other women she'd seduced, it made her body tense up with panic.

Annie obviously felt her tension when she said, "Are you okay?"

"Just some bad thoughts, nothing for you to worry about."

"We probably shouldn't be doing this, Harry."

Harry kissed her head and gently eased Annie's tunic out from her skirt, and let her hand wander inside, before simply stroking her fingers up and down the small of her back. It was so soft, and she wanted more than anything to touch more of her skin and feel Annie respond to it, just for her.

"We do a lot of things we shouldn't do, yet we keep doing them," Harry said.

Annie turned in her arms, so that her lips were at the base of Harry's throat. Harry groaned at the feel of Annie's lips, and she felt the beat of Annie's heart match the steady beat deep inside of her.

Annie whispered breathily, "Why do you think we do these things and keep doing them?"

That was the question, wasn't it. The big, terrifying question that she couldn't even contemplate. "I can't answer that question, and I don't know if I ever will. I can't do anything but tell you the truth."

Annie pushed away from her. "And that's why I have to walk away, but if you ever find an answer, you'll let me know?"

Harry's emotions were so conflicted, and so close to the surface, her hands started to tremor. She wasn't stupid, and it was a simple answer. With three short words she was convinced she could have Annie in her bed and in her home as an equal partner, and a child she had never thought she wanted.

She took a breath and shut her eyes tightly. Maybe she could do it. Take a leap of faith and know that unlike her ancestors, she could be her lady's knight in shining armour, just like Riley said. But the fear deep down in the pit of her stomach won out.

"Yes, I'll let you know if I find an answer." *Coward.*

Annie smiled and began to walk away. "Remember, you've got your first village council meeting tonight."

Harry nodded and stuffed her hands in her pockets to try and distract from the lonely, empty feeling when Annie and her touch were taken away from her. "I won't forget. I promised I would go and I will. I'm meeting Bridge at six thirty."

Annie put her hands on her hips and gave her a fierce look. "Try to behave nicely and don't be too grumpy."

The warning only succeeded in making Harry want her badly, right now, right here on her desk. The frustrating heavy beat between her legs got worse. Frustrating because it could never be assuaged.

"If you behave, you can have a treat tonight when you get home."

"Oh yes?" She was sure Annie could see the arousal in her eyes. Just as her feet took on a mind of their own and started to move to Annie, Annie took backwards steps and slipped out of the room, leaving Harry looking at a closed heavy oak door.

Her arousal was such that she braced herself against the door. "Christ almighty. What is it about this woman?"

With any other woman, they would have had sex already and be done by now.

"Annie, Annie, Annie." She moaned. "You are killing me."

She looked up to the heavens and growled, "My punishment for all my so-called immorality in your eyes is working, God. Well done."

CHAPTER SEVENTEEN

The parish council meeting was actually more interesting than Harry'd expected. It wasn't all frivolous talk about flower shows and such. They talked about real problems, and how to solve them. The council had the familiar faces of Mr. and Mrs. Peters from the village shop, Mr. Finch from the pub, Mrs. McRae, and other people she remembered from her childhood days.

They discussed the lack of social services for the elderly in the village, particularly for people like Mrs. Castle who were housebound. They voted to write a letter to the local council, and Harry assured them that if they didn't receive a satisfactory response, she would provide a village fund for the elderly to help with care needs, a pledge which delighted and surprised them all.

Mr. Peters, the current chairman, said, "So we're all in agreement. The profits from all the village stalls at the county fair will go to the running of the children's day care group. I think we all see the need for childcare for working parents in the village, and with that, I think we'll bring this meeting to a close. Next week our new chairwoman, Lady Axedale, will open the meeting."

When they exited the church hall, Bridge slipped her hand through Harry's arm, and they walked slowly in the direction of the vicarage.

Bridge couldn't have been happier. She had delivered the countess to church and to her role as leader of their small community, and all because of one housekeeper who she was sure had unlocked Harry's heart. "Clara telephoned me yesterday."

Harry stopped dead. "You? Why?"

Why was a good question. Clara and Bridget had always been like oil and water ever since Harry had introduced them. "She wanted to know if you were all right since she couldn't get hold of you."

They started walking towards the vicarage again. "Yes, I've been ignoring her calls. I don't know why but it feels wrong to talk to her here, like my country and city lives don't mix, not to mention I'm fed up feeling like a cash machine."

"I warned you about her, Harry, she's trouble that one," Bridget said.

"Hmm, maybe you're right." Harry sighed before saying, "I shouldn't be telling a vicar this but…"

"I might be a vicar but I've been your friend much longer. You can always speak frankly to me and I'll give my advice if I can, or just listen if that's what you want."

Harry nodded and they walked on. "I feel different here in Axedale. Things that have always seemed so important aren't so much any more. For one, I've never gone so long without sex in my life, but I'm okay with it. Well…I want it, but not the kind of sex someone like Clara could give me. And two, my career—I've always had this intense drive to be the best, make the next big discovery, write the best book, be the one people think of as the most learned authority in my field, but here, none of that is important any more. The Roman remains I've found in the grounds, I could have my team from Cambridge here tomorrow, have the site excavated, artefacts catalogued in a month probably, but I'm not, I'm keeping the discovery to myself so I can make painstakingly slow progress with Riley helping me."

Bridget smiled. "It sounds like your priorities are changing. That doesn't have to be a scary thing, Harry. We want different things at different times in our life. I say go with what feels right, don't let yourself be constrained by old patterns of behaviour. *To everything there is a season, and a time to every purpose under the heaven.*"

They came to a stop outside the vicarage. "Do you have a Bible verse for everything?" Harry said.

"Of course. Will you come in for a drink?"

"I can't. I'm expected at home," Harry said without thinking.

"Oh, becoming domesticated are we, Harry?" Bridge said, but regretted it as soon as she saw the look of panic on Harry's face.

"Don't, Bridge. I'm just being sociable. Like you always tell me to be."

"Very true. So? What sociable evening beckons you home tonight?" Bridge could almost feel Harry squirm.

"It's a film night. I said I would watch *Gladiator* with Riley and Annie."

Bridge burst out laughing. "*Gladiator*? The film that makes you incandescent with rage because of its many historical inaccuracies? I don't know how many times I've heard you mump and moan about that bloody film."

"Yes, well that's true, but Riley loves it. Every time we play-fight with her sword she has to be Maximus Decimus Meridius. If it makes her happy then I'm hap—"

Harry stopped abruptly when she realized what she'd nearly said, but to Bridget she had already spoken volumes. Harry had been her friend since she was twelve years old, and in all the time she had known her, only two things had been important to her friend: work and sex. She attacked both with equal fervour, but this was new. The way she was putting other people first, making sacrifices and compromises for Annie and Riley, that was unheard of.

Bridget was a woman of faith, and that faith gave her the belief that the right people would be guided to you at the right time. It was no coincidence in her view that when Lord Charles, the man who had taught Harry how much someone you love can hurt you, had died, Annie and Riley came into her life. Two people who were teaching her about love, and how to love.

Harry looked totally uncomfortable, and so Bridge said simply, "Off you go then." As she walked away she turned back and said, "Oh, Harry?"

"Yes?"

"If you get scared, read 1 Corinthians 13."

Harry looked at her strangely. "Scared of what?"

Bridget smiled and pointed at her chest. "Of what's in here."

She walked away from Harry with a feeling of surety that her friend's life was about to change, and for that she thanked God.

❖

"You're here." Riley jumped up and gave her a hug.

Harry didn't watch much television, but her father had used the music room as a TV room. It had a comfortable couch, an ancient TV next to the fireplace, and a grand piano on the other side of the room.

As she surveyed the space, she realized it had never looked like this before. The only word that she could use to describe it was *warm*.

On the coffee table in front of the couch were bowls of crisps, popcorn, and sweets. The fire was on and roaring, and there was only one lamp lit, giving everything a cosy glow.

Riley pulled her to sit on the couch. "You sit here, Harry. Mum's just getting us drinks."

"Okay."

Annie walked in with a tray of soft drinks and three steaming mugs. Harry couldn't help but smile at her. The very sight of Annie made her heart happy. She should've felt scared by this whole set-up, but she wasn't.

Annie stopped by the couch. "Hi. How was the meeting? Were you on your best behaviour?"

The earlier promise of a treat came flooding back into her brain. "Oh yes. The perfect countess. You can ask Bridge."

Annie laughed softly. "I'll take your word, your ladyship. This is your prize. Hot choco surprise."

"Yes!" Riley cheered. "Mum's hot choco surprise is the best. You'll love it, Harry."

Annie gave Riley her mug and offered the next to Harry. The mug came with a long sundae spoon. "What's the surprise?"

"Look in the mug." Annie sat down right next to her, and Harry realized why Riley was so insistent that she sit in the middle, to make sure she and Annie were close.

Harry looked into the mug and Annie said, "One scoop of vanilla ice cream in real hot chocolate."

Harry salivated at the sight of the ice cream melting into the thick chocolate. "This looks delicious."

Annie sat down beside her. "It tastes even better. Try it."

She did just that and the flavour made her literally hum with pleasure. "God, that's good. It can't be normal powdered hot chocolate. How do you make it?"

"Tell her, Riley," Annie said.

Riley sucked the spoon clean of her latest mouthful and grinned. "Mum says it's a secret recipe to make you feel loved."

"What? Are you some sort of witch in that kitchen? Making up potions and feeding them to me…I mean to *us* to make us feel things?"

Annie gave her an enigmatic smile. "Maybe. Put on the film, Riley."

A witch was a perfect description for Annie, Harry concluded. She was able to make her do and feel things no one had ever done before.

They settled down to watch the film and Annie pointed to the coffee table. "That's not some kind of antique, is it?"

"Why do you ask?"

Annie rubbed her calf and Harry's eyes were glued to where she was rubbing. "My feet are killing me. A day walking around this huge place is liable to do that. I hoped I could put my feet up."

"Of course, go ahead." Harry smiled. "It's only a hundred years old."

"A hundred years old?"

"Yes, that's modern in a place like this. Please go ahead, relax."

When Annie hesitated, Harry got up, knelt down before her and carefully took Annie's shoes off. Her hands lingered on Annie's slim legs, her fingers stroking down the underside of her shapely calf. She looked up at Annie and their eyes met. God, she wanted this woman. She had never felt anything more powerful in her life. Every day it was building up like a pressure cooker, and she was sure she would explode before long.

Even on nights like tonight, it felt like she was being seduced, not by any normal methods, but by the warmth and the food and drinks of a simple comfortable night spent together, and yet she knew Annie didn't want sex. She wanted love, commitment, and forever. Is that what she was being seduced into?

"Harry? It's starting." Riley's voice brought them both back down to earth.

Harry placed Annie's feet down and retook her seat, finishing her drink and joining Annie in putting her feet up on the table. She put her hand down by her side and felt her fingers brush Annie's, but rather than panic, on impulse, she took Annie's hand and held it through the rest of the film.

Annie rubbed her thumb over the back of Harry's hand. She had been surprised but pleased that Harry had taken her hand. It felt natural and right, and although she had seen the film with Riley a hundred times, it was a whole new experience watching it with Harry. She and Riley talked constantly throughout the film, Riley asking questions and Harry telling her the real history behind the film and the many ways the fiction played fast and loose with history.

As the film drew to a close and Annie's tears started to come, as they always did when she watched anything where someone died or lovers reunited or parted, Harry put her arm around her and pulled her close. "You're not crying at *Gladiator*, are you?"

Annie wiped away her tears. "I can't help it. I cry at everything, even Harry Potter."

Harry laughed softly and caressed her face with the backs of her fingers. "You are such a tender woman."

Annie found herself aching to run her fingers through Harry's thick dark hair. She extended her hand but they both snapped back when Riley moved to snuggle into Harry's side. She had never wanted anyone more in her life, and it was getting harder with each passing second to resist.

❖

As the credits rolled, Annie and Harry talked for a while longer before they realized Riley had fallen fast asleep at Harry's side.

"She's going to be so grumpy when I wake her up." Annie sighed.

"You don't have to. I'll carry her up for you." Harry stood and lifted Riley into her arms.

"Are you sure? She's heavy."

"Don't worry, I'm strong."

"Yes, that's true," Annie said.

Annie was watching her, and her needy gaze was as sensual as any caress. The heat returned to Harry's body, and she knew it was time to get Riley upstairs. She made her way upstairs and laid Riley down on her bed. When Annie started to get her ready for bed she said, "I'll clear away the things in the music room while you get Riley settled."

"Thanks. That would be a big help."

It didn't take long to put the cups and bowls in the dishwasher. Harry leaned against the cupboards and looked at her watch: 10:30.

She should really get an hour or so in on her book, but knew she wouldn't settle. Her body was agitated with sexual arousal and frustration. It felt like she had been on a roller coaster of excitement all day, in fact every day, and she got no nearer to the relief her body demanded. It was a frustration that would not be assuaged by her own hand.

Her body was quite clear. It wanted Annie's hands on her and no one else's. She rubbed her face vigorously and growled in frustration. "What are you doing to me?"

With a sigh she wandered upstairs to her room. Maybe she could do some work on her laptop and take her mind off things.

Just as she put her hand on her door handle she heard Annie come out of Riley's room behind her. "Annie? Is Riley all settled?"

Annie walked up to her and nodded. "Riley said goodnight and thanks for the best night ever."

"It was just a film," Harry said bashfully.

"It was the fact you were watching with her. She loves you, very much. I'm sorry if that makes you feel uncomfortable, but it's the truth."

"It doesn't. I love her too." Harry took a step back against her own bedroom door when Annie reached out and touched her tattoo.

"I'm just going to bed. I wanted to say goodnight."

Harry balled up her fists, trying to control her body that was screaming at her to touch Annie. She hadn't been in this position before, literally fighting her own needs and desires, but she knew Annie wanted so much more than sex, and she didn't want to hurt her. "Annie, don't touch me like that."

"Why? I like the way the ink looks on your arm."

"Walk away now...please?"

Annie's eyes were glazed and full of want. "I can't. I want to touch you."

To emphasise the point she slipped her hand under the hem of Harry's T-shirt, and dragged her nails softly across her muscled stomach. Harry groaned, and her heart thudded out of control. She couldn't take any more, and to hell with the consequences.

She put her arms around Annie's waist and turned her against the door. Annie looked surprised for a second, but then pulled Harry's head down to her to kiss.

When their lips came together, Harry felt a rush from the tips of her toes right to her lips, like an electrical current washing over her. It was the rawest, most astonishing feeling she had ever had, even more so than their first kiss. It was as if she had always been in darkness before, and Annie's kiss brought her into the light.

She hungrily took possession of her mouth while Annie ran her fingers into her hair and gripped her tightly, pulling her closer. The kiss was frightening in its intensity, and she felt like all the air had been stolen from her lungs.

They broke apart gasping. "Annie? I can't stop myself any more. You've made me feel madness for the first time, and I need you. Please let me touch you?"

Annie reached for the door handle, and when the door opened, Harry pushed them both into her room. When the door closed their lips came together again, and they both grabbed desperately at each other's clothes. It was like a seal had been broken on all the restraint they had used to keep apart, and now there was no going back.

Annie helped Harry pull off her T-shirt and sports bra, and she swept her hands over Harry's stomach and chest while Harry unzipped Annie's black skirt and let it slip to the ground. Annie took off her tights, and then Harry's hands were immediately on the buttons of her tunic. These breasts had tantalized her since Annie had started working here, and she needed them now. She ripped the buttons apart, and disposed of the garment.

Annie took off her lacy bra, and groaned. "Harry, touch me."

"I'll touch you everywhere, and go deep inside of you."

She lifted Annie and placed her on the bed. Having Annie naked underneath her was like a dream. *Wanted* seemed such a tame word for what she demanded from Annie. Her breathing was heavy, and her eyes zeroed in on her prize, Annie's breasts. They were so different from Clara's, or those of the other women she'd slept with, who were so concerned with their appearance and size-zero figures. Annie's breasts were plump, round, and utterly female, just as the rest of her body was.

Her slight hesitation caused Annie to grasp her hands and place them on her breasts herself, and she showed her how she liked them squeezed.

"Oh God, Harry. I've been dreaming of you touching me."

Annie's moans awoke her from her lust-filled stupor and she was back in control. She put her mouth on Annie's breast for her first taste, and gave a low, deep groan while her hips started to rock. She sucked Annie's breast, and then bit and teased her nipple.

Annie writhed and moaned and pulled her back up into a long, deep kiss. She grasped Harry's shoulders, stroked her face and hair, and basically broke every rule Harry had for her sexual encounters, but it didn't seem to matter, her mind and body told her Annie and no one else was allowed to break those rules. In this moment she was Annie's, and that thrilled her.

"Oh God, take these off. I need to feel you." Annie was fighting with her belt buckle and jeans, so Harry soon undid her buttons and struggled out of them and her jockey shorts.

Annie placed a leg between hers and Harry thrust herself against it, hoping to feel some relief from the slick heat in her centre. She wanted to thrust against Annie until she came, wanted to end her long agony.

"Harry, I can feel you need to come."

She did, she couldn't think of anything else but the throbbing between her legs, but she needed Annie too. Her hand tremored with want as she stroked softly from Annie's breast down to her hip, while she placed tender kisses around Annie's mouth. She had never taken so much time and care with a woman before, and still it didn't seem enough. Annie deserved more than she could ever give her.

"Inside me now." Annie took hold of her hand and directed it. It was such a turn-on that Annie knew what she wanted.

"Go inside." Annie groaned.

Harry gave a few strokes to Annie's clitoris before slipping her fingers down to Annie's opening. "God, you're so wet for me."

"Uh-huh." Annie's hips were moving, trying to encourage Harry's fingers inside of her, but Harry continued to tease around her opening, making her want it more and more.

"Harry, please?" Annie begged.

She circled one finger around Annie's entrance, barely dipping the tip of her finger in and pulling back out. "Tell me how much you want me inside you."

Annie delicately trailed her fingertips from Harry's hand where it rested on her sex, and up to her biceps. She took the time to trace the outline of the tattoo there, before ending by caressing her face.

Harry was transfixed by the loving gaze Annie was giving her, and her tender touch. No one had ever touched her like this, and it was crumbling the walls around her heart.

In this second, there was no fear of rejection, being trapped, or hurting Annie and Riley, there was only the deep feeling of love surging through her. *Tell her. Stop being a coward and tell her.*

Before she could Annie said, "Harry, I want you to be deeply inside me while I watch you come on me. I've never wanted anything more."

Harry didn't need to hear any more. She slid straight inside the velvety warmth of Annie, but stopped when Annie hissed. "What's wrong? Did I hurt you?"

"No, I'm fine. Just not used to it. Please keep going."

She did feel tight but Annie had told her she'd only had sex once before, so she supposed that was only natural. She slid back inside carefully and found it much easier to thrust inside her.

Harry kept her thrusts long and slow, and her own hips started to keep a similar rhythm.

Annie's hands gripped her shoulders, and her nails dug into her skin, begging her to go faster. Her thrusts sped up as her slick heat spread over Annie's thigh. Her sex was burning hot and for once she felt like she had no control over her own orgasm. She had always been able to hold herself on the edge, just until the last moment, but this time she had lost all restraint.

"I'm going to come too soon."

Annie cupped her face and breathed heavily. "Just come. I want you to."

Annie's words made her lose complete control. "Jesus, it's you. I can't control anything with you."

"Don't. Just let go, sweetheart," Annie whispered.

Two more thrusts and she did let go. Her orgasm surged through her body, and when she would normally have kept her pleasure silent, now she shouted out as if in pain as she came hard.

"Fuck." She breathed heavily as she tried to get herself back under control. "I'm sorry, I'm sorry, I couldn't stop."

Annie pulled her down to her lips. "It's okay. I don't want you to control yourself. I want you to be free."

Harry kissed her long and hard. She didn't think this woman could be any more perfect. She was everything, everything she never thought she needed.

"I am free with you, but now I need you to come for me." Harry kissed her way down Annie's neck, touching Annie's crucifix with reverence. She lingered on her breasts while she started a slow thrust with her fingers. She sucked and lavished kisses on her breasts, thinking that she could happily kiss them forever. But no, she wanted to taste her.

Annie grasped at her hair as she moved down to her hot, wet sex. "Yes, oh God. I can't take…"

Harry laved and sucked at her clitoris while hastening the thrust inside her. She could feel Annie's walls gripping her fingers in a steady rhythm. Going by that and the way Annie was groaning and bucking her hips, she would come any moment, and she did. Annie pulled Harry's hair tightly and pushed her heels into the small of her back. She called out to her God as she writhed and arched her back in her pleasure.

It was the most beautiful thing Harry had ever seen. Harry couldn't say what she felt out loud, and so she closed her eyes and let the words inside her echo in her mind.

I love you, Annie Brannigan.

Harry awoke to find herself alone, and she was surprised that she felt disappointed. The previous night, after making love for the last time, she had lain awake watching Annie as she slept. She'd stroked her beautiful hair and thought about how it would feel to have Annie in her bed every night, and she knew she would never grow tired of it.

The tight grip of fear in Harry's chest was weakening with every touch of Annie's hands, and she was surely being seduced into love.

Maybe it was that hot choco surprise that did it, Harry thought with a smile as she dressed.

Why had Annie left so early this morning? Just to get started on work? More like she was frightened awakening together would make Harry panic. She didn't know if it would have, so maybe it was better this way.

She exhaled long and loud. Annie wanted a lot. She wanted things that had always horrified Harry, but so much had changed in such a short time, here in Axedale. It was like a different world, with different rules. Maybe she could come back here during the holidays and spend time with Annie and Riley, love them as best she could. Annie and Riley would have a home and she would have a safe place to come back to when the outside world got too much. Maybe even one day she could say those three little words that Annie demanded. Maybe. But for now she couldn't wait to see Annie again.

Harry went downstairs and walked towards the kitchen door, and she saw her refurb team leaving rapidly.

"David? What's wrong?"

David raised his eyebrows. "No warm breakfast for us this morning. Ms. Brannigan is in a hell of a mood. Scrubbing the kitchen top to bottom, says it's filthy and the kitchen's closed."

Oh no. Harry closed her eyes for a second, and regained control quickly. "Okay, I'll sort it out. I want that breakfast room finished today and the work started on the stable kennel area, and the greenhouse. My estate manager is looking to get the dogs and new horses in soon, and I promised Annie she could buy plants for the greenhouse."

"Of course. We'll get it done."

Harry made her way to the kitchen with trepidation. She opened the door and Annie said immediately, "I told you. Kitchen's closed."

She was on her hands and knees scrubbing the floor with a scrubbing brush. Her hair was all messed up, and she had dirty marks on her face, to add to her look of fury. She looked up briefly when Harry entered. "Oh, it's you. Coffee's brewed. You'll need to help yourself."

Harry felt more than a little hurt that these were the first words she said to her after the special night they had shared. "I want to talk to you."

Annie kept on scrubbing and said, "I don't have time."

"That's all the response I'm to expect? After spending the night together, that's all you have to say?"

Annie struggled to her feet. "Keep your voice down. Riley might come in."

"Well talk to me like an adult then." Harry was fast losing her temper.

Annie threw her brush into the bucket of water on the floor. "I'm busy. The whole kitchen is filthy and I have the curtains being delivered back from the cleaners today. It's going to take a few days to get them all rehung. I don't have time for chit-chat."

"Chit-chat? Why are you so angry, Annie? This isn't like you. You always want to talk about things and tell me everything will be okay."

"What do *you* think is wrong? I slept with my employer last night," she snapped. "Or have you forgotten already?"

That sentence stung. That was why she didn't get involved with anyone. Her mother was right, if you had feelings for someone they had the power to destroy you.

"It's just sex. People have it all the time without this much fuss. We are attracted to each other. What's the big deal?"

Annie stepped right up to her. "The big deal is that it's not a big deal to you. I promised myself that the next time I made love with someone it would be someone who wanted me, and only me. I've waited all this time, I'd never...I mean, I let myself down."

Harry looked down at her boots. Each sentence was a new kick to her guts. *She let herself down with you.*

Annie threw her cloth onto the kitchen table in frustration. Her feelings for Harry were strong. She had been falling in love with her, but had been trying to seduce Harry into love by her continued care and attention. And now she had given Harry what the others gave her, simply sex. Everything she had done to court her had been for nothing.

Harry would be done with her, and not only would her heart break but she would break Riley's too, when they had to leave.

"I have Riley to consider. I can't take big chances. Harry? It was just sex to you, wasn't it?" Annie put her hand on Harry's chest. "Harry, look at me."

She looked up and Annie tried to read Harry's eyes.

"What?" Harry asked.

"Was it just sex? Tell me if you feel something in your heart for me, because if it was more—"

Harry had a storm of emotions behind her eyes, and after a long silence, she said, "Of course it was just sex."

Annie felt the tears well in her eyes, and her heart start to crumble. *I don't believe it. I know she cares.*

Harry took hold of Annie's hand and pulled it away from her chest. "Let's just forget it, okay? I don't want Riley to notice something's wrong. I care about her. We can leave this behind us."

Annie nodded solemnly.

"I won't need lunch. I'm going to be away for the day," Harry said, and walked out of the kitchen before Annie could reply.

❖

Harry had no idea where she was going when she left Annie in the kitchen. All she did know was that she had to get away. She walked a few minutes from the front door, and took a seat on the steps of the dilapidated greenhouse.

Annie's reaction shouldn't have bothered her. It gave her the perfect escape clause, a night that meant nothing, but instead she felt hurt. Her heart ached with the rejection. Every one of Annie's words in the kitchen played over and over in her head.

A memory from last night flashed in her mind. Annie had cried out when she went inside her. "I was her first. I was her first."

Annie had waited for *her*. Even though she had been with one woman before her in some limited way, she had kept that part of herself back for the one who would give her forever. Harry had probably been many women's first sexual partner over the years, but none had made her feel like this. Annie was angry because she believed Harry didn't or couldn't love her but she had still given of herself to her. *She's angry because she loves you.*

On impulse she took out her smartphone and dialled, but it went straight to voicemail.

This is Lady Dorothy Knight. Please leave a message and I'll get back to you.

Harry hung up and started walking down into the estate. She found herself walking to the family mausoleum, where generations of Knights had found their final resting place.

The mausoleum was built in 1715, at the same time that Axedale Hall was refurbished from its original medieval manor house to its current Georgian style.

Harry stopped at the bottom of the steps and looked up at the building that had terrified her as a young child. It was designed to be a miniature version of Axedale Hall, so that the family would rest eternally in as grand a manner as in life.

Just like the house, the family motto was engraved above the portico: *He who conquers will endure.*

She walked up the steps and opened the heavy metal door. There were times when she was younger and home from school that she would take a couple of children from the village to see the creepy place. It had always been difficult to keep friendships with the village children because they all went to school together while she was away at boarding school most of the year, not to mention the barrier created by her aristocratic position. Perhaps if Quade had been a few years older, they could have been friends.

Harry walked into the main room of the mausoleum and was hit with the damp, dank smell of the place. Although her father's body had been interred there already when she'd arrived at Axedale, she had never come down to see him. So it had been a long time since she was last in here, and it was even more dilapidated than she remembered. A few of the windows were broken, allowing the elements in, and there were leaves and twigs all over the floor, and moss growing over the stones. This was another job to add to her long lists of refurbishment tasks.

In the main room there were twenty barrel chambers, and beyond them a staircase leading to a crypt below, where the older tombs were housed.

She walked over to her father's chamber, which, like all the tombs, had a stone facing with an inscription on the front. Whereas the others had romantic and poetic inscriptions, her father's said only *Charles Knight, Earl of Axedale.*

As she looked at the stone she could see his laughing, smiling, arrogant face, and her anger and resentment roiled in her stomach.

"You made me, and not only do I look like you, but I behave like you. Because of you I'm unable to tell the best person to come into my life that I..." As much as she tried she couldn't say the words out loud, even though she was only in the presence of the bones of her ancestor. "That I...how much I care about her. I've always hated you, but I think you knew that, and you're probably somewhere in hell laughing at me. I was never quite the proper boy you wanted, was I?"

Harry walked away from his stone in disgust and stopped by her grandfather's and grandmother's stone. He had loved his wife, but as she had died so young, Harry'd never had the chance to see what a loving couple looked like. She took a seat on the stone bench in the middle of the room, and tried to gather her thoughts. Maybe her inability to have normal relationships was in her DNA.

The whole history of the Knight family and their personal lives was riddled with scandal, as her grandfather had taught her when she asked. Even though he wasn't scandalous himself, he almost spoke with a hint of pride about their family background. He'd often said it was so much more interesting to have villains in your family history than saints.

The first Earl Axedale was rumoured to have murdered his wife in order to marry the lady in waiting of Henry VII's Queen Consort, Elizabeth of York. He used his new wife's influence to gain great favour with King Henry VII. From then on the precedent was set, marriage was about position and power, and the Knights were determined to gain as much money and power as they could.

Then it hit her. There had been one exception to the rule. One person who she had always looked up to in her long line of lying, cheating, thieving, adulterous forebears.

She walked downstairs to the crypt. The crypt was even mustier and wetter than upstairs. There appeared to be a perpetual stream of water down one wall, and it had turned the wall green with algae. In the corner was the grave of a countess who the family didn't like to talk about in polite circles until very recently, but to Harry she had always been a hero.

She walked up to the double-wide chamber in the corner. The extra-large stone in front said: *Here lies Hildegard, Countess of Axedale, aged sixty-five. A well-loved master, landlord, daughter, and friend. Also her beloved companion of forty-two years, Katherine Aston, aged seventy. A Godly and charitable woman, and faithful mistress, who will be missed by all who knew her. And now these three remain: faith, hope, and love. But the greatest of these is love. 1 Corinthians 13:13.*

Harry placed her hand on the stone and closed her eyes. That was the chapter Bridge had told her to look up.

The story of Hildegard was infamous in her family's history. Hildegard had been the one to transform Axedale to its current extravagant, Georgian style. Rich and powerful, she'd managed to live as she wanted and to take a traditionally male role in life and in the running of her estate. She was an accomplished horsewoman, swordsman, hunter. *That's the way Riley looks up to me*, thought Harry.

She had often thought she was carrying on Hildegard's legacy at Axedale by refurbishing the estate as she had done. In fact, when she'd made it clear to her father that she was gay, he had remarked that Hildegard's bad blood was bound to come out one day, and it was his misfortune and shame that it was his child.

Her grandfather Henry had been happy to tell her the story of the strong woman who took on men at their own game and won. He had told her that she had been known to like the many pretty girls that crossed her path, but that all changed when Katherine Aston, or Katie as she was known, came to live with her aunt in the village. From the day they met, they were never apart.

When Harry was twelve, she had found Hildegard's diary in the library, and read it cover to cover, and to this day had kept it close.

"You settled down and got your forever, didn't you, Hildegard? How did you do it?"

She resolved to reread the diary this evening, and hoped to get some words of wisdom from its pages.

"I need to tell Riley all about you. Goodbye, Hildegard and Katie. Rest well."

When she walked back upstairs her cell phone rang. "Knight."

"Hi, Harry. It's Quade here. Stevens and I were going to look at some horses for the stables. Would you like to come along?"

That was exactly what she needed. To get away from everything for a few hours. "I'd love to. Can you pick me up at the mausoleum?"

"Will do."

Almost as soon as she put her phone back in her pocket, it rang again. She answered it without looking at who was calling, thinking Quade had forgotten something.

"Yes?"

"Hello, stranger. You're hard to get hold of."

Harry sighed. "Hello Clara. I've been busy."

"No matter. I have you now."

It actually made Harry feel angry to think that Clara thought she had any claim on her. "What do you want?"

"Honestly, what has happened to your manners since you went down to the country? Listen, I'm in a bit of a bind honestly. A bit overstretched, you understand. Maybe you could come for a visit at the weekend and—"

"No," Harry said firmly.

"What do you mean, no?"

Harry's body was rigid with anger. "I mean, I'm not paying for sex any more."

"Paying for sex? What? So I'm a prostitute for you now?"

"We both know how our friends-with-benefits relationship worked. I am not your cash cow, and I think it's time we both had more respect for ourselves."

"Respect? Are you mad? Sex is all you want. What on earth has happened to you down there?"

Annie had happened. When she thought about making love with her last night, all she could think of was that no one would ever compare to touching Annie.

"Maybe I'm just growing up at long last. We're not twenty-five any more, Clara."

"You're a selfish bastard, Harry Knight. I've got people hounding me to pay back debts. The money is just a drop in the ocean to you."

"You're not poor, Clara. Your father is a wealthy man. He's just not falling for the spoiled little girl routine any longer, and neither am I."

"You'll be back. You're not capable of anything else."

Harry ended the call. It was saddening that no one had any faith in her.

CHAPTER EIGHTEEN

There," Bev said. "Five curtains down and six to go."

Annie, Bev, and Julie had spent the morning rehanging the curtains that had been delivered from the cleaners. It was a heavy, awkward job, and had taken a lot out of them. Fortunately the hard work had kept her from thinking too much about last night. By the time they got to the ones in Harry's study, it was time for a break.

"They do look good, don't they? Julie said.

"Must have been so dirty." Annie stretched and let out a yawn. "Excuse me. I think we need a break. Why don't you both go and get the kettle on, and I'll bag up these bits and pieces the curtains came in."

"Lovely. Don't be long or Julie and I might eat that beautiful lemon drizzle cake you made all by ourselves."

Annie laughed. "I won't."

She started to stuff the plastic coverings into black refuse sacks, but the cardboard was so thick it wouldn't fold well. "Scissors, that's what I need."

Annie searched about the desk and couldn't find anything. "She must have scissors in here somewhere."

She pulled out a drawer and searched the pens and papers, and then she saw something that made her stop. It was a hardcover notebook with a flower peeking out from its pages.

Annie was well aware that she shouldn't be doing this, but she just had to look. She opened up the cover, and there sandwiched between the cover and the first page was one of every flower that she had given Harry with her food, and underneath the date and kind of flower it was.

She felt tears coming to her eyes as she slowly sank down to the seat. "She kept them. Why would she do that?"

She thought back to making love with her last night. The way Harry had touched her and looked at her had been with love, she was sure of it. It had been a magical night, and then *she* had run away, not Harry.

"I never gave her a chance. I ran, and gave her an excuse to hide behind her walls again."

It wasn't just sex.

Tears rolled down her cheeks. "What are we going to do?"

Quade was driving Harry over to the stables and filling her in on what they had come up with so far. "Mr. Stevens says we can offer scholarships in conjunction with the local college to the young people of the county. They can choose to work part time at the stables, gamekeeping department, forestry, farming, or the house side of things, whilst attending college for agriculture or hospitality. Perhaps those training in hospitality could work under Ms. Brannigan?"

At the mention of Annie's name, Harry snapped her head around. "I'd like that, for Annie and Riley to stay." Then Harry went back to staring out the truck window.

"Are you all right, Harry? You seem distracted."

"Sorry. I do have a lot on my mind. Can I ask you a question?"

"Fire away."

"Have you ever wanted to settle down? Give up your freedom just to be with one woman?"

Quade gave a hollow laugh. "It's all I've ever wanted."

So Bridge was right about you. "Can you tell me why?"

"That's not easy to explain. I suppose because I saw how happy my great-aunt and uncle were. I came to live with them when I was seven. They couldn't have any children of their own, but they loved each other dearly. My uncle Archie adored my aunt. They weren't ambitious people. All they wanted was to work together on the farm during the day, and sit by the fire together every evening. That's all I've wanted."

"Sounds nice."

Quade sighed. "It does, but unfortunately potential partners are pretty thin on the ground in a little village like Axedale."

Yet again Harry was reminded of how perfect Quade would have been for Annie and Riley, and yet the thought of them together made her feel sick inside. "You would have been right for Annie."

"No, I wouldn't. She only has eyes for you, I've told you that. The one that's perfect for you is the one your heart yearns for, and that's not me. I hope I'm not stepping out of line here, but to me it looks like you feel the same for her."

Harry knew her heart yearned for Annie. Her heart, her body, her soul, but life wasn't as easy as that. "We have different values. She wants forever and I can barely see past the next night."

"I think you above anyone can understand forever."

"Why do you say that?"

"Your family has been here for five hundred years, yes?"

Harry nodded.

"Each one of your ancestors worked to keep the Axedale estate alive for all those that came before them and all those who would come after. They believed in forever, and you must do if you're doing the same. Something to think about, hmm?"

Harry couldn't stop thinking. That was the problem, but she just nodded. She could feel the ground shifting under her feet. Whether she liked it or not, her life was changing and evolving into something that could bring her either great joy or great pain.

Quade turned into the stables, and said, "There's Mr. Stevens waiting for us. Here's hoping they have some good stock."

When they arrived at the stables, Harry watched as Stevens and Quade checked the horses out from head to toe. She had no idea what they were looking for, but so far they had chosen three pairs and dismissed quite a few more.

Mr. Holdworth, the stable owner, stood by her, commentating on the horses. "A pair of finer animals you couldn't find, m'lady. Excellent lineage if you would like to breed them."

"That'll be up to my estate managers, Mr. Holdsworth. I'm just an enthusiastic rider. My mother was the horse expert in the family."

Some of the only happy memories she had with her mother were when she'd taught her to ride. "Mr. Holdsworth, do you have any ponies suitable for a child to learn on?"

"Yes, indeed. Follow me, m'lady."

She left Stevens and Quade to their deliberations and followed Mr. Holdsworth over to the stable block.

"This lovely girl is Willow, an Exmoor pony that would be excellent for a beginner."

Harry stroked the soft velvety snout of the little pony. "She reminds me of my pony, Angus." Riley would love Willow.

"Are you interested, m'lady?"

"Yes, yes, I am." She smiled as she imagined Riley's face when she met Willow. *I just want to make them both happy.*

She had an image of Annie and her watching while her mother taught Riley to ride in the paddock. Harry stood up sharply from patting the horse. *Where the hell did that thought come from? Mother would never come back here.*

"I can't believe this is the same floor as an actual Roman walked on," Riley said.

"It still gives me a thrill and I've been doing this job a long, long time." Riley was kneeling right beside her, washing down the tesserae tiles that she was carefully scraping the soil and dirt back from. They had exposed most of the head and body of the Venus and a large part of the shell.

"Can you tell what kind of building it is yet?" Riley asked.

She had been questioning herself on that the more they uncovered. "It's a high quality mosaic, so I think we're looking at a villa, and a good quality one too."

Something caught Riley's attention behind her shoulder. "Mum! We've found a villa."

Harry jumped up immediately and stepped out of the trench, brushing down her jeans as she went.

"That's wonderful, sweetie."

The sight of Annie coming towards them smiling and carrying snacks was not what she'd expected after their encounter this morning.

"Hi, I come bearing a peace offering. And I thought you both could do with a snack to keep you going until dinner." Annie looked right into her eyes, apparently trying to convey what was in her mind without saying too much in front of Riley.

"What's a peace offering, Mum?"

Harry took off her hat and smoothed back her hair, never breaking eye contact with Annie even as she answered Riley's question. "It's when you care about someone so much that you don't want them to ever think you are grumpy with them, and you want them to know that no matter what happens, you will always care about them."

She saw tears well up in Annie's eyes, but she quickly wiped them away, before saying, "Yes, that's exactly it."

Riley looked at them both quizzically. "I don't get it."

"Don't worry about it, sweetie. Here, try these." She handed them each a white paper bag. "A little birdy told me this was a young Lady Harry's favourite."

It couldn't be. "It's not, is it?" Harry opened her bag so quickly it ripped, and she saw a piece of her childhood. "Fudgie-wudgies? Are those fudgie-wudgies?"

"They are. Mrs. Castle gave me the recipe. Try one."

Harry popped one into her mouth and groaned. Mrs. Castle always used to make her these as a treat, and she loved them. "Oh my God, they are just how I remember them."

In a rush of excitement, Harry picked up Annie and spun around. "Thank you. I'm going to savour every bite."

"I'm glad you like them." Annie held her arms around Harry's neck even when she put her down.

"Like them is an understatement. I don't know how you do it, but you always seem to know what I need."

"I try."

CHAPTER NINETEEN

That weekend came Harry's first big social engagement as countess, the Kent agricultural show.

Annie knocked on Harry's bedroom door. "Harry? The car's here."

"Can you come in a minute?"

She opened the door and saw Harry dressed in tweed waistcoat and jacket, dark blue jeans, and brown brogue shoes. *Wow.*

She didn't seem to be in charge of her own feet as she was drawn over to Harry and smoothed her hands down her lapels. "You look"—*gorgeous*—"handsome and perfectly turned out."

"Thank you. I didn't know if I looked silly in this country look."

"No." Her fingers trailed down the waistcoat buttons and caressed the pocket watch chain there.

"That was my grandfather's gold watch. I like to wear it when I can."

Annie suddenly realized how close she was to Harry and how inappropriately she was behaving, and took a step back. "I'm sorry. You look wonderful. You always wear such smart clothes, and take so much care."

"Can I add that to the list?"

Annie was confused as to what she meant. "Sorry?"

"My growing list of perfections. I always smell nice, I have nice thick dark hair, and now I'm perfectly turned out. I can't be all bad, can I?"

Annie felt the heat in her cheeks, and knew they probably were bright red. Why did she keep saying these things?

"No. You're definitely not all bad. So what was it you wanted to ask?" She tried to change the subject.

"Oh yes." Harry reached to the chest of drawers by the mirror behind her and lifted a beautiful gold handkerchief and gold silk tie.

"Do you think I should wear these, or is the full-on dapper butch look too much for the good people of the Kent agricultural show?" Harry said, smiling.

Annie laughed and took the tie from her hand. "If they're not, then they'll just have to get ready for it."

Quite naturally and without thought, she lifted up Harry's collar and started to put the tie on. When she pushed the knot up to Harry's neck, she was caught in her gaze. They stayed quite still, gazing at each other until Harry's hands came up and covered her own, and she began to lean in for a kiss. Annie knew she shouldn't but couldn't help but follow Harry's lead. There was some unstoppable, magnetic pull between them, and that force left her mind blank of all the problems that meant they shouldn't kiss or make love again.

How could fate be so cruel as to choose someone who couldn't be what she needed as her destined soul mate?

But none of that mattered as their lips came inches from each other. Just as their lips were about to meet, there was a loud knock at the door, and they jumped apart.

"Ms. Brannigan? Lady Harry? The car is due to leave in ten minutes," Bev said.

Annie was angry at herself. She had nearly kissed Harry again. She needed to leave. "I'll let you handle the rest."

"Annie, don't—" Harry called after her, but she was gone out of the room before she heard the rest.

❖

When they arrived at the show, they were escorted to the VIP tent. Harry couldn't keep her eyes off Annie in her simple pastel-coloured flower-print dress. She was so beautiful, so natural, and it felt so right to have her by her side. This was what it must feel like to have a partner, a wife. It felt warm and nice, not scary at all, not with Annie.

Riley walked a few steps ahead, excited at all the sights and sounds of the fair. It appeared to be a wonderful place for kids. There were fairground rides, all sorts of animals to see, and delicious food to eat.

They moved from the grass up onto a walkway that led to the tent. The walkway was a bit uneven, so she offered Annie her arm.

"Thanks," Annie said.

It had been hard to convince Annie that she should come with her in the first place. She didn't think it was right for the countess to take her housekeeper, but Harry convinced her that she needed Annie's support for her first big social engagement, and that Riley would love it.

So here they were, arm in arm, walking into the VIP tent, looking every inch the perfect couple. It didn't go unnoticed by Harry that she received some envious looks from some of the men they passed, having Annie on her arm. The pride she felt was something new to her. New but a nice feeling all the same.

They were met at the entrance by the chairman of Kent County Council. "Lady Axedale, how wonderful to meet you. I'm Ralph Littlejohn."

Harry could see his surprise in the way she was dressed. She shook his hand and put on her best smile. "Delighted to meet you, Ralph, this is my close friend Annie, and her daughter Riley." Annie looked surprised that she had introduced them at all, never mind as close friends.

"Nice to meet you all. Come in and get a nice cup of tea."

After meeting the rest of the dignitaries, it was time to go into the main stage and give her speech.

Annie and Riley stood just to the side of the stage and watched Harry get up to the microphone. She knew Harry hadn't been looking forward to this part, but as ever she put on that confident air that she had about herself, and started to talk.

"Ladies, gentlemen, and children, it is my duty as Countess of Axedale to encourage and congratulate those within our county who excel. I am extremely proud to be part of a community that delivers such excellent produce to the country, and the world. Keep up the good work, we are all very proud of you. So all that remains is to declare this fair open."

A cheer went up from the crowd and Annie and Riley clapped loudly.

"She did great, Mum," Riley said.

Just at that moment Harry looked at her from the stage, and she felt her heart ache with love for her. "She did. Harry can do so many things she doesn't believe she can."

After she made her speech, the three of them had a wonderful time going around the stalls and food tents. While they walked they were linked in the middle by Riley holding both their hands, and when she wandered off, Harry took Annie's hand instead. Neither made comment on it, but Annie loved it. It felt as close to a family outing as you could get.

"Mum?" Riley shouted from up ahead.

"What is it, sweetie?"

"It's the Axedale ladies' cake stall."

"We'll catch you up," Annie replied.

"Oh dear God. The Axedale ladies, sounds like a coven. It would put the fear of death into anyone," Harry snarked.

Annie chuckled and smacked her arm. "Stop it you. Be nice and try all their cakes when we get there. Besides, it would be a lovely thing to be known as one of the Axedale ladies."

Harry raised a questioning eyebrow. "It would?"

"Of course it would. Those women have lived in Axedale all their lives, or married into it. They have a home, and a community to rely on. I would say most people would give anything to have that sort of security." Annie felt a deep sadness that she wouldn't experience that. If Harry had been different, if she could love her the way she was falling in love with her, she might have what the Axedale ladies had, but that was a pipe dream.

"Oh, I see," Harry said awkwardly.

Annie released her hand and walked on towards the cake stall. "Hello, ladies," Annie said.

Minding the stall were Mrs. Peters, Mr. Finch's wife, some other members of the women's guild, and Bridget. They all replied hello back, and Bridget said, "You dragged her here, I see."

"Bridge, you're into making cakes now?" Harry said sarcastically.

"I'm into making money for the church day-care group. Everything we make is going to them, if you remember."

"I do." Harry looked around the cakes on display and noticed a label saying: *Ms. Brannigan's Death by Chocolate cake.*

"Did you make cakes for the stall?"

"Of course I did. I wanted to help."

Harry pointed to the cake and said, "I'll have a piece of that, Mrs. Peters. I adore Annie's cakes."

Bridget gave Annie a smile. "My, my, you do have our countess housetrained."

Annie watched Mrs. Peters give Harry a large piece of cake on a disposable plate, and a piece to Riley too. "No, she just needed people to care about her. She's perfectly good-natured."

"So loyal too," Bridget teased.

"How are donations going?" Annie asked, ignoring Bridge's remarks.

"Not too bad," Mrs. Peters said.

That made Harry jump to action. "Oh yes. Hold this, Riley." She handed her plate to Riley and took out her wallet. She pulled out a handful of notes and put them in the donation box.

"Oh, thank you, Lady Harry. That's kind of you," Mrs. Peters said.

Annie looked on with pride as Harry said, "Not at all. Whatever you make today, let me know and I'll triple it. Whatever you need to keep the day-care group open."

Bridget ran around the front of the stall and hugged Harry. "Thank you, Harry. You are wonderful."

Annie wanted to shout, *Yes, you are wonderful, sweetheart.* It warmed her soul to see a transformed Harry Knight opening up to the people who wanted to care for her.

❖

Why did I do this to myself? Harry asked herself as she leaned up against a fence with a bottle of water in her hand. She looked to the side and saw Annie and Riley trying not to laugh. "This is your fault."

"What's our fault, Harry?"

"Feeding me Death by Chocolate cake and insisting I go on a fairground ride called Megaspin."

Annie sighed and took another bottle of the ice-cold water they had bought and put it on the back of her neck. "Did I force two pieces of chocolate cake down your neck and force you on a fairground ride that spins you three hundred and sixty degrees while upside down? No, you saw the ride, grabbed Riley's hand, and ran off."

Riley put her hand on Harry's back and tried to rub it soothingly. "I'm sorry, Harry. I didn't mean you to feel sick."

"Don't worry, Riley. Your mum is right as usual. It was my fault. I just don't like to admit it." She heard Annie chuckle behind her.

She took a deep breath of air, and stood up slowly. "God, if my students or colleagues could see me now. They'd never recognize me."

"Maybe that's a good thing?"

That comment stopped her in her tracks. Was it a good thing? "Perhaps," Harry said.

"I hope you feel better, Harry. This has been a great day," Riley said.

Harry nodded and stroked Riley's hair. "I'm better now. Why don't we go and visit Quade in the cattle tent."

"Yeah. I hope she wins the rosette. Mabel the cow is the best looking cow in Kent, Ms. McQuade says."

How she managed to keep a straight face she would never know. Especially when she heard Annie trying to cover her laughter behind her. "Really? Well I suppose rugged farmers would know all about that."

Annie grabbed her hand and said, "Come on, your ladyship. You've got all the cups and prizes to give out in an hour."

"I'll keep my fingers crossed for Mabel then," Harry said, while being led off by Annie and Riley.

❖

As they drove home, first Riley, and then Annie nodded off to sleep at her side in the backseat. She put an arm around each of them and pulled them close. It had been a tiring day, but a perfect one. It seemed like they had laughed the whole day long. She loved having fun with Riley and Annie. Annie was just beautiful and perfect for her. She wanted her badly.

As they neared Axedale, Harry felt Annie move and slip her hand just under her belt until she felt her skin. The sight of Annie's hand there made her feel hot.

It then got worse when Annie groaned in her sleep. "Harry."

The chauffeur looked in the driver's mirror at them. She lifted Annie's hand and put it back on her own lap. Now was neither the time or the place.

She shook Annie awake when they drove up the drive to the front door, and she jumped up, clearly embarrassed at having fallen asleep in Harry's embrace.

Harry carried Riley into the TV room, while Annie hurried off to the kitchen, claiming to have some cleaning tasks still to see to. She placed Riley carefully on the couch, and pulled a blanket over her. "I love you, Riley."

It was so easy to say to her young friend, but no matter how she felt inside, it was out of the question to say it to Annie. But, oh, she wanted to. How she wanted to be with her, near her.

And she couldn't help but go to her in the kitchen.

She found Annie washing up a couple of cups in the sink, her apron worn on top of her beautiful dress. Harry took off her jacket, rolled her shirtsleeves up to her elbows, and sat on the edge of the table directly behind her.

Harry could tell that Annie felt her. She stopped working for a few seconds and flinched as if a shiver rippled across her skin.

Annie had tied her hair up when she had come into the kitchen, and there now was a tantalizing expanse of bare neck and upper back, down to the zip on her dress. It was making Harry's body ache with the want to touch, and kiss, and bite her all the way down to the small of her back.

"Is Riley still sleeping?" Annie said.

"Yes, it's been a long day for her."

Annie rinsed off her hands and began drying them with the tea towel. It felt like the air was charged with sexual energy, and she was terrified that Harry would touch her, because if she did, she didn't think she had the strength to say no, and she must.

"The day was wonderful and you were beautiful in your dress. You are exactly what I like in a woman."

Annie said nothing, but could hear Harry stand and walk the few steps to her.

She gasped and her heart started to pound when Harry's fingers trailed down her neck, shoulders, and back.

Annie was fighting against her body's wants. They couldn't go down this road again.

She felt Harry press up against her back, and she braced herself against the sink.

Harry whispered in her ear, "*You* are exactly what I like," before kissing her neck.

"Don't, Harry."

"Why?" She continued kissing down her neck and shoulder making Annie shiver. "We both know we want each other. Every time I'm with you, I want to touch you. You make me feel when I'm with you. Make me feel warm, happy to be with you."

Annie groaned. "I told you I can't do this again, Harry."

Harry turned her around so they were facing each other and said, "Our first time together was the best sex I've ever had in my life."

Annie reached up to caress her face. "Sex, yes. Making love, no. I need more than that. I've told you what I need for both Riley and me."

"I'm giving you all I can give," Harry said desperately. "I'm being with Riley, caring about her, and you, I've let you be closer to me than any lover ever has. I'm making the estate somewhere you and Riley can live and have a home. I've been working on a plan with Quade and Stevens."

"Oh, I've heard all about your plan from Bridge," Annie said with anger in her voice.

"What does she know about it? I never told—"

"A lot apparently. You've set up this grand plan where Riley and I can wait for you while you're away. Then you can come back and play at being a family for a few weeks during the holidays, and of course sleep with me. You've got it all worked out, haven't you? I'll be your country mistress—you have your London and Cambridge ones too, I'm sure."

"No, that is not it."

"It's not enough, Harry. I want…no, I need to be everything to you."

Harry grasped her face in her hands. "We just give each other what we can, while we can. I want you so much."

Harry kissed her deep and hard, and Annie pushed her away. "Don't. It's not enough. This needs to stop."

Harry looked furious now. "It won't ever stop because we both know how much we want each other, how much we need each other. Tell me you don't want me to make love to you right now? Tell me you don't want me deep inside of you making you come?"

Annie could only tell the truth. "I can't do that."

"You see, nothing can stop us wanting each other. Nothing could make me not want you every time I see you." She moved in to kiss Annie with fire and passion in her eyes, but before she could, Annie said, "I know how to stop you wanting me."

Harry looked at her quizzically.

Could she say what was on the tip of her tongue? Things had gone too far now. There was no turning back. "I love you, I love you more than I could ever have imagined loving anyone. I want everything with you, everything that frightens you. I want to be your partner, I want to have a family with you, and…I want forever with you."

Harry stopped dead, and looked at Annie silently.

Harry's silence hurt more than any words could. She'd said I love you, and laid her heart on the line and all Harry could do was say nothing. Tears tumbled down her face.

Harry reached out to cup her cheek but Annie pushed her away. "Don't touch me."

"Annie I'm—"

"No," Annie said. "I'm sick of not saying what I really feel for fear that you'll get scared. You need to face what is between us. You can't just come to me every time you want sex. I won't accept it. Tell me what's in your heart, Harry."

"You want too much. I had a terrible childhood watching two people who were supposed to be in love destroy each other."

Annie didn't think she'd ever felt more furious. "*You* had a miserable childhood?"

Harry took a step back, surprised at Annie's fury.

"Oh poor you, Harry," she said sarcastically. "Poor little Lady Harry had to run to the kitchen staff for hugs and apple pie to make it better. Meanwhile I was eating mouldy bread from the bin while my mother lay with a needle hanging out of her arm, and locking myself in the bathroom because a man came with a knife and held it at my mother's throat. Poor Harry!"

Harry opened her mouth as if to speak, but instead gulped hard. Then without a word, she turned and walked out of the kitchen.

"I told you I could stop you from wanting me." Annie convulsed in tears.

CHAPTER TWENTY

Harry kept her distance the rest of the week. She had no idea how to respond to what Annie had said to her in the kitchen. What could she say? She wanted everything Annie had said, but she knew she would hurt her somehow. The part of her that was her father would win out and she would destroy two lives, both Annie and Riley, and she couldn't bear that.

Harry dressed for the day and began to walk downstairs. It was Riley's birthday today, and she was determined to make it one to remember. She stopped on the landing and looked down at the poorly wrapped birthday presents in her arms.

She was wrong. It wouldn't just destroy two lives when she would inevitably hurt Annie. It would destroy three. It would destroy her just as much.

In one of their brief conversations this week, they had agreed to talk about where to go from here after Riley's birthday, but Harry was certain Annie was going to leave, and it would break her heart.

She took a deep breath and tried to regain control of her emotions.

You can do it. Do it for Riley.

When Harry walked into the kitchen the air was frosty. She held the birthday presents she had bought for Riley tensely. They had agreed to split the costs, choosing a metal detector and an e-reader that would suit Annie's budget. But Harry hadn't exactly stuck to the script.

The tension was eased when Harry put the packages on the kitchen table and Annie saw her wrapping skills, and started to laugh. The paper had been ripped and resealed with tape, and bits of paper added where she had underestimated the size needed.

Harry crossed her arms defensively and raised her eyebrow. "Are you laughing at my wrapping?"

"Yes, it looks like you lost a fight with the paper." Annie giggled.

"Very funny, Ms. Brannigan. This is my first attempt at the skill of wrapping, and I think the last. It's much easier paying the shop to do it."

Annie picked up the large rectangular box that held the tablet Harry had bought instead of a plain e-reader and said, "Why didn't you ask me to do it?"

Because I knew you would be angry at what I spent. "I thought it would be a surprise to you as well."

Annie examined both boxes and looked up at her suspiciously. "You haven't stuck to our budget have you. This box is too big to be the simple e-reader we picked out. You're taking us to London overnight as well. It's too much."

"Well, on reflection I thought my contribution to the budget should be more since I can afford—"

"You can't buy her expensive things, Harry. I'm your employee not your…"

Annie left the sentence hanging, but they both knew what she meant.

Harry replied, "I love Riley, and who knows how much time I have left to be in her life. Allow me to enjoy this one birthday with her."

Annie nodded and placed the package down. For the first time she realized if she left, Harry wouldn't be losing only what they'd shared together, but also what she shared with Riley, who she had come to love.

Harry looked so vulnerable in that moment that she walked around the table and pulled her into a hug. "I'm sorry. You're right."

Leaving Harry was going to kill her, but she couldn't live here and only have her part time, sharing her with other women. *She's ruined me for anyone else.*

"Morning." They jumped apart when they heard Riley's voice. Far from being shocked, Riley had a big smile on her face. "See, I told you Harry was your knight, Mum."

"It was just a hug, sweetie. Now how's my birthday girl?" Annie opened her arms and gave her a kiss.

"I'm excited. We're going to London with Harry."

The joy on Riley's face made her feel guilty. This—a life with Harry—was what Riley wanted and she couldn't give it to her. For a split second she wondered if they should stay. Could she put up with an emotionally distant Harry, to give Riley what she wanted? No. She loved her far too much for that.

Harry gave Riley a hug and said, "Come and open your presents. We've got a busy day ahead."

Riley sat up at the kitchen table full of excitement and looked at the parcels. "Wow!"

Annie said, "These are supposed—"

Harry cut in. "These are from us both." Harry handed her the long rectangular box first. "Just so you know, I wrapped these, and your mum thinks it's funny."

Riley laughed and pulled off the paper. As soon as she saw it was a metal detector she jumped up and hugged them. "This is the best present ever."

When she opened what Annie thought was an e-reader, she found the latest iPad. Riley didn't say a word, but just stared at it in shock.

Harry took the box and opened it up. "I set it up for you, look."

Annie watched a smile creep onto Riley's face as Harry told her about some of the history apps and books she had installed on it already.

"What do you think?"

Riley put the iPad down carefully on the table and threw her arms around Harry. "Thank you so much. I love you, Harry."

"That's okay. I love you too, centurion."

After it was Annie's turn to get a hug. "Thank you, Mum. I love it."

"I'm so glad. You're a good girl."

❖

Harry looked in her driver's mirror and smiled. Riley was glued to her new iPad. Then she glanced to the side and watched Annie gaze out the window. She appeared to be thinking hard, and Harry was sure she was the cause.

"Mum? Lady Hildegard is on Wikipedia."

Annie shook herself and looked into the backseat. "Who's Lady Hildegard?"

"One of Harry's coolest ancestors."

"I think books could be written about your long line of cool ancestors," Annie joked.

"There would be more villains than heroes I can assure you."

"Lady Hildegard would be a hero though, wouldn't she, Harry?" Riley said.

"Oh, absolutely, to me anyway. Why don't you tell your mum, Riley."

Riley launched into a full history of the eighteenth-century woman living and succeeding in a man's world. "She rode horses, fought with swords, everything a girl wasn't meant to do back in the old times."

"Really? Sounds like someone else I know," Annie said while looking at Harry.

"Harry said she liked girls an awful lot, but then she met her fair lady. Her name was Katherine Aston. She moved to the village and they fell in love and—"

"And lived happily ever after?" Annie finished for her.

"Yes. Lady Hildegard was Katherine's knight in shining armour."

Harry looked at her quickly and returned her eyes to the road.

"Imagine that," Annie said. "True love can hit you un-expectedly."

❖

They checked into the Savoy, and made their way up to their room. Riley was looking around at everything with awe, and her vocabulary seemed to consist of *wow* and *whoa*.

The bellboy showed them into their suite and Riley ran around checking all the rooms. Harry tipped him and they were left alone. "I hope this is all right. I thought a family suite would be a good idea. That way we can share this living space and you and Riley can take that room and I'll take the other. That way we're still together."

"It's perfect. Riley and I have never stayed somewhere like this."

Harry could feel that Annie was uneasy about her spending so much on them, so she took Annie's hand and said, "It makes me happy to share this with you. Is that okay?"

Annie smiled and nodded. "It's more than okay."

Harry clapped her hands together and said, "Right, room service for lunch, I think, and then the British Museum, here we come."

"Yes!" Riley cheered.

❖

They got a taxi to the museum after lunch, and Riley kept her face glued to the window, taking in all the many sights and sounds of the capital. Although she and Annie came from London, Riley had rarely been in the centre of town.

"Oh, I see it," Riley said as they pulled up outside the classical looking building.

"It was built to look like a Greek temple," Harry said as she paid the driver.

Annie put her hand on Harry's arm and said, "I think someone might be a little bit excited."

"She's not the only one that's excited," Harry said as they all got out. "I still get the same thrill every time I walk into the building."

Riley hurried ahead but Annie called for her to come back. "You keep beside us, Riley, and either hold my hand or Harry's."

She considered both adults and must have decided Harry was the best bet, then pulled in beside her.

When they walked through the front entrance, they were immediately greeted by the museum staff at the reception.

"Good afternoon, Dr. Knight."

"Good afternoon, Mike."

"Do you come here a lot?" Annie asked.

"Fairly regularly. That's one of the reasons I love coming here. In this world, I'll always be Dr. Knight."

Annie could see how that made sense. In this world, Harry was judged on her own merits.

"Where are we going first?" Riley asked.

Harry looked at her watch. "Well, we have to meet my colleague, Oscar, in the Roman Britain room in an hour, so why don't we start in the Assyrian and Egyptian rooms and work our way around?"

"Yeah, let's go," Riley said with excitement.

Annie found it fascinating to watch and listen to Harry as they walked around the exhibits. She didn't just tell Riley everything she needed to know, she asked questions and tried to get her to use her reasoning and thinking skills to answer her own questions.

Riley particularly enjoyed the Egyptian rooms, and it was a thrill to come face to face with the Rosetta Stone.

After an hour Harry looked at her watch and said, "We'd better be making tracks to the Roman room."

When they arrived, she walked over to an older man standing by one of the glass cases. "Oscar, good to see you again."

"Harry, long time no see. Who are these good-looking ladies?"

Harry smiled and said, "Oscar Levett, this is my good friend Annie Brannigan and her daughter, Riley."

Oscar shook their hands and said, "Delighted to meet you both."

Annie liked the man already. He was warm and welcoming.

"I trained under Oscar in the beginning of my career. I learned so much from him," Harry said.

She could feel that Harry genuinely cared for this man.

"Now, Harry. You've far exceeded what I taught you. Let's go through to the back, and I'll show you what I've put together."

Harry put her arm around Riley's shoulder. "The public don't get to see behind the scenes of the museum, but I asked my friend Oscar to put together a special display for you."

Annie was so touched. Harry was so considerate and good to Riley. It was just a perfect birthday. She followed behind the three of them as they went through a staff door and down a long corridor. They passed lots of rooms until Oscar led them into what looked like a large reading room. The table in the room was full of artefacts.

"This is a small collection of Dr. Knight's finds that we keep here at the museum. Some are usually on display, and some are so fragile that they can't be put on display."

Annie took Harry's hand. "This is wonderful."

Riley's mouth hung open in awe. "Wow. Tell us about them, Harry."

Harry began to talk them through her early finds through the later ones, but Riley was most excited by one thing on the table, a Roman helmet.

"Tell us about this one?"

"Ah, one of Harry's most important finds, and it's worth a fortune."

Harry walked around the table and carefully lifted it up. "This is a Roman cavalry helmet I found when I was excavating a Roman fort near Newcastle. We were excavating a rubbish pit in the ground, and out it came as if it had just been worn the day before."

Annie and Riley gathered in close, taking in all the intricate metalwork.

"It's the pride of our collection," Oscar added. "It's valued at two and a half million pounds."

Annie got a bit of a fright when she heard what it was worth and pushed Riley back from it. "Don't get too close, Riley."

"It's okay, Annie. Touch it, Riley," Harry said.

Riley gingerly held out her hand and touched it. "A Roman soldier actually wore this?"

The look of joy on Riley's face was one she would not soon forget.

❖

They spent another few hours at the museum, and then Harry bought them dinner, and they finished off their day with a trip on the London Eye. Everyone was exhausted when they got back to the hotel room.

After settling Riley down to sleep, Annie got changed into her nightdress and dressing gown, and walked across to Harry's bedroom door. She knocked on the door. "Harry? Can I speak to you?"

"Come in."

She found Harry standing in just her boxers and a sleeveless T-shirt looking utterly gorgeous. Her long powerful legs and strong upper body was everything that Annie liked in a woman.

"Is everything okay?"

"Yes, I just wanted to say thank you for today. I think it just might be the best day of Riley's life."

Harry draped her jeans over the chair. "I think it might have been mine too."

Annie inhaled sharply. She was not expecting that reply. "You don't really mean—"

Harry was over to her in a second and took her hands. "I do mean it. I never spent another day like today. You and Riley have brought light and laughter to my life. Before, I did my work, went to parties with people who had too much money and no responsibilities, and had sex. My life was empty."

She hadn't seen Harry as emotional as this before. Her hands were shaking and her breathing fast. Annie opened her arms to her and Harry held on to her tightly.

"Will you sleep with me tonight? Not sex, just…" Harry was struggling to say what she wanted.

"You want to be together, be close and fall asleep in each other's arms?" Annie asked.

"Yes, that's what I want."

Quietly and without fuss, Annie took off her dressing gown, and slipped into bed. Harry stood by the side of the bed looking scared, so Annie lifted up the covers and patted the bed. "Come in then."

Harry snapped off the light and got in. Annie snuggled up beside her, and lifted her hand and placed it on her hip. "This is nice."

Harry nodded. "I've never done this before, with a woman, with anyone."

Annie stroked her hair. "I'm glad I'm your first."

Lying in the dark silence felt calm, and felt right. In another world where Harry wasn't frightened of commitment, they would be sleeping like this every night, not feeling sad because they knew it probably wouldn't happen again.

"You and Riley are the only ones, apart from one woman, to give me hugs and affection without pushing me away," Harry said.

Annie felt a stab of jealousy. "Oh, was the woman a lover?"

"No, no. Mrs. Castle, when I was a little girl. She always took care of me and told me everything would be all right."

"That's why you don't like people touching you," Annie said.

"I don't understand."

It was so clear. Not only did Harry have her own baggage, she also carried both her parents' baggage. "Deep down you are afraid of being rejected, like your mum and dad rejected you and each other."

"Am I?"

"Yes. But I won't reject you." Annie gave Harry a soft kiss on the cheek. "Even if we can't be what we both need for the future."

Harry stroked her face tenderly. "You're so beautiful. Can I have one kiss, before we go to sleep? I promise nothing more, but I've been dreaming about your kiss since our last."

Annie moved forward and their lips came together. Unlike their previous kisses, Annie controlled this one. She kissed Harry sweetly, trying to convey to her every ounce of love in her heart. When she took a breath, Harry whispered, "I'm so sorry I can't be what you need me to be."

Annie felt tears roll down her cheeks. "I know. So am I."

She held Harry and stroked her hair until her breathing evened out and she knew she was asleep.

Only lightly into her fitful slumber, Harry murmured, "You're all I need."

Annie wished that were true.

CHAPTER TWENTY-ONE

As the weeks passed, Axedale was beginning to look in excellent shape, and Riley was settling in at school. Quade had started to work with Mr. Stevens on the estate, and true to her word, Harry agreed they could set the date for the celebration ball for the villagers and Riley's new friends. Annie even persuaded Harry to invite her mother, and build another bridge.

The horses had arrived, and Riley was overjoyed when she met Willow the pony. If Riley wasn't excavating with Harry, she was at the stables learning to take care of her new friend. Today she'd had her first riding lesson with Harry, and she was exhausted. Annie settled her in bed, and Harry came in to say goodnight.

She gave Riley a hug. "Goodnight, centurion."

"'Night, Harry."

"I'm just going to my study to get an hour of writing in, okay? I'll see you later," Harry said to Annie.

She sat down at her desk, and quickly flicked through the papers that her lawyer, Mr. Johnstone, had brought up. Most of them were tenants' papers and bank records, but then one folder caught her eye.

Axedale inheritance. She opened it up and couldn't believe what she was reading. "The bastard. The fucking bastard."

❖

Annie made coffee for herself and Harry hoping they could have one of their cosy evening chats by the fire. Maybe they could finally talk about their future, as Harry had kept putting it off.

"Harry I've got coffee for you—" Harry wasn't there but there was an open folder on her desk with papers everywhere. She looked through them quickly and couldn't believe what she was reading. It was a legal file from the Knight family's lawyer. Apparently, a few years before, Lord Axedale had tried to disinherit Harry, to leave the Axedale estate to a distant cousin.

"How could he do that to her?"

A few pages later she found a note from the lawyer saying that Lady Dorothy had agreed to advance her father two million pounds in lieu of changing his will. Her mum had saved Axedale for her.

She had to find Harry. Annie walked upstairs and found Harry waiting at her bedroom door. "Are you okay? I read the file." She could see Harry was rigid with raw emotion, and reached out to touch her. "I know you're hurting but tell me what you need."

Harry held out her hand and said, "I need you, Annie. I always need you."

Annie followed as she was led to Harry's bedroom. As soon as the door was shut she was pulled into Harry's arms. "You are the only thing that feels right. When I feel out of control you can soothe me."

Harry looked so desperately raw that Annie hurt for her. She wanted to wrap her up and hold her till she felt better, but she knew by the penetrating look she was giving her that Harry needed more than that.

She held Harry tightly. "It's okay. I'm here. I'm sorry he hurt you, sweetheart."

Harry reacted to that statement immediately. She kissed her feverishly, moving from her lips to her neck, while pulling at her clothes.

Annie responded immediately to her and she kissed her back with equal passion, pushing Harry backwards towards the bed.

They both pulled back from their kiss to catch their breath. "Annie, Annie, please." Harry took Annie's hand and directed it down to the silver buckle on her belt.

Annie groaned and traced her fingers teasingly along the belt. "I'll give you anything you need. Just tell me."

Harry grasped Annie's hair and pulled her closer. "Why do you keep doing this?"

"Doing what?"

"Giving everything to me, your body, your heart, when I don't give you what you demand?"

"Because you need me," Annie said simply. She could feel Harry wanted love and affection showered on her. She was emotionally drained and frustrated, and for the moment appeared content to let Annie lead.

Annie started to take her own clothes off slowly. Harry's eyes were glued to her as each layer came off. When she was finally naked, Harry licked her lips, and appeared to be using great restraint to hold herself back. Annie unbuckled Harry's belt, letting her jeans fall to the floor, and said, "Take off the rest and lie down."

Annie straddled her, and leaned over to kiss her, before pulling back and placing a hand directly over Harry's heart. "Every kiss I give you, I want you to feel it in your heart, you understand?"

"Yes, I want to feel it," Harry whispered.

Annie kept her hand firmly on Harry's chest and kissed her way down Harry's body until her lips hovered over her sex.

She looked up and saw Harry had slung her arm over her eyes in desperation. "Do you want me to kiss here?"

"*Please,*" Harry groaned.

Keeping her hand on her chest, Annie kissed and sucked on Harry's clit, until she felt her hips start to buck and Harry's hand on the back of her head.

"Oh God, Annie. I want to…want to tell you…"

She was sure Harry wanted to say she loved her, but could she take that last step? Harry gave an emotional cry and came hard. Sensing that she needed more, she coaxed her to another orgasm before climbing up her body to kiss her lips.

Harry wrapped her arms around her, and didn't let her go. "I need you so much, I can't—"

"Shh, it's all right, sweetheart. It'll be okay now."

After a minute or so, Harry had clearly had enough of being passive, and quickly flipped her over. This was a different Harry, the Harry that took control and gave her exactly what she needed. She squeezed and sucked her breasts, and without warning slipped two fingers into her, but kept them still.

"Harry?"

"Ask me to fuck you," Harry demanded.

Annie felt her excitement skyrocket. After being so emotionally vulnerable, Harry clearly needed to feel this little bit of dominance.

It made it even more exciting that the words Harry demanded were not words she would ever use. She defied Harry by keeping quiet, and moved her hips, trying to get some relief without giving in so easily.

Harry left her breasts and came back up to her lips. "Ask me to fuck you. You know you want to. I'll make you come, if you just say it."

Annie held on to Harry's hair and looked into her eyes. "Please, fuck me."

Harry groaned in pleasure, and immediately began to slide her fingers into her, while thrusting with her hips. They kissed as Annie's orgasm was seconds away, and Annie dug her fingernails into Harry's shoulders as it started to wash over her.

"I love you," Annie cried.

❖

In the dawn of early morning, they lay holding each other. Harry had been silent after her declaration of love, and she wasn't going to allow Harry to ignore the truth any longer. Annie looked into Harry's eyes and said, "I love you, and Riley loves you. Stay and make a life with us."

She felt Harry stiffen in her arms. This couldn't go on any longer. It was too painful to stay and not have Harry the way she wanted. It was now or never. "Harry, I can't take this any more. You need to tell me what you want. We keep ending up in this position and yet you don't give me any commitment. I need that commitment, and Riley deserves to know that you are going to be a permanent fixture in her life. Do you love me?"

Harry remained silent. Annie leaned up on one arm and placed a hand on Harry's heart. "I have a child to protect, and I make no apology for demanding commitment from whoever wants to be in our life. I watched all sorts of strange men come and go from my mother's home. I will not accept half measures. This is breaking my heart. If you want us to stay with you, you only have to say the word, and we will never leave."

Harry wouldn't look at her. She gulped, clearly trying to keep control of her emotions. Then a cold hardness that Annie had not seen in her since her first days at Axedale came over Harry's features. "I'm returning to work in Cambridge before my sabbatical ends. I think that would be best," Harry said simply as she got up and put her clothes on.

Annie could swear she felt her heart break inside. She had no choice now, the decision was made. There was no anger this time, just an acceptance of the pain that was facing them.

She had been putting off the inevitable for a while, but there was no turning back now.

"Then I need to leave. We'll stay until after the ball and hopefully by then my agency will have a new position for me."

Harry's jaw flexed as she tried to keep control. She nodded and without saying another word, walked out of the room.

When the door clicked shut, Annie lost control and began to sob into her pillow. She had offered the only woman she would ever love everything, and she didn't want it. The pain in her chest was unbearable. "I'll always love you, Harry."

Annie made the call from her bedroom so she'd not be overheard. "Yes, it needs to be as soon as possible. Do you have… Newcastle? No, that's not too far… Thanks, I can leave after the weekend. Monday's fine…Goodbye."

She ended the call and sighed. Riley was due home from school any minute and she was dreading this conversation.

Right on schedule, there was a knock on the door. "Come in," she called.

Riley bounded into the room. "Mum? What's going on? I can't find Harry."

Annie took her hand and pulled her over to the bed. "Sit down, sweetie. I have to talk to you."

"What is it?"

She took Riley's hand and sighed. This was not going to be easy. "I just spoke with the agency. I've got a new assignment. We're leaving Axedale."

The look of horror on Riley's face made her feel so guilty.

"We can't. We can't leave Harry. It's our home and we're supposed to teach her how to love, and I like my school, and Willow."

"It's not going to work out here. Harry and I...can't...we can't..."

Riley started to cry. "Please, Mum, we can't leave Harry. I love her. She's your knight in shining armour."

The sight of her daughter's tears was too much for Annie, and she felt her own well up and roll down her cheeks. "She's not, Riley. I wish she was."

Riley jumped up, and began to plead with her. "She is. She's Lady Hildegard and you're Katherine Aston. Please, Mum? We haven't finished our dig."

Annie's guilt started to bubble over into anger. She got up and pulled their suitcases out of the wardrobe. "This isn't a negotiation. I'm the adult and I'm telling you we're going to Newcastle after the ball."

"I'm not going," Riley shouted. "I'm staying here with Harry."

Riley ran out and slammed the door, and Annie collapsed to the bed crying.

❖

All Harry could think about was getting as far away from Axedale as possible. Somewhere where she could hide from these painful emotions inside of her. She found herself driving to London, and arrived outside Clara's exclusive Knightsbridge flat. She parked up and switched off the engine.

She had come here because it represented her old life, her life before Annie and Riley. Life was simple then. No worries, no commitments, no love inside her chest bursting to get out.

Harry took out her smartphone and opened up her pictures. The first showed Annie dressed for the county show. She was the most beautiful woman she had ever seen, and only a few hours ago, she had been making love with her. Making love, not having sex.

It had been the most intense experience of her life. They'd connected on a level that had truly petrified her, and then at her rawest Annie had demanded she convey what was in her heart.

She'd wanted more than anything in the world to say those three little words, but she physically couldn't do it.

Her mobile buzzed with a text. *I can see you skulking out there.* She looked up to Clara's flat and saw her waving to her. *Hurry up and get in here.*

Her head fell back against the headrest. "What am I going to do?"

She flicked on to the next picture. It showed Annie, Riley, and herself at the British Museum. Oscar had taken a picture of them posing with the Roman helmet. They looked like a family in the picture, a proper family. Harry traced her finger down Annie's face. Annie was right. It wasn't too much to ask for commitment. She and Riley deserved that, deserved someone to give their all, and be proud to call them their family.

She had two choices. She could walk through that door to Clara and stay safe or go back to Annie and Riley, give them everything and risk hurting all three of them.

She rubbed her face in her hands. "I love her. Love them. Why am I such a coward?"

Then she remembered what the vicar had said to her. If she got scared look up 1 Corinthians 13. The source of the inscription on Lady Hildegard's grave.

Harry quickly did an Internet search, and the answer was before her.

Love is patient, love is kind, love is not jealous, it does not boast, it does not become conceited, it does not behave dishonourably, it is not selfish, it does not become angry, it does not keep a record of wrongs, it does not rejoice at unrighteousness, but rejoices with the truth, bears all things, believes all things, hopes all things, endures all things.

As she read through the verses, the last knot of fear started to dissipate inside her, and the last line sealed it.

And now these three things remain: faith, hope, and love. But the greatest of these is love.

Everything fell into place. Faith, hope, and love were all that mattered in life. She had to have faith and hope in her love for Annie, or else her life stood for nothing. She looked at herself in the car mirror and realized that if she turned her back on Annie and Riley, history would be repeating itself, she would be like her father running off from his family in the country to womanize with his many mistresses. She has to choose to love family, and fear, or to choose safety and loneliness.

She turned on the ignition and quickly texted Clara: *I'm sorry. I won't be back. My family and life are now in Axedale. Have a good life.*

Harry's car screeched to a halt at the front of the house. She got out and hurried up to the front door. She found Riley sitting on the doorstep with her sword and shield, looking miserable, and as if she had been crying.

"What's wrong, Riley?"

"Harry, you're back." Riley threw herself into Harry's arms. "It's Mum. She says we have to leave after the ball. She's got a new job at another house. Says we can't stay here. I don't want to leave you. I love you, Harry."

Harry tried not to show Riley how panicked she was. Annie was leaving her, and she might not be able to stop her.

"Riley, I'm going to talk to your mum. This isn't your mum's fault, it's mine. It's taken me too long to realize I'm her knight, just like you said all along. I'm going to try and make things better, but I can't promise anything, okay? I love you, Riley. You be brave."

Riley wiped her tears and nodded. "I will. Make her understand, Harry."

"I'll try."

Harry ran into the house and checked everywhere she thought Annie might be. She finally found her in the newly restored greenhouse. She opened the door and saw Annie on her hands and knees, planting some of the new plants they had bought. Harry took a moment to gaze at the woman she loved, and imagined her in years to come, when the plants and trees had grown with the care and attention of her tender, loving hands. She'd never thought about growing old with someone before. She had imagined her retirement would consist of research and writing books and lots of her own company, but looking at Annie now she could see a different future. One in which she could sit in here with her books and laptop, and Annie could potter around with her plants. It was a nice thought, but one that might never be if she couldn't convince Annie of her commitment.

"Annie?" Harry walked over to her and said again, "Annie? Could I talk to you for a moment. Please?"

She heard Annie sigh but she got up and brushed the soil from her apron, and when she turned Harry could see her eyes were red and puffy from crying. She felt so guilty for causing Annie and Riley so much pain, all because she was frightened.

"What?" She reached out for Annie's hand but Annie pulled it away. "Don't, we can't do this any more."

She deserved that, Harry supposed. After all she had been toying with her emotions, and even trying to seduce her, when she had quite clearly known what Annie wanted from her.

"I'm sorry. I just want to talk and then I'll leave you in peace, I promise."

Harry knew what she had to say, but thinking it and articulating it were two different things. She let out a sigh and started with the easiest thing. "I'm sorry I ran out on you this morning, sorry for everything I never said. I'm not like you, Annie. I'm weak. After everything you've been through in life, you are still brave enough to open up your heart."

"It's not hard, you just have to want it."

"You're right, and I've been a coward all my life. I've always been so terrified I be anything like my father, and I didn't even notice I was behaving exactly like him."

Annie shook her head. "You aren't like him. Someone who cares and treats Riley like you do is not like your father."

"I'm sorry, but I was. I used women, and some of them used me too, but the worst thing I've ever done is to use you. I wanted to be with you and Riley, have the good parts of being a family, but always keep one foot out the door. It wasn't fair, it was selfish, and I know that now. I love you, Annie. I love you with all of my heart, and Riley too. If you give me a second chance I'll keep both feet in the door, in our home, and under your table."

Fresh tears ran down Annie's cheeks. Only in her dreams had Harry ever said anything like that, and it was a dream. She couldn't risk her heart and Riley's heart again.

"I appreciate you telling me the truth about what's inside your heart, but I realized this morning that I've been a bad mother. I've selfishly followed my own feelings and allowed Riley to get too attached to you. Now I have to break her heart by taking her away."

Harry took hold of her hand and wouldn't let go this time. "Then stay. Don't go, stay here with me and be a family."

Annie squeezed her hand. "I can't take a risk on someone who doesn't believe in long-term relationships. You might think you want to now, but in six months' time, when the reality of being a couple with a child sinks in, you might change your mind. I can't play with my daughter's feelings like that. No matter how much I love you."

Harry looked utterly crestfallen, and just gave a simple nod.

"We'll stay till after the ball at the weekend, so we can say goodbye to the villagers. Then we'll travel to my new post in Newcastle."

Harry reached into her pocket and took out a jewellery box. "Would you take this please? I bought it for you." She put it in Annie's hand and kissed her cheek before whispering in Annie's ear, "I love you. I'm sorry I wasn't everything you hoped I could be."

When Harry walked off, Annie opened the box to find a gold heart-shaped pendent, with a solitaire diamond on the front. On the back it was inscribed with the words, *I believe in forever...*

Annie clasped her hand to her mouth and sobbed.

Harry retreated to her bedroom and sat on her bed. She had never felt so impotent in her life. She could have had everything and she'd destroyed it, and now she would have to watch the two people she loved walk away from her.

She lifted the pillow that Annie had slept on, hugged it tightly, and inhaled Annie's scent. "How am I ever going to live without you?"

When she pictured coming back to Axedale without Annie and Riley here, she felt such deep, deep pain that tears fell from her eyes.

Her own pain was interrupted by the sound of Riley shouting at her mum, and the slamming of doors.

"I've done this." Annie and Riley had such a strong relationship, and because of her own fear and insecurities that was at risk. "I'm going to fix one thing in this mess."

She stopped to pick up her toolbox and made her way to the secret garden. Harry stood at the bottom of the tree and said firmly, "Get down here now, Riley."

Riley peeked out from the side of the tree house. Harry pointed to her and then at the ground below. "Down now."

When Riley was beside her looking sad and upset, it was hard to be firm, but she had to be. "I want you to stop being hard on your mum."

"She's taking us away from you," Riley said angrily.

Harry dropped her tools, and went down on one knee to look Riley in the eye. "Yes, because of me."

"No—"

"Yes, me, Riley. Your mum offered me everything, her love, a family, a home, and I ran away. I broke her heart. I'm not this hero you think I am. I broke your mother's heart."

Riley looked at her silently, trying to process the information.

"When I realized what I'd lost, I came back, but it was all too late. So if you want to be angry, be angry at me."

Riley threw herself into her arms and started to cry. "I don't want to be angry at Mum or you. I love you both, and I want you to love each other."

Harry rubbed her back soothingly. "I know, centurion, but I messed this up, so the best we can do is to enjoy our time together. I want you to go back inside and apologize to your mum. Then we can spend some time together at the dig site."

Riley nodded and ran off towards the house, and Harry thought, *I'm going to regret this to my last breath.*

CHAPTER TWENTY-TWO

Annie looked out of the ballroom window and silently watched Harry and Riley together at the dig. Behind her volunteers from the village were setting up tables and chairs for the ball. As she watched them, her heart told her to accept Harry's apology, but her head told her something very different. Harry had hurt her too much. She'd given her everything, her body, heart, and soul, and Harry had run away.

Her head told her that Harry might be sorry now, but when she went back to her own insular university world, family life would seem less appealing.

"Annie?" Bev called from the door.

She quickly wiped her eyes and put on her best smile. "Yes, sorry."

"The catering crew have arrived. You wanted me to let you know so you could get them started with food prep."

"Yes, thanks. I'll come now. Have you finished with the Dowager Countess's room?"

"All done. I'm sure she won't be disappointed."

Annie smiled. "I'm sure. Could you supervise the ballroom and I'll take Julie to the kitchen to help with the food?"

"Will do."

She couldn't afford to grieve for what could have been. Now she had a party for the good people of the village to organize. One last thank you for the happiest time of her life.

❖

"Will you keep digging this, Harry? After we've gone."

Harry looked down at the mosaic of Venus that reminded her so much of Annie, and ran her fingers across her face. "I might get a team in to finish it. It wouldn't feel right without you, but I'll keep you updated."

"Could I email you, maybe? Just to talk about stuff."

That would only heap more pain onto Harry as she was given a running commentary on Annie's new life, but of course Riley's feelings were what mattered. She reached out and stroked Riley's head. "If your mum lets you, of course you can."

"Will you look after Willow for me? She'll be scared when I just go away."

"Willow will be fine. I'll make sure of it."

"I'm going to be just like you when I grow up," Riley said.

Harry gave a hollow laugh. "You don't want to be like me, I don't want you to be like me."

Riley was undeterred. "I am. I'm going to go to Cambridge and be an archaeologist like you."

Harry wasn't going to argue. "I have every faith you can do that, Riley. You are a very intelligent girl. Study hard and make sure you know your subject inside out."

"I will. I promise."

She wondered if Annie would allow her to pay for Riley's education at a private school. Despite best efforts, universities like Cambridge and Oxford still had more students accepted from private schools than standard public schools.

Maybe this money of mine can be useful to someone.

"Harry? Who's that in the big car?"

She looked up and caught the unmistakable sight of her mother's vintage Rolls Royce driving up to the main entrance.

"That, Riley, is the Dowager Countess of Axedale, my mother, Lady Dorothy Knight. Come on, I'll introduce you."

❖

The Dowager Countess and her lady's maid were met at the door by Annie, and the rest of the staff lined up behind her.

She was different to Harry in many ways. Where Harry was solid and tall, she was petite and slight, but her eyes Annie would recognize anywhere. They were Harry's.

Annie approached and gave her a curtsy. "Welcome back to Axedale, Lady Dorothy. I'm Annie Brannigan, the housekeeper."

Lady Dorothy was everything you expected a countess to be, elegant and perfectly turned out, but above all, a beautiful woman. She extended her hand to Annie and smiled. "Thank you, Annie. It's wonderful to meet you. I've heard you've done some wonderful things to the house."

"I've just tried to make it as comfortable as possible for Lady Axedale."

Lady Dorothy laughed. "Harry would be comfortable in a muddy field."

"Thank you, Mother."

Annie watched as Harry kissed her on each cheek stiffly. It saddened her that a mother and child could be so awkward with each other.

"You're looking well, Harry. I think you've been eating more."

Harry looked over to her and then looked down sadly. "Yes, Annie has been feeding me well."

Lady Dorothy looked around Harry to where Riley was hiding. "And who is this little one hiding back there?"

Annie took a step forward but when she saw Harry put an arm around Riley's shoulders, she relaxed.

"This is Riley, Annie's daughter."

"Riley? What an unusual name." Lady Dorothy smiled. "You look like a little Harry with muddy jeans and shoes."

That comment seemed to break the ice with Riley. She walked in front of Harry and said happily, "I want to be just like Harry."

Annie saw something in Lady Dorothy then. A flicker of emotion and maybe regret that she didn't have that sort of relationship with her child.

"Wonderful. Well I shall look forward to getting to know you, Little Harry."

Riley beamed with happiness at that nickname and Annie felt such deep guilt that she was taking Riley away from this.

"Now tell me, Annie. Is there a drawing room refurbished enough to take tea in?"

"Oh yes, Lady Dorothy. The majority of the rooms are finished now. Harry's done a wonderful job."

She looked over to Harry and had to gulp back her emotions. "Let me show you to your room."

❖

The one thing worse than being apart from Annie was being in her company and pretending everything was fine, when all she could think about was losing her in just a few days' time. At the first opportunity, she excused herself from tea in the drawing room, and left Annie to fuss around her mother.

She began to type out an email to her lawyer asking them to make preliminary steps to set up a trust fund for Riley, when there was a knock at the door. "Come in."

Lady Dorothy popped her head around the door. "I wanted to have a talk with you, Harry."

Harry stood politely and asked her mother to sit.

"I've heard whispers that Harry Knight, the confirmed bachelor, might be finally ready to settle down."

Harry frowned. "Who told you that?"

"Bridget. I telephone occasionally to see how you are, since you never tell me anything."

Harry looked straight at her and said with a little resentment, "We don't have that sort of relationship, Mother."

Lady Dorothy looked down sadly. "No, we don't."

There were a few seconds of silence and a lifetime of hurt that hung between them. "I didn't believe it at first, I mean you've gone through women like—"

"My father?"

"No, not your father. You didn't have a wife waiting at home for you." Lady Dorothy sat back in her chair and crossed her legs.

Harry thought about what Martha had said, how the young, happy, carefree Dorothy came to Axedale and had her spirit crushed.

"As I say, I didn't believe it at first, but then I spoke to Annie on the telephone and knew she was special to you."

"How could you know that? She was just inviting you to the ball as my housekeeper."

"I'll tell you why I knew. One, because you were actually having a celebration ball with the people of the village—that was not your idea—and most importantly, you wouldn't instruct your housekeeper to invite *me*. As you said before, we don't have that sort of relationship. That's why I knew what Bridget had said was true."

There was nothing Harry could say to that. It was all true. Harry's anger was building and building, her mother just another reminder of her emotional inadequacies.

"She is the most wonderful woman in the world, and she gave me love, turned this emotionless place into a home, and I ran away from it. I ran away and broke her heart, and she and Riley are leaving on Monday."

"But surely—"

Now Harry had started, and she wasn't stopping. "Mother, you and Father raised someone who is emotionally incapable of having a normal, healthy relationship, and because of that I'm going to lose the only woman I've ever loved, not to mention my only chance of a family."

In a move that totally surprised Harry, Lady Dorothy reached over the desk and covered her hand with her own. "I know we did, Harry, and for that I'm sorry. Your father was an odious man, but the best thing that he ever gave me was you, Harry. I would go through everything again if it meant having you as a daughter. I am so very proud of you."

Harry didn't know what to say. Lady Dorothy had never spoken to her in such an open and honest way before.

"I didn't know you felt that way, Mother."

"Charles taught me to keep all my feelings tucked up inside, for fear of his ridicule by our friends and family."

"I know you saved Axedale for me," Harry said.

Lady Dorothy looked surprised. "Ah, you found out about that. I've never been able to show you much emotional care, Harry, but I would never have allowed him to take your birthright from you. Money was all he ever wanted, and he got it."

"Thank you, Mother," Harry said sincerely.

"Since your father died, I've done a lot of thinking and felt the tethers around my heart loosen."

"And what conclusion have you come to?"

"That despite your father's behaviour, I should have put your feelings first and done things differently, but since I can't go backwards in time and do it all over again, I can only plead with you to learn from my mistakes. I was wrong to tell you to never open up your heart to love. Just because Charles and I couldn't have a happy life, doesn't mean you can't."

Harry got up and walked over to the picture of her father on the wall. She gazed up at him with a mixture of anger and sadness. "I think it's too late for your advice."

Lady Dorothy stood and walked up behind her. "When I spoke to your young lady on the telephone, she sounded a warm, kind woman, and when I met her this morning I was not disappointed, and her daughter is simply adorable. Reminded me of you when you were a child."

"Annie is the kindest and most loving woman I've ever met, and Riley is a wonderful girl. I could have had it all, and I ran away. She doesn't trust me now, and I've lost them both."

"Then go and fight for her, darling. Break the cycle of misery at Axedale. Go to her and lay your heart bare."

Harry turned around and watched as her mother took off her engagement ring, and placed it in her hand. "Your grandfather Henry gave this to your grandmother, and then your father gave it to me. Take it and give Annie the commitment she needs. Make your own family, and don't take no for an answer."

"I don't know if I can change her mind, Mother."

"At least you'll know you've tried." Dorothy inclined her head to the portrait of her father on the wall. "I think we both have to leave him behind us." Then she patted the portrait of Lady Hildegard and Katherine Astor propped against the wall, waiting to be hung.

"Lady Hildegard was always your hero, and a much better role model, don't you think?"

❖

Annie jumped when Harry came into the bedroom. "I'm sorry. I was just dropping off your fancy dress costume."

"That's all right. I was looking for you anyway. Where's Riley?"

"Your mother asked if she could take her riding. Riley seemed excited to do that, so…"

Harry smiled. It meant a lot to her that her mother wanted to spend time with a little girl who she hoped would be her granddaughter. "My mother is the best person to take her riding. She is an excellent horsewoman."

Annie quickly picked up her own costume from the bed and hurried to the door. "I'll see you later then, Harry. I'll serve dinner in the dining room for you and Lady Dorothy." Harry didn't move from in front of the door. "Could I get by? I have a lot to do."

"I wanted to talk to you, if that's all right?"

Annie sighed and shook her head. "Not if you want to talk about what I think you do again. I can't, I just can't, Harry."

Harry held her hand up to stop her from leaving. She had to think of something to get her to at least talk before going over old ground again. "Not exactly, no, I wanted to ask you about an idea I had…for Riley."

"For Riley?"

"Yes, could I just talk to you for a few minutes?"

Annie nodded and walked back into the room, but wouldn't sit on the bed.

"I know you worry about Riley, and you want her to have a better start in life than you did. I wondered if you would allow me to pay for her to go to a private school."

Annie appeared surprised. "I—"

"Please, think about it. I don't have any other uses for my wealth apart from this house, and I would love to encourage Riley to be the best she can be."

"How could that work? We'd still be connected." Annie hugged herself tightly. "I can't even think about still keeping in contact with you, knowing you are sleeping with other people. It would kill me."

Harry was both confused and frustrated. Annie wouldn't stay but clearly loved her enough to be horrified at the thought of her being with someone else.

"And how do you think I'll feel? Riley wants to email me. I'll get a running commentary on your life and eventually you'll meet someone else," Harry said angrily.

"It's not the same as it will be for me. Sex is just another drive for you. It's not important."

"Not any more. Not since I fell in love with you. Sex is something special, something that I want to share only with you. You've changed me."

"Stop, you're making it so hard to leave you."

"Then don't. Stay with me and be a family."

Harry dropped down on one knee in front of Annie.

"Harry, what are you doing?"

She held up the diamond ring. "I want to give you the commitment you demand. Marry me, Annie."

"No."

"No? This is what you want. I love you and you love me."

"But it's not what you want," Annie said, her voice dripping with pain.

Harry stood up in dismay. "Of course it's what I want. I wouldn't have asked otherwise."

Annie held her head in her hands. "Harry, please don't do this. You are making everything so hard."

Harry took hold of her hands and led her to sit down on her bed, and she knelt in front. She had to make Annie understand. She was not going to lose this wonderful woman. She reached up and wiped away the few tears that had fallen from Annie's eyes. "Listen to me. When I gave you the locket, I thought it might make you understand. I believe in forever, Annie. You and Riley have made me believe."

"Harry, I couldn't bear it if you changed your mind in six months or a year, when you're sick of family life and want to go back to Clara or the other women like her. You told me what your father did to your mother. I can't—"

"I will never, ever do that to you. There will be no other women in my life. There has been no other woman since you arrived here."

"There hasn't? I thought maybe—?"

Harry took Annie's hands and kissed them tenderly. "I didn't want to since you came. I was happy, I felt taken care of. Do you know I kept every one of the flowers you gave me?"

Annie nodded. "I wasn't prying, but I found them when I was tidying."

"I tried to work out why you kept giving them to me when you knew I wasn't a flower kind of person, but then I realized only recently, just like when you gave me cakes, comfort food, or hot choco surprise, you have been courting me the whole time, haven't you?"

"Yes. In the beginning I just wanted to care for you properly, but then I began to fall in love with you, and I wanted to take care of you forever."

"That's what made me fall in love with you, Annie. No one has given so freely to me without wanting something from me."

"But Harry, you've never wanted the sort of life I want."

"I never knew it was possible. You have changed my life and all my goals." Harry took the ring back out of her pocket and gazed at it. "You've even brought my mother back into my life. We talked downstairs and cleared up a lot of old hurts. This ring has been passed down through the family. She gave me this off her finger and told me to go to you and not take no for an answer, but I know it will take a lot for you to trust me."

Annie caressed her cheek with the back of her hand. "It's not that I don't trust you, I just don't want you to commit to something that you don't want."

"Look into my eyes. I haven't courted you the way I should have, and I know I've jumped the gun by proposing to you, but whether you can accept my proposal in a few days, six months, or a year, I will court you every day until we exchange marriage vows, and to show you I'm serious about this, I've made some decisions about my life. Firstly, I'm leaving my post at Cambridge, and I'm going to become a freelance archaeologist."

"You can't do that. Your job…it's your life."

"It's not conducive to family life, but this"—Harry looked up and held her hands out—"this is. Being lord of the manor and making sure the village thrives is conducive to having a family, because every lord was meant to have her lady to help. I'm not going to be an absent landlord any more, and I want you and Riley to help me, as my family. That way I can take consultancy jobs on dig sites that interest me, and we'll go together."

Annie held her gaze, but kept her silence. It was clear she was confused and unsure.

"Annie, you asked me to believe in forever. I do, and now you have to believe in me." Harry held the ring up to her again and asked, "Do you believe in me?"

"I believe in you and yes, I'll marry you." Annie held up her hand and Harry slid the ring onto her finger.

Harry kissed her and whispered, "I will never let you down."

The next day the house was bustling and noisy as it prepared for the ball. Harry was hiding in her study, but found the crashing, banging, and voices strangely comforting. Axedale was alive again, after so long in a deep slumber. She hadn't seen Annie for a few hours, as she was so busy, and was beginning to miss her terribly, so she went in search of her.

When she looked in the ballroom she saw Bridge and Quade, who had come to help, and Riley running around already dressed in her Roman soldier's costume, but not Annie.

When Harry saw what Bridge was wearing she laughed. A tight black PVC bodysuit and tail, a cat mask, and some of the highest heels she had ever seen. "Bridge? A Catwoman costume? I think you're forgetting you're a vicar again."

"That's exactly what I said," Quade piped in.

Bridget turned to her and put her hands on her hips. "Well at least I made the effort, Quade."

Quade looked down at her dark jeans, boots, and white sleeveless T-shirt. "I have made the effort." She pointed to her stick-on sideburns. "I'm Wolverine."

"Oh, how very rugged," Bridget said.

Harry laughed. "You're in luck, Quade. Bridge tells me women love a rugged butch."

"Well if you see any, point them my way."

Just then Riley came running over. "Harry, you're not dressed yet. I want to fight you."

"I'm going now. I was looking for your mum first."

"She's over there." Riley pointed to the other end of the room where Annie was talking to one of the serving staff.

When Harry saw her she felt a heavy thud in her chest which ran like an electrical current down to her sex. She was already in her costume as Venus, goddess of love, and Harry smiled as she thought about how deeply Cupid's arrow was buried in her chest.

Without taking her eyes off Annie, Harry said, "Bridge, I'm going to go put on my costume, could you ask Annie to meet me upstairs in twenty minutes? I need to talk to her."

Bridget sniggered. "I will, but try not to keep the goddess of love occupied for too long."

"What do you have to talk about, Harry? Can I come?" Riley asked.

Thankfully Quade stepped in and said, "You don't want to talk, come and fight with Wolverine, soldier."

Harry leaned over and whispered to Bridge, "Tell Quade I'm forever in her debt."

"I will, now I shall go and seek out your Venus."

❖

Annie skipped up the large staircase. Love and anticipation made her heart flutter and her footsteps light. She paused before she turned the handle on what was now their bedroom door, held the crucifix around her neck, and she prayed.

She prayed in thankfulness to God for guiding her to Harry, the one she knew in her heart she had been waiting on. For giving her not only a home of bricks and mortar, but one of warmth, love, and community for Riley and herself.

When she walked in she found Harry waiting for her, dressed in her Roman officer's costume, and holding her helmet under her arm.

Harry looked absolutely gorgeous, and showed her athletic, strong body to its best advantage. Annie especially liked the way Harry's tattoo looked, peeking out from underneath the armour.

Harry put her helmet down on the bedside table, and walked towards her with a look that told her she wanted to do more than talk. When she took a step back against the door, Harry grinned. "Going by what I saw downstairs, I now have lost control of my own home. I am no longer its master and you are its mistress, goddess of love."

Annie's excitement was growing but she was determined to give as good as she got. "It seems so, but then I am mistress of your heart and soul, so it makes sense."

Harry trailed her fingertip along her jawline. "It does and you do. Since the goddess of love embodies love, sexual enticement, seduction, and persuasive female charm, then I never stood a chance." Harry placed feather-like kisses on her cheek and whispered, "Venus, this humble soldier is your willing slave, and I'm here to pay homage to you."

Oh God. Annie was sure she was going to melt into a puddle on the floor. "Oh? My slave?" Annie's voice came out like a squeak. Despite Harry's romantic words, she did not feel like the one in control.

Harry boxed Annie in with her arms and peppered more gentle kisses on her cheeks, nose, and lips. "Yes, your slave. This soldier once travelled through life alone, until I came under your spell of love, and now I exist only to give you pleasure, Venus."

Annie slipped her arms around Harry's neck. Each word that she whispered felt like a tender kiss on her skin. When she tried to pull Harry to her, she resisted, and smiled.

"Kiss me, Harry," Annie pleaded.

Harry did kiss her, a beautifully loving but frustrating kiss that barely touched her lips.

The point of Harry's tongue licked along the surface of Annie's lips, before she continued to tease Annie's throat with small bites and kisses.

Harry could hear as well as feel how turned-on Annie was, and encouraged by that, ran her hand up Annie's thigh. The Venus costume was split from just below the hip to the knee, giving her excellent access.

She let her hand stray to the inside of her thigh, and felt Annie open up her legs, making it clear where she wanted Harry to go.

Harry leaned her forehead against Annie's and closed her eyes. She wanted to hear and feel Annie's pleasure with her full concentration. "I love you, body, mind, and soul." Harry groaned.

Annie grasped her wrist and moved it onto her sex. Harry pushed inside her underwear, and moaned as she felt the wetness that awaited her. It was becoming much harder to control the pace, but she wanted to go slowly and show Annie that she was worshipped.

How sex had changed for her. It was no longer a simple act with one goal, and run for the door. It was to be enjoyed, hungered for, yearned for, and loved for every second they touched.

She felt Annie grip her neck and heard her breath coming heavily in her ear, as she parted two fingers and rubbed around the outside of Annie's clitoris.

Annie's hips started to move in rhythm as her excitement grew. "Oh God. Inside, just a little?"

Harry did as requested and she was rewarded by a long groan as Annie hooked her leg around hers. It was then that her eyes sparkled with recognition. "Have you got it on?"

As they'd made love last night, they had talked about things they liked or wanted to try, and she had told Annie that she enjoyed using a strap-on, but never had she used one with love. Annie had been excited to try it, and Harry thought it would give her seduction an added frisson.

"Yes, but we don't have to—"

"I want to feel you inside me. Take me to bed, soldier. I think you need to worship me completely and fully."

Harry smiled. "Anything you say, Venus."

She turned the lock on the door, and carried Annie over to their bed. She watched as Annie slipped off her costume and was left dressed only in the heart locket, her engagement ring, and a smile. "Worship me, soldier."

Harry took off her sword, scabbard, and boots. She lay down beside Annie and tenderly stroked her hair. "A lifetime will never be enough, Annie, but I will spend forever trying to be worthy of you."

They fell into a long, deep kiss, which grew more frantic. Annie shrugged off Harry's underwear, and when Harry tried to pull off her uniform, Annie said with a wicked grin, "No, leave it on, soldier."

A thrill ran through her body, unlike any she had felt before. This is what Annie meant when she had talked about making love and connecting with someone. It was so much more than sex. "God, I love you," Harry said.

Annie pulled her down into a kiss, and she parted her legs. "I want you to come while you're deep inside me."

Harry wanted to make Annie's first experience of sex this way positive and she determined to take things slowly and carefully. She rolled over until Annie straddled her hips.

Annie's eyes sparkled as she looked down at her. "Harry Knight giving up some of her control?"

In the past Harry would have seen that comment as a challenge, and met it swiftly and firmly, but not with Annie. Everything was different with Annie. She laughed softly before she reached up to cup Annie's full breasts in her hands and squeezed. "Why not? I think I get a pretty good part of the deal, don't you?"

She brushed Annie's nipples with her thumbs causing her to moan and grind her hips against the strap-on between her legs.

"I need you inside me," Annie said desperately.

Harry took hold of her strap-on and Annie raised her hips. "Take it slowly, okay?"

Annie nodded and allowed Harry to ease the cock inside just a little. Annie let out a long breath.

"Are you okay?"

"Uh-huh. It feels big."

Harry grasped her hips, connecting to and supporting Annie. "Just relax into it, darling. You're in control of it." Annie's hips started to move slowly, and after a short time, she opened up and let Harry slip fully inside her. They both groaned, and Harry began to thrust along with her.

"Kiss me." Annie leaned over allowing Harry to kiss her.

Harry hastened her thrusts, as the heat and pressure in her groin were building fast. "You feel so good."

They moved together quite naturally from then until Annie pleaded, "I'm so close. I need more."

Harry herself was too near to losing control, and had to slow and take a breath. "You...want more? Deeper?"

"Yes, yes, I need that."

Harry sat up straight, so Annie was virtually sitting in her lap, and wrapped her arms around her tightly in a lover's embrace. Annie held around her neck and appeared to love this new position as her moans became low and guttural, as she ground her hips into Harry.

Those very sounds set Harry's orgasm off without much warning. "Fuck, I'm coming." Harry kissed Annie hard as the wave of orgasm hit her low and washed down to her toes. What had once been so hard for her to say tripped off her tongue with ease. "I love you, Annie. Love you," Harry gasped.

She kept thrusting, until Annie grabbed her hair and called out, "Jesus!"

As their breathing slowed, she became aware of Annie's legs shaking. "Are you okay? Look at me."

"I'm fine, I'm fine. It was just so, so overwhelming. Just hug me."

Harry lay back and they held each other until the intensity passed. She started to feel Annie laughing. "What are you laughing at, darling?"

"Just remembering that I called out Jesus. That's never happened before. My grandma would give me a slap on the behind for that."

Harry raised an eyebrow. "I could do that for you if you like."

Annie burst out laughing and smacked Harry on the arm. "We need to get ready all over again. I've got a ball to go to."

"Shall I be your Prince Charming?"

"I don't think Prince Charming is meant to sleep with the lowly servant before the ball, but all right."

Harry lifted Annie's hand and kissed her engagement ring. "You're not a lowly servant. You are mistress of Axedale."

"Riley says we're Lady Hildegard and Katie Aston."

Harry nodded and smiled. "I'm sure their spirits will be happy two people like them now call Axedale home."

❖

Harry and Riley stood at the top of the marble stairs, just out of sight of their guests downstairs. "What's taking Mum so long, Harry?"

After a super-quick shower, Harry intercepted Riley at the door, and gave Annie time to reapply her make-up before they went down to greet their guests. She supposed this was something she would have to get used to, being part of a family, but funnily she didn't care. Instead there was an overwhelming feeling of extra happiness that downstairs there was a little girl who loved her and couldn't wait to see her.

"Your mum was helping me with my costume and she wasn't happy with her make-up and…well, you know how she is."

Riley looked at her, clearly knowing she was missing something but not sure what. She looked adorable in her Roman soldier's helmet that was just a little too big. Harry adjusted it so it wasn't covering her eyes.

"So? Are you happy that your mum and I are getting married?"

"Uh-huh. It's the best thing ever." Riley threw herself into Harry for a hug.

Harry closed her eyes and held Riley tight, savouring the joy she felt in her heart. "I'm really glad you're happy, centurion. You and your mum have changed my life."

"We won't have to ever leave here again, will we?"

Harry knelt down so she could look Riley in the eye. "This will be your forever home, and I do mean forever. There will be times we go away from here, if I need to work, or we go on holiday, but we will always go together."

Riley's face lit up. "A holiday? I've never been on a holiday."

Harry's heart ached for what Annie and Riley never had but was immediately excited by the experiences they could share together. "Well that's going to change. We'll go to Italy, Greece, Egypt, and I'll teach you everything I know."

"I can't wait to learn everything you know, Harry. Then we'll come back home?"

"Always. Axedale is your home."

"It'll be so great. Lady D says she'll come and visit all the time and teach me how to ride properly."

"Lady D?" Harry never heard of her mother being called something as informal as that, and she doubted Riley would have come up with that herself.

"Yeah, she said to call her that, but she would love to be my granny when you got married. I've never had a granny before."

Harry was lost for words. Her mother certainly had been doing a lot of thinking, and maybe a great deal of soul-searching. This new family would be a second chance for them all.

"My mother has never been a granny before, so you'll both have to teach each other as you go along."

"I can do that," Riley said quite seriously. "Mum said we had to teach you how to be friends and care about kids, and that worked."

She couldn't help but laugh. "You certainly did."

Harry immediately turned and smiled when she heard the bedroom door open. Riley ran for her mum. "Mum, I'm going to have a granny."

"That's wonderful, sweetie."

Annie leaned in to Harry for a kiss and whispered, "I feel quite naughty."

"That's because you are."

Lady Dorothy came out of her room wearing an elegant evening gown and tiara.

"Mother? Have you come to the fancy dress ball as a countess?"

Quick as a flash she replied, "No, I was aiming for duchess. I had no time to come up with a costume, so I'll need to do as I am."

"You look beautiful, Lady Dorothy," Annie said and elbowed Harry in the ribs to give her a hint.

"Yes, you always look beautiful, Mother."

"Thank you, and call me Dorothy, Annie. We are going to be family."

"Thank you, Dorothy."

Lady Dorothy stood looking a little awkward and then said, "Well, I'll go downstairs and join the guests, and let you go down with your family."

Harry nodded but then received another dig in the ribs from Annie. "What?"

Annie used her eyes to convey that she should ask her mother to join them. She suspected she would get many digs in the ribs from Annie over the years to come, as she was carefully guided through the minefield of family life.

"Mother, come down with us." She held out her arm for her mother to take. "Let's start again and make a family on our terms, not his."

She felt Annie give her arm a squeeze of approval. Her mother took her arm with tears in her eyes and said, "I'd like that, Harry."

Riley made Lady Dorothy feel even more included when she took her hand and said, "Let's go, Granny. Mum and Harry are going to dance like a Jane Austen book."

Harry looked at Annie and shook her head in disbelief. "I think you put some potion in that hot choco surprise. You've turned me into a family woman, brought my mother back to me, and are giving me a whole village of people, and I'm just nodding my head and going along with it."

Annie smiled. "I might have done, but does it really matter? As long as the outcome makes you happy."

"Oh, I'm more than happy. I never knew what happiness was until you and Riley came and turned my world upside down."

Annie gave her a kiss. "Take me to the ball then, Sir Knight."

❖

The new family stood at the bottom three steps of the marble staircase, while the guests were assembled in the marble hall. Harry waited until everyone had a glass of champagne.

"Ladies and gentlemen, first, I would like to welcome you all to the first Axedale ball in fifty years. We wanted to celebrate the refurbishment of the house with the people who have always been part of this estate's life."

Harry looked around the faces she knew and was getting to know. Bridget stood at the front with Mrs. Castle, who beamed with pride. Quade, Stevens, the rest of the staff, and all the people of the village had warm smiles on their faces.

"The estate hasn't been serving the village well since my grandfather's days. It has taken me a while, I know, but with the help of Annie, and all of you, I have come to understand my duties and role here. Axedale will no longer have an absentee landlord. The estate will be the place of employment it was always meant to be, but I can only make Axedale great again with mutual cooperation, and I ask you all for help and patience while we make this estate a going concern. We will bring in tourists, commerce, wealth, and hope to the community again."

Everyone cheered and burst into spontaneous applause.

"The other cause for celebration is that Annie has consented to become my wife."

"About bloody time," Bridget shouted and everyone laughed.

Harry looked to Annie and smiled. "As the vicar says, it's about time there was a family back in residence at Axedale. My family has been here for over five hundred years."

Harry looked to Riley, and said, "And my wish is that it will be here for generations to come, and that one day my heir, Riley, will walk these very same grounds with her children and teach them about the estate's history and the duty they have to it."

She held up her glass and proposed a toast. "I would ask you all to raise your glasses in toast to Axedale and its future."

"To Axedale," the whole room replied.

Harry turned to Annie and raised her glass. "To our forever."

Annie whispered, "To forever," and kissed her deeply.

About the Author

Jenny Frame is from the small town of Motherwell in Scotland, where she lives with her partner, Lou, and their well loved and very spoiled dog.

She has a diverse range of qualifications, including a BA in public management and a diploma in acting and performance. Nowadays, she likes to put her creative energies into writing rather than treading the boards.

When not writing or reading, Jenny loves cheering on her local football team, which is not always an easy task!

Jenny can be contacted at jennyframe91@yahoo.com

Website: www.jennyframe.com

Books Available from Bold Strokes Books

Basic Training of the Heart by Jaycie Morrison. In 1944, socialite Elizabeth Carlton joins the Women's Army Corps to escape family expectations and love's disappointments. Can Sergeant Gale Rains get her through Basic Training with their hearts intact? (978-1-62639-818-4)

Before by KE Payne. When Tally falls in love with her band's new recruit, she has a tough decision to make. What does she want more—Alex or the band? (978-1-62639-677-7)

Believing in Blue by Maggie Morton. Growing up gay in a small town has been hard, but it can't compare to the next challenge Wren—with her new, sky-blue wings—faces: saving two entire worlds. (978-1-62639-691-3)

Coils by Barbara Ann Wright. A modern young woman follows her aunt into the Greek Underworld and makes a pact with Medusa to win her freedom by killing a hero of legend. (978-1-62639-598-5)

Courting the Countess by Jenny Frame. When relationship-phobic Lady Henrietta Knight starts to care about housekeeper Annie Brannigan and her daughter, can she overcome her fears and promise Annie the forever that she demands? (978-1-62639-785-9)

Dapper by Jenny Frame. Amelia Honey meets the mysterious Byron De Brek and is faced with her darkest fantasies, but will her strict moral upbringing stop her from exploring what she truly wants? (978-1-62639-898-6E)

Delayed Gratification: The Honeymoon by Meghan O'Brien. A dream European honeymoon turns into a winter storm nightmare involving a delayed flight, a ditched rental car, and eventually, a surprisingly happy ending. (978-1-62639-766-8E)

For Money or Love by Heather Blackmore. Jessica Spaulding must choose between ignoring the truth to keep everything she has, and doing the right thing only to lose it all—including the woman she loves. (978-1-62639-756-9)

Hooked by Jaime Maddox. With the help of sexy Detective Mac Calabrese, Dr. Jessica Benson is working hard to overcome her past, but they may not be enough to stop a murderer. (978-1-62639-689-0)

Lands End by Jackie D. Public relations superstar Amy Kline is dealing with a media nightmare, and the last thing she expects is for restaurateur Lena Michaels to change everything, but she will. (978-1-62639-739-2)

Lysistrata Cove by Dena Hankins. Jack and Eve navigate the maelstrom of their darkest desires and find love by transgressing gender, dominance, submission, and the law on the crystal blue Caribbean Sea. (978-1-62639-821-4)

Twisted Screams by Sheri Lewis Wohl. Reluctant psychic Lorna Dutton doesn't want to forgive, but if she doesn't do just that an innocent woman will die. (978-1-62639-647-0)

A Class Act by Tammy Hayes. Buttoned-up college professor Dr. Margaret Parks doesn't know what she's getting herself into when she agrees to one date with her student, Rory Morgan, who is 15 years her junior. (978-1-62639-701-9)

Bitter Root by Laydin Michaels. Small town chef Adi Bergeron is hiding something, and Griffith McNaulty is going to find out what it is even if it gets her killed. (978-1-62639-656-2)

Capturing Forever by Erin Dutton. When family pulls Jacqueline and Casey back together, will the lessons learned in eight years apart be enough to mend the mistakes of the past? (978-1-62639-631-9)

Deception by VK Powell. DEA Agent Colby Vincent and Attorney Adena Weber are embroiled in a drug investigation involving homeless veterans and an attraction that could destroy them both. (978-1-62639-596-1)

Dyre: A Knight of Spirit and Shadows by Rachel E. Bailey. With the abduction of her queen, werewolf-bodyguard Des must follow the kidnappers' trail to Europe, where her queen—and a battle unlike any Des has ever waged—awaits her. (978-1-62639-664-7)

First Position by Melissa Brayden. Love and rivalry take center stage for Anastasia Mikhelson and Natalie Frederico in one of the most prestigious ballet companies in the nation. (978-1-62639-602-9)

Best Laid Plans by Jan Gayle. Nicky and Lauren are meant for each other, but Nicky's haunting past and Lauren's societal fears threaten to derail all possibilities of a relationship. (987-1-62639-658-6)

Exchange by CF Frizzell. When Shay Maguire rode into rural Montana, she never expected to meet the woman of her dreams—or to learn Mel Baker was held hostage by legal agreement to her right-wing father. (987-1-62639-679-1)

Just Enough Light by AJ Quinn. Will a serial killer's return to Colorado destroy Kellen Ryan and Dana Kingston's chance at love, or can the search-and-rescue team save themselves? (987-1-62639-685-2)

Rise of the Rain Queen by Fiona Zedde. Nyandoro is nobody's princess. She fights, curses, fornicates, and gets into as much trouble as her brothers. But the path to a throne is not always the one we expect. (987-1-62639-592-3)

Tales from Sea Glass Inn by Karis Walsh. Over the course of a year at Cannon Beach, tourists and locals alike find solace and passion at the Sea Glass Inn. (987-1-62639-643-2)

The Color of Love by Radclyffe. Black sheep Derian Winfield needs to convince literary agent Emily May to marry her to save the Winfield Agency and solve Emily's green card problem, but Derian didn't count on falling in love. (987-1-62639-716-3)

A Reluctant Enterprise by Gun Brooke. When two women grow up learning nothing but distrust, unworthiness, and abandonment, it's no wonder they are apprehensive and fearful when an overwhelming love just won't be denied. (978-1-62639-500-8)

Above the Law by Carsen Taite. Love is the last thing on Agent Dale Nelson's mind, but reporter Lindsey Ryan's investigation could change the way she sees everything—her career, her past, and her future. (978-1-62639-558-9)

Actual Stop by Kara A. McLeod. When Special Agent Ryan O'Connor's present collides abruptly with her past, shots are fired, and the course of her life is irrevocably altered. (978-1-62639-675-3)

Embracing the Dawn by Jeannie Levig. When ex-con Jinx Tanner and business executive E. J. Bastien awaken after a one-night stand to find their lives inextricably entangled, love has its work cut out for it. (978-1-62639-576-3)

Jane's World: The Case of the Mail Order Bride by Paige Braddock. Jane's PayBuddy account gets hacked and she inadvertently purchases a mail order bride from the Eastern Bloc. (978-1-62639-494-0)

Love's Redemption by Donna K. Ford. For ex-convict Rhea Daniels and ex-priest Morgan Scott, redemption lies in the thin line between right and wrong. (978-1-62639-673-9)

The Shewstone by Jane Fletcher. The prophetic Shewstone is in Eawynn's care, but unfortunately for her, Matt is coming to steal it. (978-1-62639-554-1)

A Touch of Temptation by Julie Blair. Recent law school graduate Kate Dawson's ordained path to the perfect life gets thrown off course when handsome butch top Chris Brent initiates her to sexual pleasure. (978-1-62639-488-9)

Beneath the Waves by Ali Vali. Kai Merlin and Vivien Palmer love the water and the secrets trapped in the depths, but if Kai gives in to her feelings, it might come at a cost to her entire realm. (978-1-62639-609-8)

Girls on Campus edited by Sandy Lowe and Stacia Seaman. College: four years when rules are made to be broken. This collection is required reading for anyone looking to earn an A in sex ed. (978-1-62639-733-0)

Heart of the Pack by Jenny Frame. Human Selena Miller falls for the domineering Caden Wolfgang, but will their love survive Selena learning the Wolfgangs are werewolves? (978-1-62639-566-4)

Miss Match by Fiona Riley. Matchmaker Samantha Monteiro makes the impossible possible for everyone but herself. Is mysterious dancer Lucinda Moss her own perfect match? (978-1-62639-574-9)

Paladins of the Storm Lord by Barbara Ann Wright. Lieutenant Cordelia Ross must choose between duty and honor when a man with godlike powers forces her soldiers to provoke an alien threat. (978-1-62639-604-3)